Orlo:

The Created

The Books of the Gardener

Orlo:

The Created

Lauren H. Brandenburg

Illustrated by
Jordan Crawford

KPP

KINGDOM PUBLISHING PRESS

This book may be ordered through booksellers or by contacting:

Kingdom Publishing Press
www.KingdomPublishingPress.com

Or directly at the book series website:
www.LaurenHBrandenburg.com

Cover art by Jason Dudley

ISBN: 978-0-9981600-9-2

Library of Congress Control Number: 2016919148

Printed in the United Stated of America

For My Mother,
Strength and dignity are her
clothing, and she smiles at the future.

Chapter 1

Orlo fidgeted with the pieces of metal he had collected during his travels. He squinted to place a tiny pin between two gears and then reached into the pocket of his trousers to see what else he could attach. The warmth in the crowded room made his hairless head sweat under his clean, but well-used, tweed cap. Orlo stretched his long legs out in front of him and wiggled his toes to keep them from falling asleep in his work boots. He was tall for thirteen, nearly as tall as most of the men assigned as deliverers. Tiny holes in the ground puffed a warm gentle mist of glowing steam around his feet. He slid his foot over the opening and then let it go. A burst of light shot up in front of him—eventually to blend into the hovering mist that illuminated the congested cavern.

Orlo had purposely chosen to sit on the back row so no one would sit beside him, but the Slub was busier than usual and seating was limited. He had never been told, nor had he thought to ask, why the deliverers of long ago had nicknamed the Hall of Deliverers the Slub. Since *Slub* was easier to say, Orlo had allowed it to easily settle into his vocabulary.

"Whatcha doin', mate?" the tiny boy sitting beside Orlo asked.

"Don't know. Just messin' around, I guess," Orlo mumbled, wishing the boy would leave him alone.

He honestly did not know what he was doing with the metallic pieces in his hand. His caretaker in the Hall of Orphan Care said that he was born a fidgeter. The elders of the garden must have been aware of his fidgeting as well. On the day of assigning the gardener had said, "Busy people must be kept busy. We have the perfect assignment for you, Deliverer." From that point on, Orlo spent nearly every day of the week in the Slub.

"Where did you get it?" the boy, at least three years his junior, persisted. The pale child pushed the goggles that were slipping down on his forehead back upon his greasy, matted hair. There'd been a time when Orlo thought he would never grow into his own goggles.

The boy looked around as if to see if anyone was listening. With a huge grin, he asked, "Did an inventor give it to ya?"

Orlo was shocked. "Of course not!"

"What's it do?"

Orlo squinted. "Nothing. It doesn't do anything, okay?"

"Course it does, mate! Look! Those pieces are movin' up and down." Orlo stared at what he had done. "You have the gifting," the boy said in an awed whisper.

"Listen, kid. I'm a deliverer, that's all. Deliverers don't have giftings. We make the deliveries and that's it. Got it?"

"I got it, mate," the boy said as he slumped over.

It was against the law to be unkind to others. Orlo did not think he had crossed the line into unkindness, but he remembered what it was like to be little and to have his feelings hurt by the older deliverers. He placed the gadget in his black satchel, clasped his hands together, and looked at the sad child. "So, do you have a guardian?"

"No," the boy said flatly. That was not the answer Orlo had expected. By the age of seven, most orphans were already placed in a guardianship. Orlo knew he had unintentionally hit a soft spot, so he changed the subject.

"What's your favorite garden?"

The boy perked up a bit. "The one with the green birds."

"That's a good one, but not my favorite." Orlo felt sorry for the boy. Kids in the Hall of Orphan Care had it rough, especially the ones assigned to the Slub. "What if I told you that my last delivery was to L923?"

"No way! Was it…"

"Dead and dry. I saw it with my own eyes!"

"No way! Then it's true. Their leader burned it down?"

"Looked that way. Not a thing grew. My cartagon was stacked full with crates of seeds. I guess they're planning on growing it back."

The boy sat with his mouth hanging open in awe of Orlo's journey. The garden they called L923 had become the topic of dinner conversations, teachings, and speculation among the people of the Conclusus. "Wow!" the boy mouthed.

Orlo had been overcome by the same sense of excitement when he'd received his orders to deliver to L923. He would be able to see—with his own eyes—what others in the Conclusus could only imagine. He had made many deliveries in his five years as a deliverer and had seen gardens of all sorts and sizes, but this last delivery was in a garden unlike any he had seen before. Their land was barren—rumor had spread that one of them had burned it completely to the ground. To Orlo, the idea that someone would do such a thing was unfathomable. Even though he was at the bottom of the Decorum, their social order, the Conclusus was his home. He would never do anything to upset the balance that established his way of life.

"Want to know the strangest part about it?" Orlo asked, leaning in to the boy. The boy's brown eyes were wide and eager. He had no reason to doubt the truth behind what Orlo was about to tell him. To tell a lie, whether accidental or intentionally, was against

3

the law, and would result in removal from the Conclusus. Orlo continued, "All of their elders were teenagers! Not one of them looked much older than me. Even their gardener couldn't have been but a season or two past my age!" In his heart, Orlo wondered what it would be like to live in such a place, a place where he, an orphaned deliverer, could have all the privileges and reverence of an elder.

"Wow! Can you imagine the Mysterium talking to a kid?"

"Sounds crazy, doesn't it? But it's what I saw." People in the Conclusus talked to the Mysterium all the time, but it was well known that the gardener was the one who had the gifting to hear His voice.

Orlo's guardian had once explained that in the World above them the Mysterium's name was God, and He spoke to her all the time. Even though it was against the law to lie, he'd had a hard time believing what she had told him.

Orlo looked over at the clerk to see if she was looking his way, but the middle-aged woman with her hair lumped in a knot on top her head was busy sorting a stack of disheveled papers. He tapped his fingers nervously on his slacks, sighed, pulled out his cracked pocket watch, sighed again, and put it back in his pocket. This was the longest he had ever left his cartagon anywhere. The holdup made him nervous. He did not feel that his cartagon was safe unless it was either with him or in its holding. The cartagon was his responsibility; it was entrusted to him. Usually, wherever the cartagon went, he went. Only on exceptionally large deliveries did he leave it to be unloaded—and this last delivery was his biggest yet. He could not imagine what would be taking them this long.

It had been nearly four hours.

Orlo glanced down at the boy. The boy would go back to the Hall of Orphan Care when his orders were complete, and Orlo would return to the home of his guardian. Today they were to celebrate her birthday, and since he did not have a gift to give her, he wanted to finish early so that he could surprise her by walking her home from the tower where she fulfilled her orders. Poppy was the closest Orlo believed he would ever come to having a mother. She was a product of the World above, born and raised in its ways, and brought to the Conclusus when a handsome messenger on a mission had fallen madly in love and married her. When Orlo was small, before being assigned his place as a deliverer, she would tell him stories of the World. She told him about baseball games, airplanes, and oceans. She told him about electrical devices that recorded, projected images, and took pictures—it was those tales that intrigued him the most.

It did not matter how many gardens he saw, Orlo longed to one day see the inventions of the World. That was the one place his cartagon would not take him, and unfortunately, the one place he knew he would never be able to go. Those who were strong enough and possessed the gifting to protect themselves from the evils of the World could travel back and forth. They were assigned as messengers. Orlo had witnessed two departure ceremonies in his lifetime. The messengers paraded through town in their finest attire while their apprentices followed behind collecting donations for their journey. When the messengers returned days—sometimes years later, depending on their mission to the World—they were changed, different. They seemed to have trouble functioning in the Upper Decorum of the Conclusus.

As he grew, it was not only the wonders of the World that interested him, but all of the working contraptions around him. He wanted to know why sound went higher when the strings on a fiddle were pulled tightly, and what made the hand on the clock move around at the exact same speed as every other clock in the Conclusus. He wanted the knowledge of the inventors.

For those assigned as inventors, this wisdom came with all the privileges of the Upper Decorum. If Orlo had it, he would get to sit at the front of the weekly Gathering, go to classes in the Hall of Educators, wear the purple sash across his chest, and live in one of the highest towers in all of the Conclusus.

But Orlo knew that this was never to be. The idea was as absurd as thinking he was gifted to be a messenger or a healer. He was an orphaned fidgeter, a deliverer, stuck to drive his cartagon for the rest of his days, never to be reassigned, because his parents had abandoned him to a life in the Lower Decorum. He would continue to do as he was told, he would not ask questions or complain, because his life was bound to the law of the Conclusus. *At least*, he thought, looking down at the boy whose hands were tucked under his thighs with his legs swinging back and forth, *I have a guardian*.

"Orlo the deliverer!" the clerk called. "You may receive!" Orlo stood up, stretched his back, tucked his blousy white button-down shirt securely in his loose brown pants, adjusted his belt, and pulled his own metal-rimmed goggles over his watery blue eyes.

"That's me! Good day, Deliverer."

"Good day, Deliverer," the boy called after him. Orlo felt good. Maybe he had given the kid something to talk about with the other orphans in the confines of the Hall of Orphan Care.

After spending his whole day waiting, Orlo eagerly shuffled over to the long cave wall where enormous wooden doors appeared and disappeared, forming giant entryways to the other gardens below the World. He watched, ready, for his gate—and his cartagon—to appear.

But a man with a short white beard, standing to the left of the wall, raised his left arm, palm out. Five metal fingers, connected at the joints with golden springs, demanded Orlo's attention. "That will be far enough, Deliverer." A look of concern passed over the familiar face.

Orlo realized that the door, his door, to L923 had yet to appear. He certainly hoped nothing was wrong.

Chapter 2

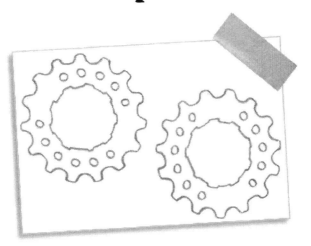

"These doors can be a bit tricky you know. You've been busy, young Orlo," Davy said, his smile peeking through his short, white facial hair. His pants were far too large for him, and a dingy red overcoat adorned with a collage of gadgetry hung heavy on his shoulders.

"Three gardens this week." In most circumstances when speaking to someone with an assignment of the Upper Decorum, Orlo would have addressed them as sir or ma'am, but not Davy.

"Ah, I remember a time when deliverers were fortunate enough to see one in a month. There are lots of needs out there these days. Something's changing in our lands; I can feel it in my bones. You'll be useful to those folks, young Orlo. You watch and see."

"I guess," Orlo answered. He was already overwhelmed by the amount of work he had done this week. If he took on more orders, he would never get to go to classes, but he did not have a choice in the matter.

"So, what were they like this time?" the man asked, leaning in. Orlo was thankful that Davy had been reassigned to the Slub and enjoyed the brief discussions they had between orders. He stood in awe, proud of his friend dressed in the soot-encrusted red velvet sash with the embroidered emblem of a burning torch—the sash that identified Davy as a messenger. He'd been exceptional at his assignment and had once served the Conclusus in the World, but then an unfortunate accident had injured him terribly—in such a way that an inventor had been ordered to repair his left arm with a mechanized replacement. To this day, the details of the misfortune were unclear to Orlo. He never considered asking because it would be rude, and rudeness was against the law. Even now, Orlo caught himself staring at the invention—not because it was an abnormality in the Conclusus, but because of its intricate complexity.

Orlo wanted to know so much that Davy could answer. He'd started many times to ask Davy about the oddities he had seen in the World. But always, he stopped himself for fear it might bring back the memory of the accident—that would be rude.

Oh! Davy had asked him a question. "They were kids 'bout my age. The gardener couldn't even have been much older than me. And there was a girl…she had a gifting I had never seen before. It was her eyes. She was blind, but she could see. I don't know how to exactly explain it."

The man laughed a deep hearty laugh. "The oddities of the gardens have never ceased to amaze me. Had a deliverer tell me that once he drove right in on one that was on the water. Did I tell you about that one?" Orlo shook his head and listened. "An underground *ocean* as far as the eye could see," he said. Orlo's eyes perked up at the word ocean. "Warriors they were. Fighters for The Way…that's what they said they called it, 'The Way.'" Davy cleared his throat and wiped the sweat off of his forehead. "Well, that's enough of that, young Orlo. Let's get this door open, shall we?"

"Sounds good to me," Orlo said, ready to get on with his day.

Davy placed the hand he had been born with on the barren cave wall and closed his eyes. In an instant, with a blink of light, a great wooden door materialized on the cave wall. With the man's help, Orlo pulled open the gate.

In the hollow darkness of the tunnel created by the door was his cartagon—a rectangular-shaped vehicle with narrow pipes running around the sides. He pulled out his pocket watch; he had time. Orlo exhaled, relieved that he would be able to return to the Conclusus in time to escort Poppy home from her orders.

Orlo crawled underneath the cartagon to inspect the gears with tiny scopes. He used a thick brown glove to locate any punctures on the hot piping. Then, he dislodged a few rocks that had gotten trapped in the underbelly and one near the front left heavy iron wheel. He leaned over the front and pulled out the cloth he kept in his back pocket to wipe down the box-like vehicle's viewing window.

"You take care of your cartagon better than any boy I know," Davy said with a chuckle.

"Thanks, Davy," Orlo replied proudly as he worked to remove a smudge from the window. Orlo boarded the cartagon and turned the crank at the center of the dashboard. With a *swish swoosh, swish swoosh*, Orlo's cartagon pulled through the door, producing a great puff of steam.

Then it stopped. No, Orlo thought, *not today*!

He turned the crank once again. This time a small puff of smoke released itself from underneath the cartagon. With a loud hiss, it stopped. Orlo hopped out and walked the perimeter of his machine.

"Need some help there, young Orlo?" Davy asked, his eyes jumping from Orlo's cartagon to the other cartagons lined up awaiting their doors.

"No thanks. I got this." Orlo continued his inspection. His cartagon had been used when it was first allotted to him and had occasionally given him some trouble. Over the past few years, he had worked hard installing upgrades he found around the Slub and polishing the brass fixtures. (Those gave it the flair that let the other gardens know it had come from the Conclusus). There! Orlo saw it—a tiny hole in a copper pipe that ran around the exterior of the vehicle. *I can fix it*, he thought.

He hurried back into the small trailer to get his tools and stepped back outside. He reached for the pipe and jumped back. *Yow!* The pain was excruciating. His hand was throbbing and red; a large blister was already beginning to form. In his rush, Orlo had forgotten to put back on the heavy leather glove that protected his hands from the scalding temperatures of the exterior pipes. He examined the area of pipe that had burned him and found that a cold white substance covered the damaged section. He had never seen or felt anything like it.

Orlo slipped the leather protective glove over his other hand and awkwardly repaired the damaged piece. He yanked his watch from his pocket, checked the time, and shoved it back. The repair had cost him the extra time he needed, but if he hurried, he could get the cartagon out of the way and into a nearby dock in enough time to surprise Poppy. Orlo tossed the tools back in the cartagon, removed the glove, and turned the crank. At first it puffed and snarled, then the swish swoosh, swish swoosh put the cartagon in motion.

"You all right there?" Davy called over the noise.

Orlo leaned out of the deliverer's side window and waved. He could not lie and say that he was fine, but he did not have time to be ordered to the Hall of Healers either. His hand stung and felt like it had a heartbeat. He took out his handkerchief and wrapped it around the wound, hoping it would keep him from bumping it on something.

Steering with one hand, he directed his delivery cart around the interior wall of the Slub to one of the cavern openings. He had docked his cartagon hundreds of times, but today his mind was elsewhere—possibly on thoughts of Poppy's birthday, or the strange gadget he had been fiddling with in his satchel—when he heard the scraping of metal against rock. His heart felt cold, sick and frightened. He carefully backed the cartagon out of the cubby, realigned it, and then pulled it straight and perfectly into its holding. He exhaled and hoped that the elders would not find out.

In all his days under the assignment of a deliverer, he had never had an offense. It would be unusual to be called before the elders for something so minor, but the thought of removal or even demotion in assignment was a fear that most everyone in the Lower Decorum carried with them daily. As an orphan under guardianship, they could not assign Orlo any lower than a deliverer. His punishment would have to be removal to The Works, or to the mines if they found his offense severe enough. He had heard stories of the heinous creatures that worked in the mines. The thought made him shiver.

Orlo pulled the lever downward to lock the cartagon in place. He removed his goggles, hung them inside the door, and hopped out to inspect the damage to his cartagon and the cavern wall of the cartagon's holding. A miniscule scratch was the only evidence that an incident had occurred. He would buff it out before his next delivery. The cubby wall on the other hand was missing a chunk the size of his fist.

He was searching the floor for the dislodged pieces when a twinkle of light caught his eye. Orlo reached down and retrieved the glimmering stone. Its shape and sparkle reminded him of the ornaments worn by the elders. Poppy would love it. Orlo carefully placed the gem in his satchel, gave his cartagon a double pat on the back, and left the holding.

Before he could step foot into the Conclusus, it was required that he bathe. A basin of water, a stack of clean washrags, and a bottle of liquid clothing spray waited for him on a table just inside the large metal doors. Orlo wiped down his face, the back of his neck, and rinsed the dust from his hand. He picked up the bottle, sniffed the top, cringed, and proceeded to spray it on his clothes. The pine scent was his least favorite of the deodorizers.

Orlo did a quick inventory of the few possessions he'd clipped to his utility belt. Then, he lifted the flap on his satchel to make sure Poppy's gift had not escaped. With the back of his arm, he shielded his eyes and pushed throgh the heavy doors, leaving the Slub behind. The light poured over him. Orlo rubbed his eyes and allowed them to adjust. He had seen many gardens in his travels, but not one could compare to the brilliant, glittering extravagance of the great Conclusus.

Chapter 3

With the rusted doors of the Slub behind him, Orlo breathed in the clean, warm, steam-filled air of the massive cavern. Despite the agonizing pain in his hand, the Conclusus had an energizing effect on him. If he was tired, the steam woke him up, and if he was sad, its glow made him smile as it did every day. The Conclusus was a happy place, and Orlo believed there was no place more perfect among the other gardens and quite possibly the World above.

As he jogged down in toward the towers of the Upper Decorum, he gazed up at the skyward gardens, taking note of the thin line of steam that had dropped from the stone roof above him to the tops of the coconut trees.

Hundreds of towering buildings constructed of sparkling quartz bricks in perfect concentric circles formed the design of the Conclusus. On the top of each tower grew a lavish garden of herbs, fruits, and vegetables, some more grand than others, but each one beautiful and full. Vines fell gently from the tops of the towers, so that they resembled stone giants with overgrown hair. As he neared the center of the towers, they became taller and their gardens more elegant.

He kept the seven front towers that created the inner circle of the Conclusus in his sight as he jogged downward. The towers beside him didn't seem much shorter than the great central towers, since they carried the groves and orchards—making them appear taller.

At the center of the Conclusus in the huge Gathering circle, water streamed down hundreds of feet from a massive stalactite into a manmade fountain. Along with what rose from the tiny openings in the ground, the fountain's warm bubbling water produced a steam that brought light to the Conclusus by day. Chiseled into the stone around the base of the fountain were the words WE WILL SERVE.

Poppy would be finishing up soon. He was certain that his presence would be a surprise. Orlo ran past the fountain and directly past the Hall of Interpreters, to the tower of the elder interpreter. He looked to the top, shielding his eyes from the light with the back of his hand. He hoped Poppy had not left for the day. He was about to begin his ascent up the back staircase when two ladies dressed in their billowing white satin daily wear stepped out of the tower's gilded front door. He immediately lowered his head out of respect and made room for them. The official golden yellow sashes draped across their chests, each embroidered with a descending dove, made him try hard not to think about his run-in with the wall in the Slub. He peeked up to see if they had passed, or if one of them had overheard his thoughts.

"Hello, Deliverer," the interpreter said.

"Hello, Elder Bednegraine." She was very kind, like all of the elders, but she spoke to Orlo whenever she passed him.

"I am delighted to see you! What brings you this way?"

"I'm going to walk Poppy home today, Madam. It's her birthday."

"How polite of you to escort your guardian home on her birthday," she said pleasantly. Orlo had always been uncomfortable with the interpreter's ability to speak what others were thinking, but Elder Bednegraine was a friend to their family. He trusted her. Orlo had been told that she had reached out to Poppy when she first arrived and invited Poppy to be her personal collector. "My word! Your hand! Her birthday can wait! You must see a healer."

"No thank you, Elder Bednegraine. I can have it looked at during a more convenient hour," Orlo said nervously.

"Sweet Deliverer, you serve us all well," the elder said, flipping open her fan and fanning away the heat of the afternoon. He had once overheard a fellow deliverer commenting on the youthful beauty of Elder Bednegraine. Although she was younger than the other elders, she adhered to tradition by wearing her thick auburn hair tucked up at the base of her neck.

"Thank you, Elder Bednegraine," Orlo replied, feeling tongue-tied at the constant repetition of her name.

"You are most welcome, Deliverer."

The elder started to walk away with one of her many apprentices by her side, but then turned back around as if to ask him another question. He did not see her speak, but would have sworn that he heard her say the word 'interesting'. Orlo was positive that he was not thinking about anything other than his wounded appendage, but he felt like she had heard something else. He did not have secrets, those were against the law, but she had definitely heard something inside of him.

They were a few steps away when Orlo heard her apprentice ask, "Is that the boy, Orlo?"

"Yes, Apprentice. He is under the guardianship of my collector. He serves well."

"I had no idea! You are too kind to take Miss *North* on as your collector."

"We must all do our part to serve, Apprentice."

"Yes, we must."

That name for Poppy made him angry, but at once, Orlo forced his thoughts to turn from the dangerous emotion and trudged up the stairs. He had known for a long time that the people in the Upper Decorum referred to Poppy as North. And he knew why they called her that. She had been brought from the North—brought into the Conclusus without the permission of the elders. She had not been approved.

Once he'd overheard a fellow deliverer refer to her in that way. He had imagined himself punching the old guy in the face, but before acting, he had pulled a piece of paper from his satchel and written out a request to the gardener for forgiveness. Had an interpreter been nearby, he might have been removed then and there.

He did not care what others thought about Poppy. She had agreed to be his guardian when no one else in the Lower Decorum was willing to step up. It was because of her that he had learned to dream—something seen as a talent by most.

Elder Bednegraine's garden was one of the most elaborate in all of the Conclusus. Orlo ran his good hand against the wall on the inside of the steps as he climbed to the top. As a child, Orlo had often come here with Poppy. He would lie on the grass-carpeted rooftop while she completed her orders. From there he felt like he could almost touch the top of the Conclusus. He would stare up into the cave ceiling and watch as the dripping water and glowing steam did their swirling dance throughout the treetops. He would imagine what it would be like to live in a garden where you did not have to wear shoes, or where you could keep what you collected and it not be divided up between the Upper Decorum and the deliverers. Sometimes, he would hang over the edge and look down at the Upper Decorum going about their daily tasks.

As he reached the tower top, he could almost see the tops of all seven inner-circle towers of the Conclusus. There were the Hall of the Messengers, the Hall of Musicians, the Hall of Healers, and the Hall of Educators (where he had classes on the rare days he did not have to work). And when he turned his head the other way, there were the Hall of Keepers (where the gardener studied and spoke to the Mysterium), the Hall of Interpreters which was directly in front of Elder Bednegraine's tower, and the Hall of Inventors. He would stare for hours, watching the purple-sashed inventors coming and going with their work securely in their arms.

Poppy's collecting basket was full to the top of plump green grapes. Her long dark hair hung loosely down her mended linen dress. She wore a belt around her waist much similar to the one that Orlo wore, and around her arm, a leather band embossed with the symbol of a guardian—two keys, one crossed over the other. Attached to her belt was an assortment of gardening paraphernalia: shears in a variety of sizes, tiny shovels, leather pouches of seeds, and a smaller basket for her other assignment-related trinketry. She wiped her forehead with the back of her draping sleeve and grinned. He was glad she had not heard the ladies call her North.

"I know you're standing behind me, Orlo. I can smell you! What was it today? Pine?"

"So much for your birthday surprise."

"Thank you, my sweet Orlo. You know it's not actually my birthday—at least I don't think it's my birthday. It was in January," she said. "It snows in January. Do you remember me telling you about snow?"

He did remember, but the idea of tiny cold white fluffs falling from the sky was hard to imagine as enjoyable.

"But," she continued, "because it is the day Knox has chosen to celebrate my birthday, how about we trade assignments for the rest of the day? I could see what is beyond these cave walls, and you could spend your afternoon daydreaming in Eden." He did not answer. "All right, spill it, Orlo. What's on that mind of yours?"

She turned to face him, bringing with her the scent of oranges and lemongrass that she carried with her wherever she went. Her dark eyes locked in on his crudely wrapped hand.

"My word, Orlo! What have you done! Let me see it." She knelt down to look at his aching hand.

"It's nothing."

17

"It is something! Have you cleaned it?"

Orlo did not have to answer. His furrowed forehead and muddled frown were enough.

"Of course you didn't," she said gently. "We'll take care of it when we get home. Be prepared, though. Knox will want you to see a healer." Poppy had made her opinion on the capabilities of the healers in the Conclusus more than clear. She was only permitted to distill and use oils as a hobby, but often, she knew more than the healers—she'd learned it up in the World. "It's more than the hand, isn't it? Come on, spit it out." She said the strangest phrases, most of which Orlo had deciphered. The first time he had heard her say 'spit it out', he'd spit a blueberry on Knox's boot.

"Speak, talk. What is on that brain of yours?"

All he could think was of the interpreters calling her Miss North. It was a horrible nickname that she would carry as long as she lived in the Conclusus.

"Hmm," she said, with her hands on her hips. "You won't lie, and you won't tell me. Did you pass Elder Bednegraine on your way up?"

Orlo bit the inside of his cheek. It was her birthday and he did not want to upset her.

"All right then, silence it is, but remember this: A joyful heart is good medicine, Orlo, but a broken spirit dries up the bones."

"Happy Birthday!" he said, changing the subject.

"Not my real birthday," she reminded him jovially.

"Well, it is the day you first came to the Conclusus, isn't it?"

"It is, and since I have completely lost track of how old I am, and there is no such thing as January here, we're going to celebrate!"

"Oh," Orlo nearly shouted, "I almost forgot. I have a present for you. Would you like it now or later?"

"Let me think," she chirped. "If I receive it now, the moment will be over and all I will have left are the memories. In and of itself, memory is a beautiful thing. But, if I wait, I will have time to guess what it is you have hidden in your satchel. Then there will be the moment of receiving it, and I will still have all the memories.

I will wait." She bent over and lifted the collecting basket into her arms. "Shall we exit?"

At the edge of the tower, a dumbwaiter was in position to lower the harvest down. Poppy placed the day's harvest in the wooden box and pulled on the roping. The pulley at the top squeaked as the contents descended to a large wheelbarrow at the bottom where another worker would take it to be processed and divided. Orlo let Poppy walk in front of him as they took the trip together down the back staircase. From high up he could see other collectors ending their day's orders and returning to their towers.

On their way back to the far edge of the Conclusus, Orlo and Poppy weaved in and out among the movement of workers. Some of the other collectors, as well as water bearers, planters, and pickers, smiled at them as they walked by. Those of the Upper Decorum and the elders continued with their conversations as if the Upper and Lower Decorum did not live side by side.

There'd been a time in Orlo's life when he saw the only differences in the Upper and Lower Decorum as top hats and towers. Now, he tried to overlook the separation and see the possibility. He dreamed of the life that the inventors in the Upper Decorum had—days filled with building, designing, and fixing. That would be the closest he could get to the innovations Poppy described in the World.

Chapter 4

The Lower Decorum home of Knox and Poppy was small, a three-level tower with a modest orchard on top. The small garden barely produced enough to provide for the household of four, unlike Elder Bednegraine's garden which produced enough for twenty families and extra to use for trading in the Mercor.

Orlo had been to the Mercor once—the vendor-filled street that divided the Upper Decorum from the Lower. There was nothing in their household to trade, so he doubted he would have a need to return. The Decorum took great pride in their gardens, especially the Upper who delighted in the extras they were able to produce and have delivered to the other gardens.

This tower had been Orlo's home for the past seven years. At six, in the Hall of Orphan Care when he had learned that he had been placed with a guardian, his first thoughts had not been of a life with two adults to care for him, but of a tower that he could call home. In most towers, the first two or three levels were for entertaining, the next levels were resting rooms for each member of a family. Above that was the preparation room, and at the top, the dining area—to allow the hot steam from the stoves to rise out into the Conclusus. Like the higher towers, their room for entertaining was on the first floor; unlike the others, the four residents had to share the middle floor, which Knox had cleverly divided into four separate rooms, and the dining area was in the middle of the preparation room.

Knox was waiting on the third level when they arrived. In the tradition of the Lower Decorum, he dressed much like Orlo in a baggy white shirt and suspenders. However, his long black overcoat was nicer than any piece of clothing the others in his tower possessed. A nice patch on the sleeve indicated his assignment as the aeronaut, a pilot of the steam-powered transportation balloon.

Before greeting Orlo, he hugged his wife and kissed her. "Happy birthday, my lovely bride!"

"Hello to you as well," she said, smiling cheerfully.

"Hello, Orlo. How was the new garden?" Knox asked.

"Completely dead! It was like a…what did you call it, Poppy? You know, that place with the sand?"

"You mean a desert," she answered.

"Yes, it was like a desert!"

"The stories were true? Do you believe the boy burned it down?" Knox asked.

"Looked that way." Orlo took off his satchel and hung it by the door. He peeked inside to see that his gift was safe.

"I have prepared all of your favorites to celebrate the day you made me the happiest man in your world and mine." He kissed her on the check and returned to the stove where pots bubbled and steam rose.

Poppy had once told Orlo that windows in the World had glass to protect people on the inside. Glass in windows sounded ridiculous to him, but he had to admit that the glass in his cartagon protected him from rocks that might fly out from underneath his wheel. "Like in my cartagon?" he had wondered.

"Exactly!" she had responded.

He remembered asking Poppy if people threw rocks at windows. When she had answered with yes, Orlo was relieved that she no longer lived in a kind of place where glass was needed to protect people from rock throwers.

"And how was your day?" Poppy asked the woman with graying hair seated by the open window of their tower.

"Did you find my R? I have looked everywhere, and I can't seem to find it. Have I lost it?" Knox's mother reached up and touched her hair, braided into a high bun.

"No, but if I find it, Avia, I will be sure to return it to you." Poppy kissed the old woman on the forehead.

"You are a kind girl. Do you think my R is with the others? Oh dear, I must have misplaced them all."

Orlo struggled not to laugh. Whenever Knox's mother decided that she had lost her letters, it turned into an interesting, yet confusing, conversation. Orlo had sat with her for nearly two hours one evening trying to explain that a person could not lose a K, but she had insisted that at one time it had been in her possession along with all of the others.

"No, Mom," Knox called, setting the last steel plate on the dark wood table. "They are safe." It was the only thing they could say to keep her from rambling on about them. "Come to the table. Let's enjoy the dinner you have prepared for us."

Orlo had assumed Knox had retired the steam-powered balloon early so he could come home and help prepare Poppy's birthday dinner. He could by no means be considered a cook. In fact, most of what he prepared did not taste very good, but it was filling, and Orlo was thankful to have it. The baked broccoli, boiled potatoes, and slightly burned biscuits were standard to their evening meals. The addition of homemade tomato sauce on wheat flour dough topped with oregano was the treat. Poppy had attempted to explain pizza to them, as well as the need for cheese and pepperoni, but it was a concept of the World that repulsed Knox and Orlo.

Still, tonight it did not matter what was served—Orlo was hungry.

"Mysterium." As Knox opened in prayer, the others joined hands. "Thank You for those You have brought into my life. Thank You for our home, for our food, and for our future. Amen."

Orlo mumbled the word "amen" under his breath, not understanding the point of talking to someone who was not going to respond. He was surprised at how hungry he had become over the day. He had spent most of it waiting for his cartagon to be returned and was unable to come home for lunch.

"So, Orlo, was it true that there were no adults?" Poppy asked.

"No, there were adults, but they were not the elders," Orlo responded while attempting to eat with his less dominant hand.

"Did you meet their gardener?" Knox asked.

"I did."

"What an exciting life you have, Orlo!" Poppy said enthusiastically. "To meet so many different types of people!"

"I never thought about it that way."

"When are you going to tell us how you hurt your hand?" Knox asked.

"Oh, dear boy," Avia said nearly jumping up from the table. "You broke my fan?"

"No, Avia," Orlo said, continuing to restrain his laughter. "I burned my hand. My cartagon had a leak today. I wasn't thinking and grabbed the pipe without a glove."

"You shouldn't be driving that old thing," Knox muttered.

Intentionally changing the subject, Orlo asked, "How was your day?"

"About the same, flying the Upper Decorum all over the place. Got to talk with a musician about his new baby, and had an observer tell me about some new uses for banana peels. Orlo, I talked to your educator today. She's expecting you on your next day off, and by the looks of it, you may have a few of those coming your way until that hand heals. You will see a healer tomorrow."

"Yes, sir." He cast a glance at Poppy who was holding in her giggles.

Knox brought forth a somewhat lopsided cake, drizzled with a coconut-chocolate sauce and topped with a sprig of lavender from their garden. Poppy acted surprised, but he baked her one every year. It was his yearly gift to her. Even as an aeronaut, he did not earn much by the standards of the Conclusus. Still, they were content and happy with what they had.

"My dearest Poppy. I do not know what I would do without you. You have chosen a life with me away from everything and everyone you once loved." Knox looked over at his aging mother and then back to Poppy. "I love you, and I have a gift for you."

"What are you talking about?" she asked. "You've made me a, well, a pizza. And the cake! The delicious cake!"

"You deserve more!" he shouted as he ran from the room. Poppy's face went from curious to concerned. "Knox?" He returned with a package wrapped in brown paper and tied with a pink satin bow. Tears formed in her eyes.

"How?" Orlo had seen many ladies in the higher order carrying those packages. He knew where it was from, the clothier in the artisan sector of the Mercor. As far as he knew, Poppy had never so much as peeped inside Madam Vesti's Ladies' Boutique.

"Open it," Knox urged, acting as if he would unwrap the gift if she did not.

"All right then." She untied the bow and twirled it into a neat circle to be reused. Orlo leaned over the table to get a better look. This was the first time in his life that he had ever seen a gift opened. She peeled back the top layer, then the bottom, and gasped.

"Knox! They're beautiful!" She lifted from the paper a pair of satin gloves, black and glossy, and long enough to cover her hands and forearms.

"They're to wear to the Gatherings—like the other ladies. I'm sorry you have not had them sooner."

She jumped up from the table and hugged his neck as tears trickled down her cheeks.

"One day, I will buy you a dress. It will be a real Gathering dress. The most beautiful dress in the whole store. I promise!"

Her smile faded.

"You don't like them? There are other colors. I will take you, and you can pick them out yourself."

"I adore them, but Knox. We can't afford them."

"Did you trade my Y?" Avia asked.

Orlo almost spit the cake from his mouth. The tension in the room was released.

"No, Mother." He looked back at Poppy. "I traded a few bits of our Bosweilla tree." The awkward tree that grew from their rooftop was the most contorted tree in the Conclusus and the only one of its kind. "I took some of the resin to the healers. You said yourself that it has medicinal properties."

"But I'm not a healer, Knox. It was a hobby I had in the World." Hobby. Orlo did not know the word "hobby". He would ask her about it later.

"Yes, of course, and if you were a healer, the gardener would have assigned you to apprentice. But nonetheless, I do not see why we cannot benefit from the wisdom you brought from the World."

"Oh, Knox, you sweet man! So they took it?"

"Well, not much of it, but enough to trade! They said they would assess it to see if it indeed had the capabilities to serve the Conclusus."

"That is delightful! What if it is useful? That in and of itself has to be worth something!"

"Yes, but let us not get too excited. Happy Birthday, my dear!"

Orlo knew that not everyone in the Conclusus would agree with Knox, especially the elders. Even Knox separated Poppy's *hobby* from the giftings of the healers. Until this moment, Orlo had forgotten about the time Poppy handed him a cup full of bitter plant juices in the middle of the night claiming it would settle the cough that had kept him awake. The next day he returned to the Slub without even so much as a tickle in his throat.

"And now, Orlo. I'm ready for my moment," Poppy said, turning her attention to him.

"It's not much. Truthfully, I came on it by accident," he said, thinking back to his run-in with the cave wall. "But when I saw it, I thought you would enjoy it."

Orlo lifted his satchel from the hook by the door, but as he did so, the strap became stuck, spilling the contents of the bag all over the floor. Orlo hurriedly tried to collect the items, but it was too late. Something other than the gem had grabbed Poppy's eye.

Chapter 5

"Orlo, it's magnificent." Poppy stooped down to lift the gadget in the palm of her hand.

"Looks like I am not the only one who has been trading," Knox said, stepping back and putting his hands in his pockets.

"Orlo! How delightful!"

"What exactly is it?" Knox asked.

"Knox, it's a ladybug!" Poppy explained.

Orlo stared blankly at the item that had occupied his time waiting in the Slub. To him, it was merely a concoction of screws, coils, springs and gears—a plaything made of scraps he had found lying around the Slub.

"Ladybugs are tiny flying creatures we have in the World."

"Like bees?" Knox turned the object over in his hands.

"Similar. They fly like you, Knox." She giggled without taking her eyes away from the metallic bug. "There are those who believe they bring good luck, and there are those of us who simply marvel at the Mysterium's creation of them. Where in the Conclusus did you find such a wonder, Orlo?"

"I guess the better question is, what did you trade for it? Your spare set of goggles?" Knox laughed.

An uncomfortable fear struck Orlo. Knox thought he had traded for it, and Poppy thought he had found it. He could not lie; it was against the law. "I...I...I..." he stuttered. This was not how he had imagined the evening. He was going to give her the gem, and she would love it. It was supposed to make her happy, and because she was happy, Knox would be happy. It was her birthday. "I made it," he confessed.

"Looks like he's lost his letters, too," Avia chuckled.

"Orlo! You are a deliverer, not an inventor! Are you telling us a lie? Because if you are..." Knox said sadly.

"I'm not lying! I put it together with parts that I found!"

"You do not have the knowledge to do such a thing! You were not given this gifting!" Knox said angrily. Orlo had never seen him upset before.

"I was fidgeting, like the gardener said. I didn't know it was making a woman's bug. You have to believe me! I will write a letter to the gardener immediately to seek the forgiveness of the Mysterium."

"That will not be necessary."

"It was something to occupy my time. Here," he said rummaging through the broken bit of trinkets in his bag. "Here is your gift."

He handed her the clear stone, but her eyes were fixated on the mechanical bug in her hand. She studied it intently. "Orlo, this is amazing. The detail is so lifelike." She turned it over in her hands.

"Orlo," Knox said with hushed frustration, "if the elders hear of you working above your assignment, we could all end up in The Works, Mother included!"

"Maybe that's where I left my letters," Avia said, unaware of the tension around her.

"He could possibly have a talent," Poppy suggested. "Maybe the gardener was wrong."

Orlo wanted so much to hope she was right, but he was so confused. Knox said he was working above his assignment, and Poppy said he had talent. Orlo had never connected his mindless fidgeting with his secret desire to be an inventor. *What if Poppy was right?* No, he could not allow his mind to assume there had been a mistake in his assignment.

"Please, dear, guard your tongue! Not here. It is not how it is done. What if we all ran around saying that the gardener and the elders had gotten it wrong? Healers would start acting like musicians, and messengers would try their hand at inventing! And the guardians creating doors...what a mess the Conclusus would be!"

If Poppy were no longer a guardian, then Orlo would have to wait for a new one. He had no desire to return to an isolated life in the Hall of Orphan Care. "It was a mistake. We will toss it away. Right now," Orlo stammered softly as he twiddled his thumbs nervously. "It wasn't meant for anyone to see. I thought it was a toy. I didn't mean to cause a problem."

"Oh, Knox, we can't toss it away; it is far too lovely. Please, he meant no harm. You know how he fidgets." Poppy gently removed the ladybug from Knox's hand and clutched it to her heart. "If it is okay with Orlo, may I keep it?"

"Well, as Orlo said it was play, we are under no law to report this. So...yes, Poppy," he said, looking into the pleading eyes of his bride, "if you can keep it out of the sight of the elders, you can keep this reminder of your World. Orlo, is it good with you?"

Orlo nodded, relieved that Poppy was happy and that his contraption would not end up in the waste bin.

"Good. And Orlo, no more doing whatever you have done. We will not talk of it anymore. Tomorrow is a new day. How about we all go up to the garden and watch the mist settle?"

Orlo did not feel like going to the garden that night.

"Did Orlo find my letters?" Avia asked.

"No, Mother," Knox said, taking his wife by the arm.

"Maybe the Mysterium has my letters!" she said excitedly.

"Mother, please do not add disorder to our evening. Good night, and may you dream."

"Why would I scream?" Avia asked. "You can hear me fine, can't you?"

Orlo heard a muffled giggle escape from Poppy as they climbed the stairs to the garden.

He thought about his own dreams, his desire—had he invented on purpose? Had he known what he was doing? No, it was an accident. It had to be. He was not an inventor. He was a fidgeting deliverer. Orlo had never shared his dreams with anyone, not even Poppy. At classes, it was a popular sport to decipher one another's dreams. Orlo did not care for anyone to know what was going on in his mind, especially now.

Poppy and Knox left the room leaving Orlo alone with Avia.

"*Psst.*" The older lady practically spit on Orlo. "Orlo, come closer. I have a secret for you." Orlo did as she had requested. In a voice that was stern, clear, and free of disorientation, she said, "The Mysterium told me so. He said it. I heard Him. You will find my letters."

Chapter 6

As Poppy had predicted, Orlo found himself in the Hall of Healers instead of fulfilling his orders the next day. The combined scents of oregano, lavender, orange blossom, apricots, cinnamon, and fragrances he could not discern had nearly knocked him down when he stepped inside the door. At first, the overwhelming aromas had made him dizzy, but as time passed, he became pleasantly entranced by the scents.

He wriggled his bottom in the plush blue velvet seat. Because he had never sat in something so soft before, he was having trouble finding a comfortable position. Poppy sat next to him with her hands in her lap. He wondered what she was thinking. Was she trying not to notice the stares the two of them were getting?

All around him, people from various levels of the Decorum waited for their names to be called. Some were coughing, others held their heads in their hands as if they had a headache, and a few moaned in discomfort. Orlo held his burnt hand and yawned a full-mouth yawn that caught the attention of the messenger a few seats down. The throbbing from his burn, Avia's strange comment about hearing the Mysterium, and the idea that maybe he had invented something had kept him awake most of the night. There could be absolutely no truth in it whatsoever, since he clearly recollected the day when the other ten-year-olds had been assigned their apprenticeships, and his assignment was a deliverer. The gardener and the elders were never wrong. It was like Knox had said, if everyone started to think they had been wrongly assigned, the Decorum would collapse. There had to be a way for him to know for sure without breaking any laws.

The scent of rosemary and lavender drifted from among the many plants in the room. Every now and then the fragrance of pine that lingered on his clothing would overpower the room's scent, but not often. Orlo had never been inside the Hall of Healers before, but on his way home from the Slub, he often stopped in front of the hall to smell the scents escaping the opening and closing door.

Orlo watched as healers' apprentices, their blue clothing neatly covered by stark white aprons, called for and escorted various ailing patients up the blue-carpeted staircase at the center of the room.

"How's your hand?" Poppy asked.

"Still hurts," Orlo said, cradling it.

"There's no reason for us to spend our morning around all of these sick people. I could have taken care of this back at our tower," she said with a sly grin. Orlo did not respond. His mind was stuck on the ladybug. How had he done it? "Come on, Orlo! What's with you?" She nudged his side.

What's with you? It was another one of her phrases from the World. If someone from the Conclusus had asked him that same question he would answer with, "my satchel," or "my goggles." But he had come to know what she meant. She could see that something was on his mind.

"Is it about last night?" she continued. "Because I absolutely love it!"

Her statement did make him feel better, but before he could tell her, a short girl with long blonde hair twisted up into a braided knot emerged below the staircase. "Orlo the deliverer," she called across the room with her clipboard in hand.

His legs had grown stiff and his bottom sore from sitting down for so long. "I'm Orlo," he replied, raising his hand.

Poppy stood with him. "Do you want me to go with you?" she asked.

Unfortunately, this produced a few cackles from apprentices waiting in front of them. Apprentices did not have to be escorted by a guardian to the Hall of Healers. Even though Orlo was older than most of them, he was technically considered an orphan and had to be under supervision.

"No, thanks. I've got it from here," he replied.

"Orlo the deliverer," the girl asked, "are we correct in our records that this is your first time in the Hall of Healers?"

"Yes," he answered.

She jotted a few notes on her clipboard and asked, "And your ailment, is it internal or external?"

Orlo looked at the hand he was holding. "External?"

"Here's your map in the instance you are redirected." She handed Orlo a square piece of paper. "Follow me." The wide, winding staircase went up through the center of the twelve-story tower. At each floor, the stairwell leveled off before beginning its ascent to the top. As they ascended to the second floor, Orlo stopped to read the sign that hung in front of the elaborately adorned double doors—APOTHECARY. He checked his map. It agreed with the sign.

"Please keep up. We are very busy here," the healers' apprentice said. As Orlo continued to climb the stairs, he caught a peek at the next two floors—PRESERVATION and ADJUSTMENT.

"We are here, Deliverer." The sign above her head read OBSERVATIONS. "Please have a seat and a healer will be with you." She walked away leaving him alone in another room filled with more plush blue chairs.

Orlo started to sit down, but reconsidered after his lengthy wait. He found a wall that was not covered in plant life and leaned against it. He never realized the Hall of Healers had so many different sections. He had always thought that all the floors were for healing people. He read from his map the levels above him—Recovery, Experimentation, Separation, and on top, like every other tower in the Conclusus, Garden.

"Orlo," another apprentice called. His voice was squeaky, and his clipboard unsteady in his pale hands. "Orlo the deliverer!"

"Yes, that's me," Orlo answered.

"Come with me, please," he said, without making eye contact. Orlo followed the nervous apprentice down a door-filled hallway to the last door on the left where he was ushered inside. "Have a seat and wait here, please."

Orlo climbed up in the elevated chair at the center of the room and waited. On the white walls a plaque read WE WILL SERVE. Minutes later, the door opened, and in walked a healer. Her blue sash was embroidered in gold with the symbol of the healers—a grouping of wild flowers within a circle. Her accessories perfectly matched the chairs and drapery in the other rooms.

"Orlo?" she said in a voice that was drawn out and sweet.

"Yes, ma'am."

"Your guardian sent a message to us this morning requesting treatment for a"—she paused, looked at her own clipboard, and continued—"a burn. May I take a look at it?"

Orlo unwrapped his hand and held it out for her. She gently took it in her own hand and then pulled a magnifying glass from the pouch on her leather belt. She turned his hand over, examining both sides, and then inspected his elbow. "Yes, it is indeed a burn. Are you in pain?"

"Yes ma'am, a great deal."

"Hmmmm," she said, continuing to inspect it. "I can see that you are in pain."

Orlo was confused; he had already told her that. "All right then, Orlo. I am giving you authorization for treatment." She scribbled something on a pad of paper and handed it to him. "Take this to level two. The healer in the Apothecary will fill the prescription. It should take the discomfort away." Orlo took the paper and hopped down from the chair.

She did not show him the way out or say good-bye as he left the room. He looked back at her to see if maybe she had more to tell him, but she sat on her stool scrawling words her clipboard. Orlo walked down the door-filled hallway, through the sea of blue velvet in the waiting area, and to the wide spiral staircase. He looked down at his map—realizing that this must have been why the first apprentice had given it to him. From the looks of it, the Apothecary was two floors below the Adjustments and Preservation floors.

With his prescription and map in one hand and the burned hand lifted to his chest, Orlo began his descent to the Apothecary. When he came to the floor labeled Adjustments, his curiosity overcame him. He knew what it meant to adjust his cartagon, but what under the World could it have meant to adjust a person? He had never had an adjustment before, but had heard that many in the Conclusus had them done on a regular basis. He knew he might never again have a chance to see for himself, so he leaned in to have a look.

Blue velvet covered tables spread across the room, nearly empty with the exception of a light-blue-garbed musician who was lying face down with a blue sashed healer standing over her. The healer took the palms of his hands and pressed into the musician's back. A loud pop startled Orlo. Then the healer moved to the neck. With a loud crack, the healer twisted the neck. Orlo gasped. He wanted to take off down the stairs and never look back, but he was frozen. Before his heart could be heavy for the poor musician, she jumped up from the table, brushed the loose strands of her long hair back into place, and shook the hand of the healer.

Orlo would have insisted she had been murdered at the hands of the healer had he been called as a witness, but she looked great.

By the smile on her face, the popping and cracking were as normal to her as the swish swoosh of the cartagon was to him. Still, he vowed that he would never purposely seek out an adjustment. It looked morbidly painful. *People trade for this service*, he thought. *I wouldn't trade a dirty sock for that kind of treatment.* The musician walked past him, nodded in a way that was polite, but not meant to strike up conversation or suggest that they were equals. Orlo waited for her to pass and then continued toward the Apothecary.

He did not feel the same curiosity on the Preservation floor; he already knew what it was—mostly. All the apprentices at classes talked about it. One would say, "My day of preservation is Friday." Another would say, "I went to preservation twice this week." Once a girl in his class said that she only went to preservation when she had an assessment.

What he really knew about preservation treatment was that it was an injection privileged to the apprentices of the Upper Decorum. The cost of the lavish luxury was—too much for him to imagine. No member of the Lower Decorum even considered them. Besides, he did not like the thought of someone purpose-fully sticking him with a needle, but he considered how he would feel after the prick and sting of the injection was over. The apprentices said it was better than chocolate crepes.

He had never had those either.

The door to the Apothecary was closed. His hand was hurting more now than when he had come in. There were no instructions suggesting that he walk in or knock. So, to be safe and avoid rude-ness, he knocked.

"Come in!" called a shaky voice. Orlo turned the brass knob and entered a room filled wall-to-wall, ceiling-to-floor with dark wooden shelving, filled with neat rows of tiny vials—thousands. The fragrance in this room took hold of his ability to breathe. It was like a cacophony of sage, oregano, citrus, and eucalyptus infused in one warm swirl. He had never smelled anything so fantastic in his entire life. In the back, an elderly woman clung tightly to one of the wooden ladders that pressed against the shelving. "What's ailing you?" she said without looking at him. "Allergies? Pollen gotcha?" she gurgled.

"No ma'am." Orlo stepped towards her.

"Ah." She turned to look at him. "Young one. Hmmm…preservations are upstairs. Ya missed a floor." Orlo glanced down at his plain clothing. She had not noticed that he was not an apprentice.

"It's my hand, ma'am." He looked around the room to see if someone else with more clarity might be able to assist him.

"Your hand?" She stopped her chaotic arranging to climb down the ladder. The lady hobbled over to him and lifted his wounded appendage. "What they say upstairs?"

"She said you would have something to take the pain away." Orlo handed her the authorization for treatment.

The older healer snatched the paper out of Orlo's hand with a smirk. She twisted a nob on her spectacles to adjust the vision, and then handed the paper back to Orlo. "This won't heal a paper cut." She turned towards another ladder.

"But, the healer said—"

"Healer, schmealer," the woman mocked.

Orlo nearly gasped at her blatant frustration and disrespect. His hand pounded. The pain had turned from annoying to excruciating. "Please, you must have something for me." The woman fidgeted with the vials from atop the ladder, shooing Orlo away with her free hand. He turned helplessly and walked toward the door.

"Where are you going, Deliverer? First you want me to help, then you chitchat away as I'm searching, and now you're walking out on me? You younglings make my mind all bubbly!"

Orlo gaped at her. He tried to formulate the words to explain, but before he could begin, the door swung wide open. Three inventors' apprentices burst into the room boldly—this was not their first visit. Their confident presence commanded the room. It was like they knew they possessed knowledge far above the reach of the other assignments. Even as a small child in the Hall of Orphan Care, they had intrigued Orlo.

"Knock!" the woman shouted.

The teens rolled their eyes and then backed out of the room, shutting the door behind them. From the other side a hard, rhythmic knocking sounded from the door.

The healer shook her head, placed her hands on her hips, and grinned with white teeth showing. "Come in," she said in a sickeningly sweet tone. "Don't touch anything! I'll be with ya when I'm done with the deliverer."

Orlo wished she had not pointed it out. The apprentices jerked their heads towards him and began their snickering. He watched as they walked the perimeter of the room, leaning in to sniff the liquid-filled vials and then glancing back to see if he was still there.

"Here," she said, returning Orlo's attention to his hand. "This is what you should use." Orlo took the small brown bottle from her hand and pulled out its tiny cork. "Careful there, Deliverer. It's all you get! Two to three drops a day on that hand until the oil's gone."

Orlo sniffed the vial, expecting it to be a rotten-smelling concoction, but instead it was pleasant, reminding him of how Poppy smelled when she brought in cuttings from their garden.

"Lavender," she said with a nod. "It will help with that stinging, and it will give you a doozy of a sleep." She leaned in close, looked back at the inventors, and then at Orlo—her cold nose nearly touching his cheek. "But be careful, Deliverer, it will deepen those dreams of yours."

Orlo turned to look at her. How could she know about his dreams?

"He, he, he," she chuckled. "Gets them every time." As she walked away from him, Orlo clearly heard her say, "Healers treating burns with bergamot! What's next? They'll be telling me not to use oregano on warts!"

"Thank you," Orlo said, dabbing a bit of the prescribed liquid on his hand. The oiliness seeped into his skin and soothed the rage of the burn. "Thank you," he said again with relief. For a second, he thought he saw a genuine grin seep from the wrinkled lips of the Apothecary healer.

"I've decided to enter the tournament!" Orlo overheard an inventors' apprentice brag—the girl.

At the word *tournament*, Orlo whipped his head around, accidentally dropping the vial on the marble floor.

The healer scowled at him. He lunged for the container, heaving a long sigh of relief. The vial was neither broken nor cracked. The inventors' apprentices sniggered at his clumsiness.

Orlo turned to one of the many vial-filled shelves and pretended to look at the alphabetically arranged oils, so he could hear the conversation that had trapped his attention. But he glanced over occasionally.

"What's the point, Lyla?" a boy asked. He wore purple—but still very masculine—attire with leather strapping secured around his thigh to hold the tools presented to the inventors. "You are already apprenticed. It is a waste of your time. Your assignment is guaranteed."

"I'd rather win than give a Low Deco the chance," the girl answered. She could've been the boy's twin were it not for her dress.

"Why should the Low Decos be allowed to enter?" the other boy said. His eyes wandered across the expanse of oils.

"That's the point!" she said emphatically. The other two boys looked at one another for clarity. "We have been assigned! We are inventors! If one of us wins, then some Low Deco won't be able to take the open apprenticeship. The elders chose us. We are gifted! A person of the Lower Decorum does not have the right to hold such a position."

"But it is tradition," the other argued. "Why not give someone the chance?"

The girl ignored him. "If you think about it properly, it is an act of kindness. I will be giving the Conclusus a chance to applaud someone who is truly worthy of the apprenticeship. It will be proof that this tradition is absurd and antiquated. The Conclusus needs inventors who can actually invent and not come up with some useless, hair-brained idea in an attempt to enter our Decorum. Besides, I'll win!"

"Wait a minute!" the twin argued. "If you enter, then I can't! One per household!"

"May the fastest step first!"

The Festival of Sevenths. Orlo had forgotten about it. Once every seven years a festival was held to honor the seven assignments held by the seven elders—the seven assignments that were deemed as the most important to the function of the Conclusus. The highlight of the festival was the Tournament of the Inventors. Three weeks prior to the tournament, during the Gathering, one member from each tower would be invited to declare their entrance before everyone. At the tournament, each candidate would present an invention that would serve the Conclusus. The winning candidate—a factor determined by popular vote and confirmed by the elders—would be permitted to advance into the Upper Decorum as an inventors' apprentice. It was the only way a member of the Lower Decorum could rise to the upper.

Orlo's heart raced. This could be his chance to find out if he had the gifting to invent or if the ladybug was merely an accident. He couldn't have dreamed up a better opportunity. If he won, he could change the lives of Poppy, Knox, and Avia forever. They would never have to worry about not having enough to trade ever again. The aromas of the oils began to overpower Orlo and make him dizzy. He turned the knob to the double doors, clutching the vial in his hand. He raced down the stairs, knowing Poppy would be at the bottom. He had to tell her right away.

He slowed, remembering what she had said about enjoying the moment. Actually, he would wait to tell her, and let his entry be a surprise.

Chapter 7

Orlo leaned back on the highest branch of the boswellia tree. Its crooked arms held him safely above the bricked streets of the Conclusus. Everything would change if he could win the tournament. He thought back on the ladybug. He had trouble believing that the thing had a name. He had fidgeted, tinkered, and searched for miniscule gears to add to it. There had been no plan in the design. Poppy had told him of many beings in the World, but not once had she talked about ladybugs. How had he known? Had he seen it in another garden? That had to be it. Had he been under the guardianship of anyone else, the incident could have ended badly—without question, removal from the Conclusus.

Working above your assignment was against the law, but now that Orlo planned on entering the tournament, surely practicing a bit would not hurt anyone. He had to know if what he had done was a strange coincidence or if there were more to it. He allowed his musings to take him into a land of gears, springs, and coils—a place where he knew what to do with them.

Orlo dug into his pocket to see if there were any leftover bits that he had not used in building the bug. He pulled out a piece of flexible copper wire he had wrapped around a bolt to form a ball. It would not be as easy to work with one hand. Using his teeth to hold the loose end, Orlo unwound the wire. The glow of the lingering day-mist dimly lit the night sky.

As Orlo twisted the wire, he thought about what Poppy had told him of the World. In the World, she said, stars materialized in the sky at night. Above him here was cave ceiling; the concept of a sky that bled into a star-filled vastness was overwhelming. He wondered what stars looked like and if they sparkled like Poppy had described them. She said that God—that's what she called Him—had made them along with a great orb to give some light to the night. By day, a hot continuously burning star shone on the World. She had also told him about sunsets, waves, and snow. During the month of her birthday, it would snow.

Orlo bent and molded the wire, forming symmetrical triangles and right angles. He wrapped the orange wire around his finger to form spirals. Until that instant he had not realized what he was doing. In his hands, he now held a symmetrical item with points jutting out from all sides. He had never seen one before, but he knew what he held—an intricately detailed snowflake. A sense of fear mixed with the excitement growing in his brain. He gasped and let it drop to the ground.

Poppy spoke of snow often, how it would blanket the ground in white, how you could catch it on your tongue and build men out of it, but that was all he knew. It was something that he could not comprehend. If snow was freezing, and freezing was the opposite of warm, and freezing caused people to be uncomfortable, then why would the Mysterium have created it? Was it because the people in the World were fallen, like those in the mines? Was it a punishment of sorts? But Poppy had described it as beautiful. He deliberated all of this until he heard footsteps climbing the steps to the garden.

"Orlo? Are you up there?" Knox called. Orlo looked down where the orange snowflake gleamed against the green grass. He turned to see that Knox had entered their garden. He hurriedly reached for the branch above him to swing down. Forgetting that he could no longer use his left hand, Orlo slipped off of the branch, landing on his back at Knox's feet.

From here, Knox looked exceptionally tall and slim in his ankle-length black coat. On the left shoulder of his work attire, the seamstress had embroidered the symbol of the aeronauts—a pair of wings wrapped in a circle. Orlo wore the symbol of his assignment around his wrist. The symbol of a compass was embossed into the leather bracelet he had been given on the day he was assigned. It often reminded him of the compass welded into the dashboard of his cartagon. Without it, Orlo feared he would never find his way back home.

Like all the others in the Decorum with the exception of Poppy, Knox had been born in the Conclusus. His father had been a messenger. In the tradition of his father, Knox started his apprenticeship at an early age. Like the other messengers, he was trained to look past the evils that lingered in the World, so he could freely pass communication between those that served in the World and those that lived in the Conclusus. It was there that he had met Poppy, and there that his life was changed forever.

"You all right?" Knox chuckled after seeing that Orlo was okay.

"Yes, sir." Orlo rubbed his elbow.

"I do not think that did any favors for your hand."

"No, sir," Orlo chuckled with him.

"Here, let me help you up." Knox reached his arm out, and Orlo extended his good hand. As Knox assisted him from the ground, Orlo felt a sharp stab in his lower back—he had landed on the snowflake.

"If it's all right, I'll sit for a bit," he said, rubbing his elbow again.

"Mind if I sit with you?" Knox asked. Orlo enjoyed his talks with Knox. Poppy said it was good for them to "hang out." The phrase had escalated into a series of jests that included references to hanging out the laundry and hanging outside from a tree branch.

"Orlo, I am sorry I snapped at you last night. I should not have said what I did. You are not a punishment. We are a family. You are a part of our family." Orlo fidgeted with the thin piece of leather on his wrist—the physical reminder that this was his life. He was told who to live with, what to do, how to act, and what not to say.

"We have a…a different kind of family, Orlo. It is not always easy—especially when we have to keep Mother from telling every person she encounters about her conversations with the Mysterium."

Orlo raised his eyebrows.

"You are not the first person she has told," he said. "I do not know what she thinks she heard, but it was not Him." Knox was keeping true to his word; he was not bringing up the ladybug.

"How were your orders today?" Orlo asked, changing the subject and moving the conversation forward. If it had not been for the snowflake stabbing him in the backside, he would have been happy for Knox to stick around.

"I did not tell you, did I?" His voice became mysterious and quiet. "I transported the gardener today."

"Are you certain it was him?'

"Can I lie?" It was a household joke; the laws forbid them to lie. "Strange fella. I have known him since we were small, but he did not say a word. He looked tired. Maybe he felt strange around me because his first act as gardener was to reassign me as aeronaut. Guess I cannot blamed him—your first day on the job and you have to demote a man for bringing in a woman from the World." They both laughed. "Poor fella, I would not take his assignment for anything."

"But wouldn't it be great to hear the Mysterium?" Orlo asked openly—this was okay, when it was he and Knox.

"Maybe, but I am afraid He might tell me something I do not want to hear. Then what would I do?"

It was a hard question. Orlo wondered what he would do, too. Would he do what the Mysterium had asked? It was against the law to disobey, so he figured he would have to do whatever the Mysterium was asking even if he did not like it.

Orlo wondered what the Mysterium thought about Poppy. By bringing Poppy to the Conclusus, Knox had broken the law. The gardener should have had Knox removed to The Works, but for some reason, he did not. Orlo figured the Mysterium must have told the gardener that it was okay for her to stay.

"There goes your brain again, Orlo. I can see it in those blue eyes of yours. Spit it out, but not on my boot this time."

"Ha ha, very funny. I was thinking…you broke the law, but the gardener didn't send you away." The wire dug deeper into Orlo's skin. He tried to wiggle it free, but the snowflake felt like it was wiggling with him.

"Let's just say, it helps if your father was an elder." Orlo had never heard that piece of information about Knox's father. He knew that at one time Knox lived the life of lavish meals and fine clothing, but he did not know that Knox's father had been an elder before his passing.

"If you knew it was wrong, why did you do it? Why take the chance? You could have wound up in The Works…or worse!"

Knox grinned. "Love. Love is stronger than the law, Orlo. I did not want to break the law, but it was the only way to be with her." There was silence between the two for a few seconds. "Get some rest. No orders for you on Monday. I have worked it with the Slub for you to have the day off. It will be a classes day! You have to let that hand heal."

Orlo raised his eyebrows. He liked classes but was rarely able to attend. When he did go, he was usually behind the other students, and did not know what the educator was talking about that day, but he did not care. It was a day out of the Slub, a chance to be with the others his age.

Knox stood up and brushed over the backside of his coat. "Knox," Orlo asked, "why did you let her keep it?"

Knox ran his fingers through his shaggy brown hair and smiled. "I believe it would break her heart if I took the thing from her. Daily living is hard enough on her as it is. Simple pleasures mean a lot. Wish there was a way that I could give her more, but my decision was my decision, and I would not change my life with her for all the towers in the Conclusus."

There was a long silence before either of them spoke. Orlo could sense that Knox was thinking about his past. "Thank you," Orlo said, breaking the quiet.

"You are welcome, Orlo. Do not stay up too late. Poppy would like us to leave early for the Gathering."

"I won't," Orlo answered. He watched as Knox climbed down the stairs and into their tower. Once he was out of sight, Orlo removed the object from behind his back. The once nicely proportioned snowflake was now a smashed mess of copper.

Orlo laid his head back on the soft grass and listened to the steady drip from the stalactite above—a metronome keeping the rhythm of life in the Conclusus. Most of the time, he never paid attention to it. It had always been there, but tonight everything seemed clearer. The rich smell seeping from somewhere underneath the tree's bark and the fragrance of lavender bleeding through his bandage lulled him into a trance. What was it the healer had said about lavender, nighttime and dreams? *Oh yes*, Orlo remembered. *Deeper dreams.* His eyelids grew heavy, challenging the oil to take him to the place where he held his dreams captive. His mind gave into rest as he stepped into what life would be like after the tournament.

He saw himself in a long purple coat with silver buttons lined down the front. Across his chest he wore a darker purple sash, and on the shoulder, the tool that represented the symbol of the inventors. He did not know how the inventors used the gadget with a gear like head and two legs decorated with tiny pipes, but he longed to make it a part of his life. Knox was standing beside him at the center of the Gathering circle, dressed in the finest clothing in all of the Conclusus. A shiny pocket watch dangled from the side of his brocade vest, and a pouch, containing enough to trade for whatever Poppy wanted, swung from his belt. Poppy wore a formal Gathering dress larger and grander than any he had ever seen. It was blue with a billowing crinoline of a lighter blue pouring over layers of more blue taffeta. Her jacket was striped in black and white with a high ruffle collar. On her arms she wore the elbow-length gloves that Knox had given her for her birthday. Across her chest hung the blue sash of the healers. She was stunning.

The fountain behind them billowed steam, moistening the plant life that grew high above them. The fine beads of water sprinkled down upon them, evaporating in the humidity of the cave as it always did before making contact with the Decorum. Knox took Poppy in his arms and spun her around. The silken layers of her dress shifted and crinkled, creating a melody of their own. In the distance, a musician pulled at the bow of his violin generating a tune that warmed Orlo from head to toe.

He was enjoying the warmth, embracing the comfort, and ab-sorbing the luxury of the moment when his hands became icy cold. He removed the white gloves from his fingers to see a tiny snow-flake embedded in each palm.

Knox and Poppy continued to dance; the mist continued to billow. Orlo's arms felt light, as if they were floating like the great balloons driven by the aeronauts. A shiver traveled from the bot-toms of his bare feet to the tips of his outstretched fingers. Then, as if the tips of his fingers were miniature fountains, tiny snowflakes burst forth from them. He shivered.

Knox and Poppy's dance went on, the music hypnotic as the delicate snowflakes settled on their shoulders and in their hair. *Love is greater than the law*, he thought. A glimmer of light jumped from Poppy's chest. He looked at her more intently...there it was again. The ladybug she wore around her neck began to move. Its tiny wings fluttered as if brought to life by the moment.

Orlo blinked and found himself sitting atop the Hall of Inven-tors with his feet hanging over the edge of the tower, able to see the events taking place below. Onlookers dressed in an array of colors watched longingly as the couple, lost in their own joy, danced as if time belonged to them. In the crowd, he could see everyone he knew—Elder Bednegraine, the healer, Avia, and even Davy. The snow no longer escaped from his fingertips but fell from the sky like sparkling lights in front of a black curtain.

Then in the tapestry of colors below, Orlo spotted an unusual movement. His eyes followed a strange dark shadow as it passed among the spectators, unaware. It stopped suddenly and looked upward to where Orlo sat. He squinted his eyes to get a better look, but he could not make out the image of the figure below him.

Suddenly, he heard a load *crack* followed by terrified screams from below. "The fountain!" someone yelled.

Orlo leaned forward, bracing himself with his right arm so as not to fall. The fountain had split into two crumbling chunks; hot bubbling steam billowed up from the ground, and moving closer, someone in a brown hooded cloak. Orlo craned his neck, this time losing his seating. His body slid off the ledge. With one hand he snatched hold of the wall's knobby surface. His heart pounded, and the ground seemed suddenly farther away. *Oh no!* He was losing his grip!

The cloaked figure stretched out its arms and called his name. "Orlo!"

Orlo sat up straight, panting and sweaty, shadowed by the leaves of the tree. Had he fallen? Was he hurt? No, it was a dream.

And what a dream.

The colors, the music, the cold, the strange figure…it was like he'd truly existed in the reality his mind had created. Even the smell—lavender—had been strong. He touched the palm of his hand, expecting to feel the cold remnant of the icy flakes. He closed his eyes to see if he could return to that place, but it was gone. His heart pounded. Never in his life had he had a dream that realistic.

"Orlo!" Avia's scratchy voice called from the level below him. *Had it been her voice in the dream?* "Have you found my letters yet?" He did not have the words to respond to her. His mind was elsewhere, floating in a haze of memory. "Orlo? Are you up there? Knox said you were up there. Did you find them?"

He shook his head to clear it and chuckled at her persistence. "On my way, Avia!" With the wadded wire shoved into his pocket, he got up to peer over the brick wall that kept the garden in and the eyes of passersby out. Below him the steam-filled streetlights dimly lit the bricked avenues of the Conclusus.

His heart raced. He wanted the moment to come back. He wanted it to be real. *I can make it real*, he thought.

Chapter 8

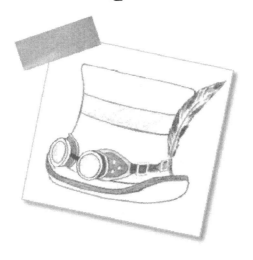

On the morning of any other Gathering, Orlo would have stayed snuggled up under the patchwork quilt Avia had sewn for him when he first arrived at the tower of Knox and Poppy.

But today's Gathering was different—it would change everything.

Although he awoke disappointed that his bizarre dream had not been repeated, his nervous excitement for his imagined life as an inventor pulled him from his bed. After he had officially announced his entrance into the tournament, under the law of the Conclusus, he would be permitted to work on his invention. And if he won, not only would he know that the ladybug had not been an accident, but he would be placed in an apprenticeship away from the Slub and among the Upper Decorum.

He imagined himself dressed sharply as he had been in the dream. A long purple coat with big gold buttons and shiny magnifying spectacles would replace his tweed waistcoat and goggles. He would stand among the other apprentices laughing, showing off the gadgets he had designed to make life in the Conclusus easier. He would go to Preservations in the Hall of Healers as many times as he could—and classes every day! If the inventors did it, then he would overcome his uneasiness of needles. The anticipation welled up inside of him. All he had to do was stand up. He would shock them all! Orlo the deliverer! He could feel his new life beginning to take form.

Orlo reached in his trunk for his nicest trousers, white button-down shirt, and brown velveteen blazer. He noted the worn elbows on the jacket, the threadbare knees of his pants. Poppy kept all of his hand-me-downs mended to the best of her ability. He knew they did not have extra to trade for new Gathering garments, but that was about to change.

"Orlo?"

He jerked around.

"Why, Orlo," Poppy asked, "what must you have been thinking about to be struck with such astonishment?" He gazed at her compassion. "Were you thinking about roller coasters? Airplanes maybe? Knox would say that is precisely why I should not tell you stories about the World," she rambled delicately.

"Actually…" He started to tell her. She would understand. He knew she would. More than anyone else, she would be excited for him, but he'd planned to wait and give her a moment to remember.

"Yes, Orlo. Go on," she pressed cheerfully. "I can see it in those clear eyes of yours. It must be something wonderful. Did you receive orders for a new garden? I love to hear about those, you know."

"I know," he started. "You will find out very soon. It's a surprise."

"A surprise?"

"Yes, for you and Knox, and for Avia. You will see!" He was glad he did not tell her. He could not wait to see their faces when he proudly stepped forward and represented their household in the Festival of Sevenths.

"You are unique, Orlo. Finish dressing and come on up. Avia is in the kitchen making breakfast. We can't be late for the Gathering!"

Orlo reached for the vial of lavender oil by his bedside table. Poppy inhaled the soft flowering fragrance as Orlo lifted the cork.

"I put that on my pillow every night," she said. "It helps me sleep…and gives me the most lovely dreams."

Orlo wondered if she dreamed about the World. When she'd first arrived, the elders insisted she be assigned. Orlo remembered watching from the roof of the Hall of Orphan Care with the other curious children as she presented herself to the elders and gardener on the steps of the Hall of Keepers. He was sure that everyone in the Conclusus was watching in anticipation as the woman from the World was assigned. He did not know her then, and at the time, even he thought she was an unwelcomed addition to the Conclusus.

The gardener assigned her to be a collector. If Orlo were free to second-guess him, which was against the law, Orlo would have thought Poppy to have the gifting of a healer. But even if she had shown the gifting of a healer, she could not be assigned as such, because she was from the World. In his dream, though, she'd been dressed in blue like the healers. It was hard to see her otherwise now.

Orlo had no more than sat down at the table when Avia shoved a plate of ripe blueberries and grilled bread in front of him. "Eat," she commanded. He quickly piled the fruit on top of his toast and took a bite. He loved the way the berries popped inside of his mouth when he ate them. Orlo checked the clock on the wall. They needed to leave in a few minutes if they were to arrive early.

Orlo went to take another bite when he felt Avia observing him. When their eyes met, she went back to deseeding a brilliantly red pomegranate. She did not have the gifting of interpretation, but she did have an uncanny ability to read his emotions. Today, he knew she was reading the excitement that was spread over every millimeter of his face.

"You had a dream, didn't you, Orlo?"

How she determined that by the way he ate his toast was beyond him, but he would not lie. "Yes." He hoped she would not ask him any more questions. Knox and Poppy would be coming up any minute.

"Did you dream about my Q? Such a lovely thing is the Q. It fit snuggly by my U, but then they took them away, Orlo. Is that what you dreamed about? Did He show you where to find them?"

"No, Avia, I'm sorry, but I didn't dream about your letters."

"Well, that's all right. The Mysterium will help you find them." Orlo did not respond, he continued to chew his toast, hoping Knox would walk in and give him reason to change the subject of their conversation.

The crashing of Avia's chair against the floor made Orlo jump. She reached across the table and grabbed his pale cheeks with her pomegranate-stained fingers. Her eyes were fierce and her lips quivering. "They don't know what they have done, Orlo. It's all wrong. You will find them, He told me, Orlo! He told me!" She released his cheeks, but it still felt wet where she'd grabbed him.

"Is everything all right in here?" Knox ran into the room. "Mother, are you okay?"

"Oh, I'm fine," she said as if the confrontation had never happened. "I slipped on a seed, that's all."

She had lied. Orlo was stunned. Now, he was to report her to the elders, but what would they do to her? Send her to The Works? She would die in her loneliness without Knox and Poppy. She often spoke unusual statements and confused her wording, and when she did it was passed off as a mistake of the elderly. Orlo hoped this was the case.

"Isn't that right Orlo?" she asked.

If he agreed, then he would also have lied and broken a law. If he disagreed, he would have to do his best to explain what had happened. His eagerness melted into worry, but worrying was against the law, so he tried to think of something else.

"Are you in a hurry this morning, Orlo?" Knox asked with his usual chuckle. Orlo breathed a sigh of relief, thankful that he'd been spared an impossible decision. Knox dressed in his finest garments for the Gathering, which also happened to be what he wore to fulfill his daily orders. His work attire was nicer than any of the Gathering attire worn by the other men of the Lower Decorum. With a few exceptions, his goggles replaced by a charcoal gray top hat, and his brown work gloves exchanged for black ones, he looked the same as he did every day. "How's the hand?"

"Much better, thank you."

"Mother," Knox said, "you look lovely as ever. I'm glad you are well."

"Humph," she grumbled. "This dress gets tighter every week! Tight sleeves, slips and girdles…I don't believe the Mysterium would care one bit if I tossed the whole lot of it off the roof!"

"I do not believe it is the dress, Mother. Maybe you have been sneaking a few too many peaches from the garden," Knox added.

"Mind your own, son," she said as she sucked her stomach in tightly.

"It's not so bad," Poppy said, entering the room and adjusting the simple hat that was positioned at an intentional tilt on her head. "I think Gatherings are quite lovely."

Orlo thought she looked beautiful in her Gathering attire, even if it was plain and colorless. Her dress was a fluffy version of her work clothing, but despite its rugged beauty, she was the most beautiful in all of the Conclusus—more beautiful than Elder Bednegraine. As was required of all ladies, especially at the Gatherings, she had her hair bundled and off her neck as best she could—for her, a simple braided knot at the back of her neck. If she had been born in the Conclusus, he believed her hair would be as long as the other women who were able to twist and pile their locks into extravagant works of art on top their heads. On her arms, she wore the gloves Knox had given her. All the women of the Conclusus wore gloves on Gathering Day. The wearing of gloves fell somewhere under the laws governing women, but Orlo had never understood their purpose.

"Are we ready?" he asked excitedly.

"Don't you want more to eat?" Poppy asked.

"No thanks," Orlo said, brushing the crumbs off of his cheek with the back of his sleeve.

"Orlo, not hungry?" Knox asked. "Stranger and stranger you are becoming." Orlo bit the insides of his cheeks. His excitement was returning. Today was his day. How could he possibly eat when the thought of a life of feasting was merely a tournament away?

Orlo grabbed his hat, pulled on his boots, and opened the door for the ladies to pass before him. Knox followed behind, giving Orlo a questioning glance.

To Orlo, everything seemed brighter today. The cave ceiling glowed with the rising mist, the lush gardens overflowing from the towers above them were greener, and the air smelled fresher. In the far distance the rhythmic banging and clanging of instruments had already begun, beckoning participants to the fountain. All around them, the Lower Decorum emerged in their finest clothing. From the back of the Conclusus, the colors of tans, whites, creams and ivories filled the streets.

Orlo was amazed that a pair of gloves could make a lady feel more important. Poppy looked brighter today with her glove-adorned arm nestled in the crook of Knox's elbow. She held her head high and nodded pleasantly to their neighbors. Knox didn't have to work today, nobody did. It was against the law. The elders at one point had debated that particular law, since without Knox doing his job, they walked.

The closer they neared to the fountain, the bigger and brighter the dresses of the ladies in the Upper Decorum became: the interpreters in their canary yellow, the educators in citrusy oranges, the messengers in ruby reds, the healers in cobalt and royal blue, and the inventors in deep velvety purples. For the men of the Upper Decorum, the hats were higher and their colored vests embroidered with golden threads and adorned with brass buttons. From head to toe, they were all covered in embellishments of their assignment's coloring.

The Conclusus had been constructed in such a way that on Gathering Day, should every person conscious of the law be on time, the Lower Decorum would never have to pass the Upper Decorum.

"You'd think we could have a bit of food before all of the hullabaloo. I might starve before the day is done," Avia groaned, gripping Orlo's arm tighter.

"Did you not eat breakfast, Mother?" Knox whispered.

"Of course not," she said, loud enough for the Upper Decorum to hear, "why would I do that?" Orlo bit his lip to keep from laughing.

Orlo was not envious at the site of all the apprentices emerging with the Upper Decorum; he was anxious—anxious to be one of them. Sitting through the Gathering was going to prove difficult, because he would not be able to pull a few trinkets from his pocket to satisfy his anticipation.

He watched the orange bustle of an educator bounce from side to side. He chuckled—louder than he had intended—but it was not he who the educator saw and suspected, it was Poppy. A swift elbow to the lady by her side and the two puffy balls of tangerine taffeta were casting glimpses back to Poppy with snickers and giggles, but she did not seem to care or notice.

Knox, however, lifted his chin and escorted her unashamedly into the Gathering.

Chapter 9

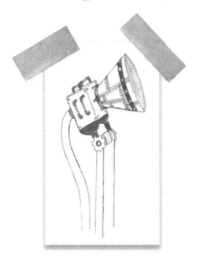

As they entered the Gathering, Elder Bednegraine greeted them. Orlo held tightly to his thoughts. "Good day, Poppy," she said, extending her yellow-gloved hand. "You look absolutely lovely! Oh and your gloves! Are they new?"

"They were a gift," Poppy replied, smiling up at Knox.

"A wise choice from our aeronaut."

"You look lovely as well, Elder Bednegraine. I do not believe I have seen a Gathering dress quite like it!"

Orlo thought she looked like a gigantic lemon. The brightness of the yellow combined with bits of golden beads that had been sewn throughout every layer was blinding. "Are those buttercups from your garden?"

"Yes!" she exclaimed. "I am so thankful someone noticed. It would have been a complete waste of my designer's time had someone overlooked them. It took her five hours to sew them on. She serves so well. And do you recognize this?" she asked, tilting her head. Her reddish hair was twisted into what Orlo thought resembled a pineapple, and attached to the side was a giant sunflower.

"Remarkable! Is it the one I collected yesterday?"

"It is the very one," she whispered as if Poppy were the only person who should hear.

"You are sure to catch the eye of everyone who passes."

"And you are too sweet, Poppy!" Her eyes shifted to Orlo. "I see you have been with our healers. Are you well?"

"The lavender seems to be helping," Orlo answered hesitantly.

"Lavender? Are you certain this is what the healer prescribed?"

"Yes ma'am. I mean no. The healer prescribed something else, but in the Apothecary—"

"I see," she interrupted. "No need to explain further. Poppy, I would like to meet for tea this week. Would an afternoon suit you?"

"Of course, that would be lovely," Poppy said excitedly. "We would be honored."

"Then it is settled." She calmly fanned herself with one hand. "Enjoy the Gathering."

The four found their way into the Gathering where long rows of wooden benches had been arranged the night before in a grand semi-circle in front of the fountain facing the Hall of Keepers. The seven back rows stretched from the Hall of Educators to the Hall of the Interpreters. Among the Lower Decorum, it was nearly impossible to see who was sitting on the far end of the rows.

Because Poppy worked for an interpreter, and their tower was in line behind Elder Bednegraine's, they usually sat on her side of the circle. In front of the benches, organized into seven sections by assignment, were seven more rows of hand carved chairs for the Upper Decorum. At the top of the hall's wide staircase, colorfully upholstered chairs were lined up for the elders. For the gardener, a podium had been positioned at the front. If Orlo stood, he could see the green of the gardener shaking hands with the elders—specifically the purple clad inventor with shadowy eyes and sunken cheeks, Elder Archivald. Orlo studied the inventor, watched the conversation take place, and imagined what his life would be like if the elder knew him by name. The two talked a bit longer and then the gardener turned to casually wave at an acquaintance in the audience down below. Gatherings were the only occasion at which Orlo got to see the gardener.

The gardener appeared once a week for the Gathering, spoke at the festivals, and oversaw the Ceremony of Assignments. His apprentices and the elders were the only ones permitted to speak to him. His life was private, separate, and in Orlo's mind, lonely. If the Decorum knew that Knox had transported the gardener outside the Hall of Keepers, it would have created as much controversial conversation as the burning down of L923.

Orlo wondered why they called it the Hall of Keepers instead of the Hall of Gardening. Maybe it was because, unlike every other tower in the Conclusus, nothing grew on top of the Hall of Keepers that he could see. No flowering vines cascaded over the edges of the brick walls, no landscaped hedgerows and decoratively arranged plant life. The building was as much a mystery as the life of the gardener.

Knox shook hands with those in their Decorum who were near them. He appeared to know many people, both in the Upper and Lower Decorum. Poppy delicately extended her arm to receive a kiss of welcome on the back of her gloved hand from their neighbor, James—a timer whose assignment it was to determine the best time for planting in the gardens. Orlo could not take his eyes off of Poppy. He was completely intrigued by her elevation of spirits. She was rarely in a foul mood, but this was different. If she had been dressed in blue, she would be the Poppy from his dream. He surveyed the area hoping that Elder Bednegraine, her apprentices, or any of the other interpreters had not heard his thought.

Sounds of chatter and the warm hum of the stringed instruments filled the air. Elder Manis, the elder of the musicians, stepped up to the podium with his light blue sash draped across his suit and tied into a fluffy knot at the top. The knot fell in front of his face when he moved. He raised his hand and flicked his wrist dramatically. As the Decorum, Upper and Lower, rose to their feet, the knot fell back into place. Even at his height, Orlo could barely see over the sea of hats in front of him.

The twenty-two musician's apprentices filed up to the top two steps in two rows of eleven. Their soft blue Gathering attire glittered and sparkled in the fountain's mist that swirled around them. The elder flicked his wrist again, the music swelled, and all the Decorum joined in singing an arrangement of words in a haunting melody that Orlo knew well. His mind felt numb and his heart steadied as he was pulled into the trance created by the music. In his raspy voice, the elder sang with them, flipping his wrists back and forth. The song came to an end, leaving the Decorum awestruck with silence.

Orlo had once learned in classes that if the musicians were successful in their leading, the Mysterium would be with them. Poppy had told him that this was not true, and that God was always with them. Knox had gently quieted her by clearing his throat. Her beliefs on the Mysterium seemed somewhat unlawful to Orlo.

He looked across the valley of colors to see if the Mysterium had appeared, but no sooner than the song had ended, the elder flipped his wrist and the Decorum sat back down. The women fanned away the steamy humidity, and the Lower Decorum craned their necks in anticipation of the gardener's presence.

The musicians' apprentices returned to their seats in their section of the Gathering, and the elder took his seat behind the podium beside his fellow elders.

A girl Orlo had seen once in classes stepped up to the voice amplifier in her crimson Gathering dress. Her pursed lips boasted a confidence worn by the apprentices of the Upper Decorum. "Conclusus—" Her small voice projected across the crowd. "May I present our 143rd gardener!"

The Conclusus rose to their feet once again with controlled pride. They clapped their hands; a few of the men took off their hats and bowed as the gardener stepped to the podium.

His black top hat was banded with a green satin ribbon, his matching coat embroidered with tiny golden bees. Across his chest, he wore a green sash, elegantly adorned in a swirling pattern of gold and silver beadwork. His sophisticated attire and gleamed under the glowing mist that surrounded them, but his cleanly shaven face showed no signs of arrogance. His smile was pleasant and approachable. When he spoke, his words were so controlled and pointed that it was as if the towers leaned in to hear the correct enunciation of his every word.

His words were the words that the people of the Decorum, both Upper and Lower, would embrace as their personal message for the week. The oration would push them through their days, give them topic for conversation, and for some, debate. It was a bit of wisdom they reflected on and reminded one another to put into practice until the next Gathering.

Nine years earlier, when the previous gardener had publicly stated that he was retiring to the Hall of Resting, the entire Conclusus went into a tizzy. He had no children among the apprentices to step into the assignment, and there was no system in place for selecting one without an heir. Orlo was a child when it had happened, but he remembered the tension as the ten apprentices were confined to the Hall of Keepers with the elders for three days. Then, for the first time in the life of Conclusus, the apprentices to the gardener believed that they had a chance for succession despite having no blood relation to him. When the new gardener was finally chosen, his ascension to the assignment had created such a stir in the Conclusus that when it was all said and done, the elders made a law that all private discussion regarding the new gardener stop.

The Decorum waited with eyes wide for their gardener to speak.

"Decorum of the Conclusus," the gardener started. He looked uncomfortably across the rows of seated spectators, up to the height of the fountain where it spewed the steam that lit their days and kept them warm, and then back down to those seated in front of him. He hesitated, cleared his throat, and glanced over to the area where the messengers were seated.

Orlo shifted in his seat. This disappearance of the gardener's confidence was unsettling. By the rustle of taffeta, Orlo could hear that others were also disturbed with the gardener's seemingly unrehearsed presentation.

The gardener cleared his throat again. "We know that the Mysterium causes all things to work, um…" he stopped and scanned the group. *Who's he looking for?* Orlo wondered. A sheen of sweat glistened above the gardener's eyebrows. He adjusted his posture. "For, um, good to those who love…um, the Mysterium." There were whispers behind him from the elders.

Orlo had never heard anything like this. *Love the Mysterium?* What was he talking about? Where was the lesson on obedience and adherence to the law? The anticipation of the tournament's announcement was making it too difficult to concentrate on this new teaching. The teaching of the gardener rarely varied from the Decorum's responsibility to the Conclusus—with an occasional focus on a specific law. The gardener shifted back and forth on his feet. He removed a silken green handkerchief from this chest pocket, wiped the sweat from his forehead and continued. "And anyone who does not act on the words that the Mysterium speaks is like a…like a man who builds his house on sand," he stuttered.

What is he talking about? Orlo thought. *We don't build houses. Maybe he isn't well. Maybe he should see a healer.*

The gardener stared into the multitude, cleared his throat, and started again. "We are one, brought together under these walls to serve the Conclusus." Instantly, the murmuring ended and the people sat up straighter in their seats. This was normal. This was right. "As the settlers of this garden embedded it around the fountain, we will serve. We will serve with gladness, with a kind heart, not forgetting our Decorum in order that we may grow and thrive," he said flatly and without expression. "And let us not worry, for it is against our law."

He closed his eyes; the people followed his lead.

"Impenetrable Mysterium, thank you for the light by which we live. May that light live within each one of us as we dwell upon Your word."

What? Orlo thought, looking up from his meditation. *Your word?* In all of his years, he had never witnessed a teaching that strange. By the reaction of the Conclusus, he was not the only one that thought so.

The gardener sat down beside the other elders. At every other Gathering, a proud supportive clapping would have praised the teaching, but this time he received a handful of muffled pats. "That was rather odd," Knox whispered to Poppy. She smiled but did not respond.

"I thought it was entertaining to watch them stir," Avia tried to whisper.

Orlo had to admit it was interesting.

The announcements were next. Orlo rubbed his sweating palms on his pants as he waited for the messengers to take the stage. He wished he had something to tinker with—the passing time was making him anxious, nervous, and excited all at once. Announcements could take a long time, depending on which apprentice was giving them.

And he knew they would save the announcement of the tournament for last.

The apprenticed messenger returned to the stage. "Thank you, gardener, for that lovely presentation." It was clear to Orlo that her words had been rehearsed. The gardener's words were anything but lovely. It was clear that in the ears of the Conclusus, his message was awkward, puzzling, unrehearsed, and different.

"Ladies and Gentlemen," she said, her smile wide and her arms outstretched, I present to you…the elder of the messengers!"

With more clapping, the Decorum returned to their feet once again and welcomed a man dressed all in red—from the ascot he wore around his neck to his pointed shoes. The man held his hand up in the air, palm out. He clenched it tight, and before Orlo could blink, a door appeared out of thin air.

The Conclusus cheered wildly. The messengers were the door creators to the World. Had Knox not returned with Poppy, he might be the one standing up there. The man knocked on the door. The handle turned slowly. Orlo could hardly stand it. He knew this was it. They were bringing the announcement. He scooted to the edge of his seat, ready to stand up.

The door swung open. Orlo was on his feet struggling to see the display in front of them. The elder's wife squeezed her wide, red glittery dress through the door on the stage. With her arms out to her sides, she twirled around and shut the door behind her. It vanished from sight.

Again, the Conclusus cheered as the couple did their best to portray humility before a hungry audience. "Gardener, Elders, Decorum of the Conclusus…we hold in our hands an invitation!" she spoke into the amplifying device.

"My dear, the proclamation," the husband said, giving her a gentle bow and a wink. The wife handed him the envelope, her wide eyes focused on the audience. He gently lifted the golden wax seal and read:

"It is hereby decreed that every seventh year within the seventh month, a festival shall be held to honor the giftings of the Decorum in our fair Conclusus, and shall be known as the Festival of Sevenths. It is on this day that we will honor the giftings given to us by the Mysterium through exhibition and demonstration. It will be a day of celebration and joy to honor the kindness He has gifted us to serve.

On this day, we shall not overlook the lesser assignments of our Decorum, those whose giftings are not as present, but are necessary for our survival. In their honor, we will hold the Tournament of the Inventors. To the victor, an apprenticeship. One representative per household may participate until the next seventh.

We will serve,
The elders of the Conclusus."

Orlo waited impatiently for the word to stand. His feet tapped the ground; his clutched hands shook. He imagined the joy on the faces of Knox and Poppy when he jumped to his feet. They would support him and be proud of him. He would make their lives better.

The husband folded the envelope, and looked at his wife lovingly. She nodded and grinned. In unison they said, "Let the participants stand!"

Orlo pushed off proudly, but then felt a slight tug on the back of his jacket from Avia. She nodded to where Knox stood.

He was already on his feet, proud to represent their household.

Chapter 10

Orlo slumped on the bench in shock as men, women, and children, all around him stood to represent their household. Nearly all of them were from the Lower Decorum, with the exception of a few children—musicians, artists, and observers—who most likely had been identified with a practical gifting, but whose parents were encouraging them to compete for the prized apprenticeship. *It was supposed to be me*, Orlo thought. *This is wrong.*

"Ladies and Gentlemen," the messenger's wife squealed with delight. "We have our participants!" As was tradition, the Upper Decorum turned around to face those standing from the Lower.

Orlo fought back tears. Crying was not something he had been allowed to do in the Hall of Orphan Care, so he had not made a habit of it when he came under guardianship. Everything he had built up in his mind vanished. He would have to spend seven more years in the Slub, delivering. *Maybe the gardener had gotten it right,* Orlo thought, accepting that his fate was pre-determined. *It was fidgeting. That's all it was.*

The elder grabbed his wife's hand. They raised their clutched hands declaring their own victory as the Decorum continued their praise. "Would the participants," the wife started.

"And your household," the husband continued.

"Join your elders at the front of the Hall!" the messenger's wife finished. As if on cue, the elders in the back rose to their feet, the gardener stepped forward, and the messengers stepped back in line with the others.

Orlo watched as Knox took Poppy's hand in his and kissed it. She was crying. This had been as much a surprise to her as it was to him. Knox linked his arm inside Poppy's and lovingly escorted her to the aisle that led to the Hall of Keepers.

"Let's go," Avia stated. "We are household!"

Orlo did not move. His mind was stuck in disbelief.

"Hmmm," Avia frowned, "disappointment, sadness—those aren't good for you, Orlo. It'll sort out. He'll sort it out. Come on now, we're going to have to catch up! I've got some words for the gardener!"

"Oh," Orlo said. He foggily moved out of his row with Avia holding onto the back of his jacket. He pushed through the crowd until they were directly behind Poppy and Knox. Nearly the whole Lower Decorum stood in line with their participants. For some, this was an opportunity to speak into an amplifying device, or to shake the hand of the gardener—there was no intention of entering the tournament. Therefore, there would be no way of telling how many participants there would be until the Festival of Sevenths.

As a household they climbed the steps, one by one, inching their way to the top. Orlo could hear the murmurs of the Upper Decorum conversing with one another and not giving attention to the voices of participants being projected through the voice-amplifying device. He did not want to be there, not like this, not as an orphan placed in guardianship. He had envisioned himself walking proudly up the steps as Orlo the participant, not as Orlo the deliverer.

"Earl Afterly, collector." The voice reverberated over the Decorum.

There was a minuscule break, and then another name. "Toby Smith, deliverer." Orlo recognized him from the Slub. He was a year or two older than Orlo and had more dints and scrapes on his cartagon than any of the other deliverers.

The names continued as they climbed—a timer, a water bearer, and even a guardian, announcing that they would compete for the chance to apprentice as an inventor in the Decorum. All it would take was one marvelous invention that would serve the Conclusus.

They were next in line. Orlo watched as Knox pointed out the Hall of Inventors to Poppy. Her glow made it evident that she was proud of her husband's decision to increase their order. *It could be good for them*, Orlo thought. *It could be good for all of us.* Despite his attempts to convince himself to be happy for Knox, his chest ached with disappointment.

"Lyla von Smoot, apprentice to the inventors!" The proud pitchy voice, the same one he'd heard in the Apothecary, halted the babbling. She grinned smugly in her purple dress. She kissed her hand, extended it to the inventors, and bowed.

"She can't do that," Poppy whispered. "It's cheating!"

"Dear, what is this *cheating*?" Knox asked.

"The proclamation stated that the tournament is for those of the Lower Decorum. If someone enters who is already trained as an inventor then she has an advantage. You know…misleading, tricking, cheating!" she explained.

"One day I will understand all of your funny words. If the gardener approves her entry, then we must accept it," Knox said, nodding to the elder of the inventors who had stepped up to shake the hand of the gardener.

By the time Knox had approached the amplifying device, the Decorum had lost all interest in the rest of the participants. Orlo had an odd temptation to bump him out of the way and shout his own name to the Decorum. He quickly pushed the thought away and glanced up at the section of interpreters to see if Elder Bedne-graine had heard his thoughts.

"Is it allowed?" Orlo heard a healer ask.

He hoped his thoughts had been covered by the confusion that Knox's entrance had created. His candidacy was apparently more controversial than the apprenticed interpreter's.

"Surely not," another gasped. A few more forthright comments, and Orlo realized that it was not Knox creating the ruckus, especially when he heard them call her "North."

"Knox Dumont, aeronaut," he said, leaning down into the cone shaped mouthpiece of the device. His name echoed across the Conclusus. Poppy held tightly to his arm. From the top of the stairs, Orlo could see the water that dripped from the colossal sta-lactite creating ripples in the small pool on top of the fountain as well as he could see the Upper Decorum watching his household. Like Orlo, they saw the man who had once been one of them, who was now competing to be one of them again. If he won, he would be bringing the woman from the World with him. They would have to accept her.

Orlo understood why Knox had to compete. He, like Orlo, sought more for his life and for Poppy.

Orlo's head swam as the whispers and gossip whirled up to him. He forced his body to move behind Knox, Poppy, and Avia to where the gardener stood with a messenger and a girl he had never seen before.

"Allow me to introduce my family," the gardener said with a smile. "This is my wife, Evangeline, and my daughter, Sima. We are pleased with your willingness to participate."

"Thank you, Gardener," Knox said. There was an awkward si-lence between them.

"Well then, please, introduce your family," the gardener said.

Orlo's mind was on his future. He was not in the mood for fancy introductions from the reclusive gardener.

"Of course. This is my bride, Poppy, my mother Avia, and our..." Orlo was accustomed to uncomfortable introductions. Most of the time he did not know what to call himself either.

"It is Orlo—Orlo our deliverer—is it not?" the gardener interjected.

He knows me?

For gracious sakes! Shake the man's hand! The voice came, not from his ears, but inside his head. *Shake his hand!* The girl at the gardener's side glared at him. It was her—his daughter.

*But you're a...*he started to communicate back.

"Is everything all right, Deliverer?" The gardener flashed a warning look at his daughter.

Knox elbowed him in the side. "Yes, sir. I apologize, Gardener. It is my pleasure to meet you."

"The Mysterium desires the best for your household. Well wishes to your participant." Orlo took his hand and shook it, but he couldn't tear his eyes from the gardener's daughter.

He tried to talk to her again the way she had spoken to him. *Your father, he's the gardener, and you're his apprentice...*

The apprentice rolled her eyes. *Mind your own, Deliverer.*

This girl intrigued Orlo. She was the gardener's daughter and apprenticed to be his successor, but her gifting was that of an interpreter. For a minute, the music seemed to have ended, the voices silenced, and the gentle hiss of the steam pouring from the fountain was without sound. What if she were like him? What if she could do something else? What if the gardener had gotten it wrong with his own daughter? Could it be true? If he had given his own daughter the wrong assignment, it would make sense that Orlo had been wrongly assigned as well.

Then, she was in his head. *Stop thinking, now!* she insisted. *If you must, think on what you know is true. Do you understand?* She glared at him. *Change your thoughts!*

But, you're breaking the law! The idea of the daughter of the gardener being removed from the Conclusus was unimaginable.

Deliverer, there are things beyond your knowledge. For the last time...mind your own! He absorbed every detail of who she was—afraid that he would never see her again. Her black hair was pulled off her neck, sprouting in twisted curls that stuck up like tree branches on the top of her head, and her dress reminded him of an

75

oversized garden shrub. Like her father's vest, her gown was embroidered with tiny gold bees. Her eyes were a shade of blue that could easily be mistaken for purple, and her cheeks were flushed with pale pink.

Stop looking at me, Deliverer. You are drawing attention to yourself! she hissed in his head.

What do you mean beyond my knowledge? You heard my thoughts? Can you help me? Orlo thought back, but Avia's wise voice interrupted his thoughts and unintentionally projected out into the onlookers.

"You know where they are don't you?" she asked the gardener firmly.

"Mother!" Knox nearly shouted. "Now is not the time!"

"He does," Avia said with her hands on her hips. Poppy had her hand on Avia's back, trying to usher her away gracefully, but Avia planted her feet firmly in front of the gardener. "I know he does! He knows where they are! He more than said he did! Didn't you hear him say it?"

"Mother, there is no telling what you heard," Knox said cautiously. "Gardener I am terribly sorry. We beg your forgiveness."

Make her stop, the girl begged Orlo. *You must make her stop!*

But Orlo didn't know what was best to do or say.

"Avia, will you tell me about the letters when we get back to the tower?" Poppy asked softly.

Avia jerked her arm away from Poppy. "No! Listen here. I can hear as well as the lot of you. I heard what you said, Gardener!"

"Mother, please," Knox begged. "Not now, let's go."

"He knows where they are," she grumbled. "I don't know how, but he has found my letters. Orlo is going to help you get them. He told me." Knox and Poppy turned their heads to him questioningly.

"I didn't say that. Avia, you've made a mistake," Orlo insisted. The Decorum was latching on to the scene being played out before them. Their eyes were glued on his household. Orlo felt the interpreters tuning into his thoughts.

Avia's voice softened to a whimpering plea. "It's true, Gardener. Orlo will find my letters, won't you, Orlo?"

Silence fell on them. It was as if the Conclusus were waiting for him to answer.

"Avia, I'm sorry, but I can't find your letters."

She stomped her foot. Her crinkled lips turned downward into a sorrowful frown. She choked on her words. "It was a pleasure to meet you, Gardener."

"You as well, Madam." Orlo could see the sympathy in his eyes. After all, he was the gardener. He understood matters that no one else could, or perhaps he had seen this with his own mother.

Orlo trudged behind his household as they stepped down the long staircase. All eyes were on them. No one seemed to be aware that more participants were announcing their entry or shaking the gardener's hand. He glanced back at the apprentice who was pleasantly shaking the hand of an observer.

She did not look at him, but he heard her. *Mind your thoughts, Deliverer. They can hear everything. They know everything. Think on what you know to be true.*

Chapter 11

Orlo sat in the back corner of the classroom—his thoughts a muddled mess of what could have been and what was true. With his left hand bandaged and resting on the desk, and his right in his pocket fidgeting with fragmented pieces of metal, he fought against the bitter reflections of the day before. "Think on what you know to be true," she had said. "They know everything."

The whole day, including the apprentice's thoughts, had not made a bit of sense. What had she meant by, *They know everything?* Who were they, and what did they know? Maybe they knew that he was supposed to be representing their household in the tournament, not stranded for another seven years to work in the Slub.

He sighed. Even his future in the Slub was not guaranteed if his hand did not heal soon. However, the longer it took his hand to heal, the more days he would get to spend in classes.

From his seat by the window he could see Knox's balloon floating over the tops of the towers. Orlo wondered whose voice sought Knox's listening ear today. This was why Orlo liked to sit in the back of classes—here, he had the best view of the Conclusus. Orlo craned his neck to see if he could see Poppy working in Elder Bednegraine's rooftop garden.

Before he had walked out the door, Poppy reminded him to be home in time for tea. Elder Bednegraine had sent word by one of her apprentices that she would be stopping by for tea in the afternoon, and she would like Orlo to be present. The memo said it was a routine visit to see how Orlo was adjusting to his guardianship. In all the years Orlo had been under the guardianship of Poppy, they had never had a "routine visit."

This was another thing to add to his list of the unexpected: Knox had announced his participation in the tournament, Avia had declared in front of the Decorum that Orlo was going to find her missing letters, and the gardener's daughter who was assigned as his apprentice had the gifting of the interpreters.

He looked around the room to see if any of the interpreter's apprentices were in classes today. The excitement of the Festival of Sevenths overtook the chatter of the students dressed in their classes attire. The boys wore black vests with their nicer slacks. Around their necks and neatly tied under their collars were silken scarves depicting their apprenticeships. For the girls, color coordinating their outfits was as much fun as it was for their apprenticeship. Orlo could have guessed the assignment of the girl in front of him without looking at her blue attire, though. He could smell her—a healer. Her herb-scented clothes decorated her with blue from top to bottom—from the mini-top hat that was tied on with a large blue bow to the blue spats that covered her boots. Like all of the other girls under the age of thirteen, her skirt was permitted to rest at knee length, unlike their mothers' which covered the ankles and at times dragged the ground behind them.

The room was as colorful as the students in it. Banners depicting the symbols of each of the apprenticeships lined the walls, and at the front a gigantic wooden plaque read: Laws of the Conclusus. Along with every other child in the Conclusus, Orlo had memorized them before he was of the age to be assigned. There were other sets of laws, some specific to women, some to men, and others exclusive to the assignments, but these were the laws for everyone.

The clock on the Hall of Keepers struck. Orlo, along with the other students waited until the full nine chimes rang out, then moved out from behind their desks to recite the Laws:

Do Not Lie

Do Not Complain

Do Not Show or Speak Rudeness

Do Not Ask Unimportant Questions

Do Not Keep Secrets

Do Not Worry

Do Not Disrespect the Elders

Do Not Break the Law

Do Not Work on Gathering Day

Do Not Be Late

Do Not Work Outside of Your Gifting

Orlo adjusted his brown jacket and sat down. He tried to focus on the words of Elder Stockhart, but the inconsistent ticking of the classroom clock—*tick, tick-tick, tick, tick-tick-tick, tick* replaced her words until all he could hear was the clock's error. He looked out the window toward the Hall of Keepers and back at the clock hanging on the wall. It was off by two seconds. His mind began to swirl with the possibilities of the timekeeper's ailment. *No*, he thought. *Think on what is true. You are a deliverer. You make deliveries. You don't have the gifting to solve the problems of the inventors.*

Elder Stockhart stood proudly at the front of the bricked room. The light gleamed in on them from the rising steam outside, illuminating the tiny wrinkles that spiked out from the corners of her eyes and lips. Her plump frame was layered in white taffeta from head to toe. It was not full and frilly like a Gathering dress, but hung long and straight like most of the ladies' daily clothing in the Conclusus. Across her chest hung a wide orange sash embroidered with the symbol of the teachers—an oil lamp with a flame protruding from its lip. The hat on her head matched her sash perfectly. Kennedy Wells, a girl at least three years younger than Orlo, sat in front of him wearing the same orange coloring. One day, she would stand before her own class and teach them about the current events of the Conclusus.

"Apprentices," Elder Stockhart said, "Oh, and Orlo! I nearly forgot you were with us today. Welcome. Class, let us welcome Orlo the deliverer."

The class of seventeen turned in their seats to face him. "Welcome, Orlo the deliverer," they said in forced unison. As fast as they had said it, they turned back around. He had known most of them before he was under guardianship, not by name, but by recognition and now assignment. The Greysons—Jax, Catcher, Finn, Lulabelle, Holiday, Petunia, and Rocky—usually sat in front of his household during the Gathering.

"Today's discussion will center on current events," she said with a pleased grin. Normally, the class would groan, but with the forthcoming tournament, there was a stir of excited chatter at her announcement. Orlo leaned his back on the wood railing of his desk chair. Current events was his least favorite subject—especially today. He knew what had happened during the Gathering and was trying hard not to think about it. On the one day he was able to be in classes, he had hoped to be hearing a lesson on science or mathematics.

"Class," Elder Stockhart began, "let us review our current events. Can anyone tell me what the gardener spoke on at the last Gathering?" The class was hushed as students looked from side to side. Orlo knew the answer, but he did not dare raise his hand. He was there to listen.

The teacher-to-be raised her hand.

"Edda, you may rise and speak."

"Elder Stockhart, our beloved gardener, however muddled yesterday, told us that the Mysterium wants us to build towers and live in them; He wants us to plant gardens and eat their produce. He wants our men to have wives and become fathers to sons and daughters. In summary," she said with a smirk, "he wants us to seek the wellbeing of the Conclusus."

"Very well said, Edda. You have unquestioningly been gifted with memory. Class, as Edda has reminded us, we are to seek the wellbeing of the Conclusus."

Orlo did not claim to have been gifted with memory, however it was hard to forget the strangeness of the gardener's message. And as he recalled, the gardener had said very little of what Edda had recited.

"Larry, what can you tell the class about the current events of travel?"

A short round-faced boy with his black scarf tied snugly around his neck wiggled out from behind his desk. On his hat he wore goggles. They were much nicer and cleaner than the ones Orlo wore when he drove his cartagon. Andrew would one day take Knox's assignment. "The inventors are working to increase the size of our balloons. They call them ships, and they will carry up to ten people at one time!"

Orlo was impressed. Knox had not shared this information with him. At most, a family of four could travel comfortably by balloon, and that was if the apprentice was not on board.

"That is most exciting, Larry! We will look onward to that day! Let's see…how about you, Shirley. What is current with the musicians?" Orlo knew she was waiting to call on an inventor's apprentice last.

"Yes, Elder Stockhart. With the help of the inventors, a new instrument has been added to our collection. It has a lovely sound, like a repetitive whistle. The musicians will be debuting it at the next Gathering. Of course, the gardener and the elders must approve it first. But if you ask me, they will not refuse. It is too lovely!"

"Thank you, Shirley, but we must not speculate on what your gardener will approve. His wisdom exceeds all ours, and he knows what is best for the Conclusus."

Shirley plopped down at her desk. Her red face displayed her embarrassment.

Orlo listened attentively as apprentices explained the current events of their assignments. Every time one of them mentioned the inventors, his ears tuned in. Even those students serving with their parents in the Lower Decorum, like the planters and timers, told of marvelous inventions that would make the work of the others easier. Lyla von Smoot smirked with her arms folded in her lap, taking in the accolades of her fellow apprentices. Orlo clenched his fist, struggling not to be angry. Lyla was apprenticed. Her chance at winning the tournament was better than anyone else's. Unlike Orlo, she had nothing to lose. If Lyla lost, she was still an apprentice and he was still a deliverer.

"Let's hear from one of our healers..." Elder Stockhart started. Before the apprenticed healer could get his hand in the air, one of Elder Stockhart's second-year apprentices stepped into the room.

"Pardon me, Elder. I must speak with you...urgently." The older teen glanced over to Orlo and then back at his elder.

"Yes, of course," she said to the teen. "Class, I must step away. Please mind your behavior." Elder Stockhart walked briskly out the door.

"What did the deliverer do?" someone in the front of the room asked without concern for Orlo's being there.

"Don't be daft," Edda butted into their conversation, "deliverers don't do anything. They drive those dirty cartagons all over the place dropping our leftovers off at other gardens."

"I heard a deliverer got trapped in another garden once and never came back," someone else said.

"I heard she decided to stay, and when she came back, they put her in the mines, and she's been there ever since."

Elder Stockhart walked slowly back in front of the room. She forced a smile. "Orlo the deliverer," she said with a tight smile. He could tell that she was doing her best to look unshaken. "Your presence has been requested at the Hall of Keepers. My apprentice will escort you."

The whispering stopped, and silence swept over the students. Every eye in the class watched as he stood up, adjusted his jacket, and walked numbly to the front of the room. The Hall of Keepers was where the gardener's apprentices were trained, where the elders convened, and where the gardener prepared his messages for the Gathering. No one, except the privileged few, had seen the inside of the Conclusus's oldest building. Orlo's heart sunk. Being called before the gardener meant that something was very wrong.

What had he done? Did the gardener know about the ladybug? Had his thoughts been overheard? How much did the gardener know? Orlo had not meant to break the law. It was an accident, a mistake—a mindless attempt to fill his boredom. Or, did the gardener know that Orlo had questioned his assignment? *It was a passing thought. I didn't mean to do it,* he thought.

Orlo could not stop his mind from spinning. The gardener's daughter's words rang in his ears. *They know everything.*

Chapter 12

Orlo followed the apprentice into the light of the Conclusus. If he did not know that he would be breaking the law, Orlo would have turned around, run back to his tower, and hid in the branches of the boswellia tree. How would he explain this to Knox? Orlo had already shocked Knox with the ladybug, and then there was Avia's outburst at the Gathering. What was next? Would he be apologizing from the platform during his own removal ceremony?

The Hall of Keepers stood directly across from the Hall of Educators on the other side of the fountain. It was not a long walk, but to Orlo, it felt like it miles. In the thirteen years of his short life, he had never heard of anyone being called to the Hall of Keepers.

The educator's apprentice stopped at the base of the grand stone steps and looked to the top. "I am not permitted to go farther. An apprentice to the gardener will take you the rest of the way." He nodded to the girl at the top of the stairs.

Orlo started to ask the apprentice if he knew why he had been called, but feared the question would be unimportant to the apprentice and therefore unlawful. "Be well, Orlo the deliverer."

Orlo watched as the young man in orange hurriedly shuffled back to the Hall of Educators. He did not look back. *Here goes,* Orlo thought. He lifted his foot to the first step, and then pushed himself to continue to the next, and the next. As he climbed, he wondered what was going to happen to him, and if maybe Knox and Poppy had already been informed of his summons. What if the Gardner removed him and they were not told? They would believe he had run away. No—removal ceremonies were a public event—they would know.

When Orlo reached the top, a redheaded apprentice to the gardener greeted him. "Orlo, the deliverer?" she asked.

"Yes, ma'am," Orlo replied politely.

"Follow me." Attendants flanking the grand double doors swung them open wide. As soon as Orlo and the apprentice stepped through, the entry slammed shut behind them. Doors lined both sides of the long hallway—each door gilded in glistening silver with one of the symbols of the Upper Decorum. Orlo passed a torch for the messengers, a single flower for the observers, a harp for the musicians, a tool for the inventors, and a dove for the interpreters.

At the end of the vestibule a vault-like door loomed large and unwelcoming. A huge lock with gears and pipes sealed it shut. Above it hung a banner of green silk. Orlo guessed that was where the gardener worked because the beehive of the gardener had been intricately sewn into the fabric by a needle worker or seamstress, along with the words WE WILL SERVE. Everyone in the Decorum lived by those words—to not only seek the wellbeing of the Conclusus, but also to serve their assignments for the preservation of the gardens, so they may be seen as pleasing to the Mysterium.

Orlo had to remind himself to breathe—the grandness of the room was overwhelming. It was far more luxurious than the Hall of Healers—and to him, that had already been a far stretch from the simplicity of his tower. A series of glass balls hung suspended by long poles from the vaulted ceiling, pulling and trapping the steam above him to bring light to the room at any hour of the day. It was the most amazing invention Orlo had seen—a way to harness the steam for light all day long. It could end the need for candles. He wished he could study the plans and learn how they worked.

Orlo followed the gardener's apprentice through a mechanized door where ten desks—five on each side of the room—provided training space for the ten gardener's apprentices. It was said that on any day, one of them could be chosen as the new gardener, but most people knew that unless a gardener was forced into the Hall of Resting, he or she would never let go of the revered assignment. Nonetheless, honor accompanied an apprenticeship to the gardener.

The apprentice turned sharply to him. "Welcome to the Hall of Keepers," she said. "Stay in the area of the hall designated to your visit. Under no circumstances are you to speak to the gardener unless he is directly speaking to you. Touch nothing. Do not disturb the apprentices. Do you understand the terms of the Hall?"

Orlo's mind fought to catch up to the regulations. "Yes, I believe so," he stammered. Her eyes rolled up to his hat. He jerked it off his head and pulled it to his chest.

"Very well, we can proceed."

Orlo started to ask why he had been summoned to the Hall, but the apprentice answered before he could ask. "You have been requested by one of the gardener's apprentices, for what reason I do not know, nor can I imagine. Do you have any questions?"

Orlo shook his head. He did have questions, more than he thought the apprentice would care to answer. Like, did the gardener live here? If Orlo saw him, should he bow? And most importantly, why have a Hall of Keepers when there was no *keeper*?

"Wait here," the apprentice instructed.

Nervousness welled up inside Orlo as he watched the other apprentices busy at their table studying the different aspects of the assignments with intense curiosity. The future gardener would have to know everything in order to properly assign and be able to orchestrate every movement of the growing Conclusus. Orlo watched as one of the apprentices busily sniffed and applied oils to his skin. Instantly, the apprentice was scratching and blowing on the area.

Another apprentice tinkered with what at, one time, might have been pieces of a clock. The hands spun wildly backwards as he dug into the layering of gears. "Crazy thing," the apprentice muttered.

Orlo knew one of them was going to escort him to his fate. He wished they would hurry. The waiting was making him jittery. He reached in his pocket for the fragments he had been tinkering with early in the day, but—realizing that this habit might have led to the ruin he now faced—he crossed his arms across his waist.

At the end of the desks, nearest to the gardener's door, Orlo saw her stand up. It should have occurred to him that she would be here. The gardener's apprentices never, as far as he knew, went to classes. She looked different—her hair was curled and pinned up in such a way that it looked like the coiled wires on the inside of his cartagon. Her black hair reminded him of Poppy's; however her skin was much darker, except for the cheeks, which looked as if she had dabbed them lightly with a strawberry.

The green embellishments on her black taffeta dress swished and jingled as she sauntered towards him.

"What are *you* staring at?" the apprentice snipped.

"I—"

"Mind you own, Deliverer. Of course I do not wear face color! It is forbidden for me, or did you not know that? You probably did not." She rolled her eyes. "Stop trying to figure me out!"

"You're an interpreter?" Orlo asked, confused.

"Of course not, Deliverer! Do you not see my garments? Did you not see where I was sitting?"

"I...um..." Orlo stuttered. He had no idea what to say, what to think, or what not to think. "But your gifting?"

"It is not a gifting. The elders would have assigned me to apprentice an interpreter if I had the gifting, wouldn't they? It is simply a talent. Like your talent." She glanced at his pocket. She knew. That was why he was there. "That is not why you are here," she said more gently. "We shall agree between us two to not make assumptions based on what we do not know. Do you agree?"

"I guess—"

"Good. Would you mind if we talked outside?" Orlo did not have to answer; she had heard him. "If you will be patient, I will explain. This is of utmost importance and is meant for your ears alone." She spoke into his mind, *When we walk through those doors, ask me a question…something about my apprenticeship. Do not think about anything else until we get to the fountain.*

Okay, Orlo thought, becoming more intrigued. She took him by the arm, as if he were intentionally escorting her, and pulled him back toward the door through which he had entered. The large doors swung open. With the apprentice a foot in front of him, Orlo stepped out into the brightness of the Conclusus.

She cleared her throat.

"Oh, right. Do you like it? I mean, being an apprentice to your father?"

"Of all the questions, that is what you came up with?" As they strolled across the circle and to the fountain, they weaved in and out of people in the Upper and Lower Decorum fulfilling their daily orders. "Of course I do. Do you like being a deliverer?"

Orlo had to be careful how he answered her. "Well, I—"

"Of course you do not," she jumped in with a chuckle. "Who would?"

When they arrived at the fountain, the girl surveyed the area before sitting down beside Orlo. The hissing of the pipes pushing the mist up through the fountain was so loud that Orlo had to lean in to hear her. "Orlo the deliverer, there is something you must do for the Conclusus. Will you do it?" she asked.

Orlo knew he did not have a choice. "Yes, Apprentice, um…"

"Sima. You may call me Sima. Do you promise that you will refrain from telling anyone what I am about to ask you to do, including the aeronaut Knox and your guardian, the one they call North?"

Orlo frowned.

"Poppy. I forget that she has a name. I apologize for that error. A good name is to be desired more than great wealth you know."

Where had he heard that before? He wished she would quit reading his thoughts and get on with her request. Interpreting made him uneasy.

"We need you to make a delivery. Actually, it is more of retrieval than a delivery. It once belonged to the Conclusus, but was…it was taken. Can you get it for us?"

"I don't know," Orlo said, looking at his bandaged hand.

"It is not big. Therefore, you will not be driving your cart wagon."

"Cartagon."

"Right, cartagon. You will be going in on foot." Orlo was baffled. Deliveries were never, ever, under any circumstances filled on foot. "This is…different." She looked around, her eyes darting from one passerby to the next.

"How am I supposed to get into this garden?"

"The messenger will let you in."

"But the orders. I have to get my orders, and the clerk, she'll ask why I'm not taking the cartagon."

"This is unlike any delivery you have done before. No orders, and no…no garden."

"Where am I going?"

She looked around nervously once again. "The Works, Orlo."

"The Works!" he nearly yelled.

Orlo's heart raced, his chest tightened, and he felt dizzy. Nobody who had ever gone to Works came back. Once a person was removed, they were gone and never spoken of again. The Works was the place for criminals and lawbreakers. It was directly under the Conclusus, and it was from there that the entire Conclusus was powered. Great pipes and mechanisms churned to create the steam that powered, lighted, and grew everything around them. Now, he was being asked to walk right into the heart of it.

"Orlo, calm down," she said sternly.

"Is it dangerous?" Orlo asked. His mind dove below The Works to the lands known as the mines where dark creatures supposedly roamed. When he had described the stories from his childhood to Poppy, she had called the beings wolves.

"They are not of your concern," she said, once again reading the images created by the stories of his classmates. "The messenger will let you in. Get the package and leave. It should not be difficult."

"Get the package and leave," Orlo repeated. Less than an hour ago he had thought he was being escorted to some unknown miserable fate. Now, he thought he might prefer the miserable fate to this trip to the Works.

"You can do this. I believe that you can, so does my father."

"Your father!"

"Yes." She looked around to see if anyone had heard Orlo's outburst. "Do not let your brain get big," she said with a smirk. "You might start growing hair."

Orlo rubbed his hairless head. He often forgot how different he looked. Knox had once suggested that they take Orlo to see a healer, but Poppy said that God had created Orlo the way he was for a reason. To this day, Orlo did not have a clue as to why the hair on his head would not grow.

He knew, though, that refusing to fulfill the orders was against the law. Nobody ever denied orders. "I'll report to the Slub first thing in the morning. You'll have to let Poppy know that my hand is better and I have been cleared for orders. But wait, that's a lie. What will I tell her?"

"You won't tell her anything," she said. "The messenger is expecting you within the hour. You must go. We do not have much time." Her blank stare told Orlo that she had more on her mind. "They know everything, Orlo. They know about you."

"Who knows what about me?"

"I have to go." She glanced up at the clock on the Hall of Keepers. "So do you."

"Please—what do they know about me?" She nodded towards the pocket where he kept the spare parts. "It's my fidgeting, nothing more!"

"You do not believe that do you, Orlo?" He was caught between telling the truth and exposing himself. "They do not believe it either. Your future depends on that package, Orlo. All of us depend on it."

His mind spun. She was not making sense. She started to walk away, leaving Orlo by the brilliance of the fountain but then turned back. He could not believe what he had heard. But he had heard it, and it had come from her.

You would have won the tournament, Orlo.

Chapter 13

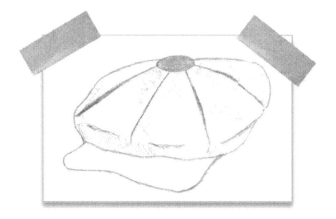

From the fountain, Orlo's walk would be at least half an hour. The Slub was the furthest point from the fountain, and on the complete opposite side of his tower. It felt strange making the walk without his satchel. It felt as much a part of his assignment as his goggles and cartagon—and today he would have to do his job without any of them—unless he could get his goggles at the Slub. He was partly tempted to run back and get his satchel. Orlo checked his watch; there was not enough time.

The mist was at the highest and brightest point it would be all day—collecting above the rooftops before it descended back into the ground to bring in the night. Poppy would be expecting him home for tea with Elder Bednegraine after classes. He would have to make this trip a quick one. A normal delivery, if the other deliverers were on schedule, could take him less than an hour, but that was with his cartagon. On foot, he would need to allow at least three. As he neared the Slub, the large fronds of the coconut trees on the shorter towers partially shaded the walkway. The doors to the Slub were not much further.

His mind bounced back between the secrecy of this assignment and her final thoughts to him: *You would have won.* She had not said you *could* have won, or *it might have been possible* for you to win, she said that he *would have won.* How could she have known such a thing? Maybe she knew the same way "they knew everything." The more he thought about it, the more he considered the idea that the *they*, whoever they were, knew more about him than he knew about himself. She had seemed concerned that someone would hear her. Maybe she was nervous *they* would overhear the conversation. Whatever was going on, he was ready to have it over with and move back to his normal life—the way it used to be before he had learned to dream.

Despite the stories he had heard, Orlo was curious to see The Works. He could not help but speculate as to the type of engines that must be used to push the steam up through the ground. It was something he would normally have shared with Poppy—she would have listened to every detail. The complexity of the Conclusus fascinated her, but the apprentice had warned him not to mention this assignment to anyone. He wondered why something that was good for the Conclusus was being kept secret. The gardener always shared good happenings at the Gatherings.

Orlo approached the large iron doors. Roots burrowed out from the walls breaking and covering the brick archway that had once surrounded it. He pulled it open and stepped inside. The clerk sat shuffling papers behind the counter, and all of the benches were empty except one. *They all must be on break*, Orlo thought, recounting his daily treks home for lunch.

"Hey, mate!" the small voice called. Orlo's talkative companion from a few days prior wildly waved his hat back and forth in the air. Orlo pretended he did not see him. "Mate! It's me! From the other day! You was tellin' me bout L923! Now I got somethin' to tell you!"

Orlo stopped. Sima had said the delivery was urgent; he did not have time for the ramblings of young deliverers, but Orlo feared the boy would interfere with his orders if he did not acknowledge him, so he waved back.

"I thought you weren't seein' me, mate," the boy said, putting his cap back on his sweaty head. "I got some news for ya."

"Is that right?" Orlo asked, looking around nervously. Somewhere in the Slub's dreariness a messenger would create a door to The Works.

"I got a guardian!"

"I'm sorry, what was that?" Orlo asked, distracted.

"Ya asked me if I had a guardian. Well, I got one. Real nice lady…she can't cook, but she's real nice. What ya think?"

"Um, I think…" Orlo could feel the gaze of the clerk on him. "I think I should go."

"Weren't ya listenin'?" he said with hurt in his voice.

Before this got out of hand, Orlo needed the attention off himself. "You got a guardian! That's great!"

The clerk eyed Orlo over her spectacles. The gardener's daughter had said no one could know. Orlo could sense that the boy was a few words away from asking how he planned to drive his cartagon with a burned hand. "What are you doing here?" Orlo asked. "Looks like everyone's on break. Aren't you going back to lunch?"

"Nah, I'm good."

Orlo had a good idea as to why the boy would be there. "She wasn't at her tower was she?"

The boy frowned. "She trades in the Mercor…silk scarves and such. Real nice stuff."

"My guardian used to forget, too. You need to let her know." The boy smiled. "Listen, Avia is in our tower—the back tower to the left, in interpreters' row. If you run, you can make it back in time for your next order."

"The one with the funny tree on the top?"

"That's the one! Have her fix you some lunch, but whatever you do, when she starts talking about her letters, don't ask her any questions. Got it?"

"Got it, mate! Thanks! That's real kind of ya. Thanks again. I owe you one!"

The boy ran off before Orlo could respond.

Orlo checked his pocket watch again. He had to hurry. Since there was no sign of a messenger, he did what he would normally do, check with the clerk.

"Orlo the deliverer, ma'am."

"I know who ya are, Orlo. Ya been here long enough." The lady looked at him oddly. "How's the hand, Deliverer? Didn't expect to see you back for a week or more."

Her cluelessness let him know right away that she was not privy to the gardener's order. He could not lie—he absolutely could not. "I didn't expect to be back either," he said honestly.

She looked down the list of names in front of her. "I don't see ya here, Orlo. There must be a mistake. Where did you say you were going?"

A knot formed in his throat. If he made up a garden name, she would know, and it would be a lie.

She continued to study him. "Whatcha hiding, Orlo? I don't need ya getting me in any trouble with the elders. They'll send me to The Works, that's what they'll do."

"The Works?" Orlo nearly shouted.

"That's right, Orlo…The Works. That's where they send all the ones who mess up, unless ya turn—and then it's off to the mines." Orlo gulped. He had a good idea of what she meant by turn. "So, about ya telling me why you're really here, Deliverer?"

A cold metal hand rested on his shoulder. "You're gonna want these," the man said, holding up Orlo's goggles.

"Davy!" Orlo said, relieved.

"I've been given his orders. I'll take it from here."

"You got his papers?" the clerk asked.

"I must have misplaced them," Davy said, leaning in on the counter. Because of the nature of the orders, Orlo was positive that there were no papers to be misplaced. Unless Davy had carefully crafted his words, he had lied.

"All right, Davy, I'll go along with ya this time, but if you two get me sent to The Works, I'll make sure the both of ya are coming with me."

With his mechanical hand resting on Orlo's shoulder, Davy guided him to his cartagon. "But I don't..." Orlo started to explain the situation.

"Trust me," Davy said.

"You're the messenger!"

"Of course I'm the messenger!" Davy chuckled. "I don't see any of my other kinsman hangin' around the Slub, do you?"

"No, I guess not."

When they were far enough out of her earshot, Davy asked, "So, young Orlo, this is out of your normal. What'd you do to earn the favor of the gardener?"

Orlo did not know how much Davy knew. "I didn't do anything."

"Well, it must have been something good. They don't trust many people."

"They trust you."

"I guess they do," he chuckled.

"Davy, you broke one of the laws, for me. You shouldn't have done that."

"I know better than to break the law, and it ain't because I'm afraid of what the elders might do to me." Orlo could not imagine what it would be like to not fear the elders. "I'd rather please Him, if you know what I mean," he said, pointing his finger to the cave ceiling above them.

"Oh," Orlo said. He had never thought about it that way.

"Truthfully, I did misplace those papers. I misplaced them where nobody else could find them." He patted the chest of his long coat.

Orlo's cartagon was parked securely where he had left it the afternoon of Poppy's birthday. That day seemed far away. "We got to do this one different. I'll make the door here. Once you're gone, I'll drive your cartagon through another door, see?"

"I got it." His nerves must have been evident.

"Orlo," Davy said, glancing back to see if the clerk was looking their way. "Ain't nothin' to be scared about. They're just people down there, like you and me. They can help you if you need it. Tell 'em Davy says hello."

"You've been there?" This was news to Orlo. There had never been a removal ceremony for Davy, and had he been removed, he certainly would not be serving the Conclusus as a messenger.

"Well, I've done opened my mouth too wide. Know this young Orlo, it ain't what you've been told. Remember…"

"They're just people," Orlo said, more as a reminder to himself than to Davy.

"That a boy. I'll create your door straight way. You be ready. Keep a check on the time. I can give you two hours. The Slub should be cleared out about then. I believe that should be enough for whatever they have you doin'."

Two hours, Orlo thought. That should be enough time to get back to Poppy and Elder Bednegraine without suspicion. Orlo considered asking Davy if he knew what he was supposed to pick up, but he decided not to mention it.

"Go ahead and start her up for me while I make the door," Davy instructed. "Then, we'll make the switch."

Orlo nodded.

Orlo opened the door to the cartagon. He pulled knobs and pushed buttons. He checked the water tank. It was three-quarters of the way full—enough to get Davy wherever he was planning to go. He turned the crank. Steam billowed out from underneath and from the top. He hopped out and joined Davy at the front of the cartagon.

"You ready?" Davy asked.

"I suppose I must be," Orlo replied.

"Young Orlo, there's always a choice. Once you're in, keep walking."

"But how will I know what I'm looking for?"

"Beats me," Davy said with a shrug. That was not comforting to Orlo.

Davy placed his hand on the wall. A rapid popping and flashing of light outlined the emerging door. The simple metal door held a heavy wheel, similar to the one that steered his cartagon.

"Give it a push and you're on your way, young Orlo."

A push, Orlo thought. He pushed the door open with his good hand, then looked back to see Davy slowly backing his cartagon with a swish swoosh, swish swoosh.

The door slammed shut behind him before Davy had completely pulled the cartagon out of its hole. As he had expected from his deliveries to the gardens, there was a moment of darkness. He anticipated The Works to be dark and dreary, cold and isolated with people trudging along with great chains wrapped around their ankles as they worked the pipes, praying to the Mysterium that they could return to the comforts of the Conclusus. It was in these thoughts that Orlo felt guilty for wanting more than his life as a deliverer provided.

He moved toward the light until the stone surface of the cave walls changed into massive pipes that pierced the cave ceiling above him. Like he had on his visit to L923, he was seeing something that those walking above him had only heard about in stories. The clean steam that rose up from the mines traveled through the pipes on each side of him into the Conclusus. It was said that the Removed regulated the steam through the day and night—controlling the amount of light and warmth that filled the Conclusus. Their work was supposed to teach them how to be good citizens of the Decorum once again.

Orlo walked on, cautiously looking for a friendly body. Then he could see it—a city, lit from top to bottom with steam-filled bulbs similar to those he had seen in the Hall of Keepers. Poppy had once described a carnival; this is what he imagined it would look like. Large wheels like the one he had seen on the door turned, and long bars moved up and down around and above him. From where he was standing, the entire city seemed to be in motion. It was like a dance of moving parts. The buildings were very similar to the ones in the Conclusus, however not as shiny—as if covered in a thin layer of gray dust. A glass dome dotted in tiny windowpanes sat upon the top of each tower like miniature greenhouses. This was nothing like the stories he had been told. This was more like an entirely different garden.

"Hello!" he called gently. *I must not be close enough,* he thought. He cautiously advanced and reminded himself, *They are just people.* He could not help but think, *They are just people who broke laws of the Conclusus!* He wondered what kind of people they would be. He knew the types that were removed…thieves, liars, worriers, desirers, and those who worked outside of their gifting. In an instant Orlo realized how easily—if an interpreter had overheard his thoughts or someone had misunderstood his fidgeting—he could have been sent to The Works.

He thought about turning back, and then he remembered his situation—it was not like Poppy had asked him to wash the dishes. Sima had given him an order. She said his future depended on it. And somehow, it was for the good of the Conclusus.

Orlo shivered; he had an odd sense that he was being followed. As if they had popped out of the pipes, people began to emerge. The farther into the city he went, the greater the amount of people he saw. There were masses of people moving from one place to the other. It was unsettling to Orlo that this many people had broken the law. There were mothers holding hands with children, men chatting with one another in what Orlo guessed were their work coveralls. In the far distance, he could see an enormous tree trunk bursting through the cave ceiling. It was larger than any tree he had ever seen in the Conclusus—and for that matter, any of the gardens he had visited.

All around him workers twisted and turned giant wheels to monitor the flow of steam coming up from the mines. *Without them,* Orlo thought, lost in his musings, *there would be no light, and not even a wild blackberry would grow.*

"Excuse me." Orlo whipped around to find himself face to face with a youth who, by appearance, was not much older than he. The boy wore trousers and a waistcoat much like Orlo's and had a head full of dusty blond hair that peeked out from under his cap. The boy confidently extended his hand toward Orlo. "I've been expecting you."

Chapter 14

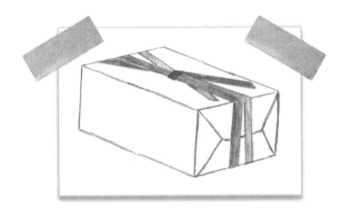

"**Y**ou were expecting me?" Orlo hesitantly extended his hand.

The boy gave it a firm, confident shake. "Name's Banyan! And you are?"

"Orlo. Orlo the deliverer," Orlo replied cautiously.

"Aye! The delivery arrived late last night."

"Delivery? Someone else delivered…to you?"

"That's right, mate! Came by boat, too! Not too often we see that. It was a great big one, with a sail and everything. Flew right in, it did! My pa said it's the water ship that travels the waters of the caves. Only the leaders can sail it ya know. The parcel's waiting for you over by the postal. I'll take you, mate."

A water ship making deliveries? Orlo had never heard of such a device before. His journey proved more mysterious by the minute.

"So," the boy continued to talk, "what's it like up there? I hear they got lots of rules and such. But boy, I'd still like to see it. Can't imagine a whole city with a garden growing freely right on top. My ma would think that was the best thing since the light bulb! We have to keep our gardens covered; it gets too hot. Aye, but you probably already knew that. I hear you all know way more about us than we know about you."

Orlo was trying to process what Banyan was saying. Had he said that his mother was here, too? Had they both broken the law? Had she broken the law and brought him with her? Maybe it was the other way around. And what was a light bulb?

Orlo continued to listen to him as they walked down the stone streets. The harshness of the pipes gave way to rows of short brick towers similar to the one that Orlo lived in. People walked in and out of them grinning and laughing with one another. There did not seem to be a Decorum, or the presence of elders. Their multi-colored clothing made it difficult for Orlo to determine who had once been a puller or who had been a healer. The Works did not have the majesty of the Conclusus, but it was not at all the dungeon Orlo had expected.

"My pa was born in the Conclusus," Banyan rambled. "He don't talk about it, says things are better this way. That's why we stay."

"Wait a minute," Orlo said. "What do you mean *stay*?"

"You know, mate," Banyan said, stopping Orlo in front of a door. Hanging above the door was a sign that read: POSTAL. "Instead of going back up, to the Conclusus."

"But, you can't go back, unless he's learned his lesson."

"Sure we can. Mate, my pa would say you've had your head messed with."

"You didn't break the law? You weren't removed?"

Banyan started giggling so hard that what came out was more of a snorting sound. "Stop it, mate! You're too much!"

Orlo had no idea what he had said that was funny. He was neither laughing nor smiling.

"You're serious, mate," Banyan said, containing his amusement. "You believe we were sent here because we broke the laws. I guess maybe you don't know as much about us as I thought. Sorry, Deliverer. My parents chose this. They wanted this life for my brothers and me. We aren't lawbreakers. Our laws are the same as your laws…for the most part. We all have the same God, right?"

There it was, the name Poppy had given to the Mysterium.

Orlo did not believe a word of what he was hearing. He took his cloth out of his coat pocket to wipe the sweat off of his face. He assumed it was the heat of the steam pipes causing his face to drip like a leaking pipe, but he could also be coming down with something. Either way, he had less than an hour to get the delivery and return to the Slub. He checked his pocket watch, frustrated by Banyan's lies. "Where did you say I could get the delivery? I'm on a tight schedule."

"Right through this door, mate!" Orlo stepped through the doorway of the Postal. Inside, from floor to ceiling, the walls were lined with tiny boxes. Each box was labeled with a tiny, numbered brass plate, and in each box were neatly folded papers—some holding more than others.

"What is this place?"

"My pa's shop. He works at the postal."

"I've never heard of a postal assignment. What is the gifting that goes with it?"

Banyan leaned over and placed his hand on Orlo's forehead. "You don't have the fever." Orlo pulled away. "It's where we put our letters."

"Wait, did you say letters?" The only time Orlo had heard the word letters was from Avia. He considered the notion that these might be the thieves who had taken her infamous letters.

"That's right, mate. You sure you're all right? The great Conclusus must have a postal for letters."

"Not that I've seen." Still, Orlo supposed it might be possible that the Upper Decorum had a Postal and he was not aware of it.

A few days ago the chance of finding out what those of the Upper Decorum experienced had been as real as his cartagon, but now it felt hundreds of feet away. Orlo walked around the room examining all the cubbies. The ticking of the clock on the wall reminded him that his time was short.

"The package—you said it was here?"

"Back here." Banyan led Orlo to another room. In the far corner was a giant locked metal box—big enough for Orlo to climb inside. He had never seen anything like it before.

"Is that…the package? There must be a mistake!" Sima had told him to go on foot, and there was no way he could get this back.

"No, mate," Banyan said with a concerned expression. "It's inside the safe. We never use this thing, but when we heard a delivery was coming for the Conclusus, Pa thought we shouldn't take any chances."

Orlo went over and touched the metal box. He rubbed his hand across the intricate locking mechanism. His mind was totally consumed with the working of the box.

"Your mom needs help upstairs with the babies, then you got to finish your classwork," the voice said.

Orlo turned, surprised by the voice, and saw a man come down the last step of a spiral metal staircase.

"Yes, sir. Nice to meet you, mate!" Banyan said, tipping his tattered hat to Orlo.

"So," the man, an adult version of his son, said, "let's get you on your way, shall we?"

"Yes," Orlo said uncomfortably.

The man slowly turned the handles on the mechanism to the right, then back to the left, and with one final spin to the right. A thud resonated in the room. The man pulled the door open to reveal a small package tightly wrapped in brown paper and tied with a leather cord.

"Whatever is in this package must be right important for them to send you to all this trouble," he said, handing the package to Orlo. "Must not have come from a garden, or they could have sent you to get it the normal way. Wanna know my guess?" It seemed unlawful to make speculations about what was inside the package. "I figure it came from the Binders," the man said, closing one eye tightly with a smile.

Orlo had never seen anyone do that with their eye before.

"What Binders?" Orlo asked.

The man slapped himself on the forehead. "I've said more than I should have. I think we both know what they'd do to me if I said more."

Did he mean the mines? Orlo looked at the small parcel. How could something so small be connected to something so important? According to Sima, whatever was in the package could change everything,

"Paaaaa," a tiny voice called from above the stairwell. "Momma wants to talk to yaaaaa!"

"Deliverer, I've got to go for a minute. If you can wait, I'll walk ya back."

Orlo checked his pocket watch again. "I think I can make it on my own."

"Paaaaa" The voice called again louder.

"All right, Deliverer. It was a pleasure to meet you. If you're ever back in here, be sure to stop in. I know my Banyan and you would get right along. It'd be good for him to have someone his own age around here."

"Thank you," Orlo said, knowing he would never be back. In a way, he felt like he was betraying his household by being down here. Knox would have never let him go if Orlo had been permitted to ask. Maybe that was why Sima had forbid him to tell anyone.

Orlo left the Postal with the package secured tight enough in his good hand to keep it from dropping, but gently enough to keep from damaging it. He considered that what he carried might be from the people called the Binders, but had to remind himself that Banyan's dad was possibly a liar, so his talk of Binders was most likely make-believe.

He sensed that time was running short. He tucked the package under his arm and reached for his pocket watch. Thirty minutes until the door would vanish. Panic whipped through Orlo. He had to get to the far side of The Works—the place where the tunnel led him in. Davy would not be able to hold the door open; it was too dangerous. Anything could come out into the Conclusus. There was no telling what mysteries were lurking in The Works.

After having been down here, part of him did not believe that The Works was quite as bad as he had always been told. It was possible that its foulness had been exaggerated. Then again, that would mean everyone he had ever known in the Conclusus was a liar. *Think on what is true*, he reminded himself.

Orlo sped up, protecting the package by holding it tighter. His chest pounded and sweat poured down his cheeks. He found the tunnel that had led into The Works. It was dark, but he trusted that on the other side there would be a door. He wished he had been permitted to bring his cartagon. No matter where he went, he felt protected when he was on the inside. Now he was open, exposed to whatever unknowns surrounded him. He quickened his pace anticipating the door that would usher him into the Conclusus. But the closer he got, the darker it became, until in front of him was a barren cave wall.

He was too late. Davy had shut the door.

He felt around in the darkness, pounded on the wall with his good fist. He thought about going back to see if Banyan knew of a way to contact the Conclusus, but the thought was ridiculous. Why would Banyan know? Orlo had to remind himself that even though they seemed like friendly people, they were lawbreakers. Being stranded in the dungeon of delinquents had not been on his agenda for the day.

Davy would have to wait until the next workday before the deliverers arrived to create a new door. Poppy and Knox would be so worried tonight. How would Orlo explain this to them when he got back? He would not lie to them, but telling them the truth would mean disobeying an order.

Then he remembered—his stomach churned. He would miss tea with Elder Bednegraine. She would ask where he was, but Poppy would not know what to say. He did not want to think about what they would do to Poppy—would they send her back to the World or separate her from Knox? And Knox, would they send him straight to the mines?

Orlo sunk down against the wall with the package stuck under his arm. There was no one who could help him and nowhere to turn. The one person that he thought might hear him was the One that he knew would not answer him back. But he tried it anyway.

"Mysterium," he said out loud. *This is ridiculous*, he thought, but he kept going. "Sir, I know that You won't answer me, but I don't know what to do. I don't believe that I have broken any laws. Maybe I should have petitioned the gardener to seek Your forgiveness for the ladybug. Is this my punishment? But You see, it's not just about me. My guardian and Knox, they might be in trouble... because of me. If I can get back to the apprentice, she can explain." Orlo waited in the silent absence of light for the answer his heart believed he would not receive. "Mysterium!" he yelled. "Do You hear me?"

In anger, Orlo tossed the package to the ground. The instant he did it, regret filled him. He picked up and inspected every inch of the small parcel. On the corner was a minor tear. What had he done? Even if he made it back, the gardener would never forgive him if he had damaged the valuable inside.

"Deliverer! Orlo!"

"Davy? Are you there?"

Then, he heard it again, like a gentle hum in his ear, and he knew with certainty it wasn't Davy. He looked around, hoping for the door to the Slub to burst into light and appear in front of him.

"Orlo..." the voiced whispered in the darkness, instantly filling him with fear. What if...what if it was them, those who lived in the deepest parts of the Earth—those who had never been seen? "Orlo..." it called again.

111

Truth, Orlo reminded himself. *Truth*. If no one had seen them in the Conclusus, maybe no one had seen them in The Works either.

"Orlo..." it called. Orlo spun around. The voice was coming from The Works. He had nowhere to run. His best chance was to face it head on. As the voice lured him back from where he had come, the light from The Works brightened his path. Orlo blinked to adjust his eyes. In front of him he could see a figure moving rapidly towards him. He briefly thought about turning to run the other way, but he knew there was nowhere else to go.

As the figure moved closer, he could see it waving something back and forth in the air. *A weapon?* Orlo wondered. Then he could see clearly, and his shoulders sagged in relief. It was not a creature. It was Banyan. Orlo's heart slowed down, and his grip on the package loosened.

"Mate!" Banyan called, waving a paper back and forth in the air. "Mate!" he called again. When he caught up to Orlo, Orlo gave him a minute to stop panting and get a hold of himself, but Banyan did not stop talking. "This came for you, mate, by messenger. Door opened right up in the Postal. Glowing thing scared the wits out of Ma, but Pa, he knew what it was. The messenger, she said to give you this straight way, mate! I ran as fast as I could. Here." He handed the envelope to Orlo.

Orlo turned the neatly folded paper over. On the back was the seal of the gardener. "Pa knew who it was from when he saw that symbol on the back. He told me to run as fast as I could. I was afraid I wouldn't find ya. 'Go to the tunnel,' he said." Banyan coughed with his body hunched over and his hands on his knees.

Orlo lifted the seal and opened the note.

You must stay, Orlo. We will send for you.

Sima

Chapter 15

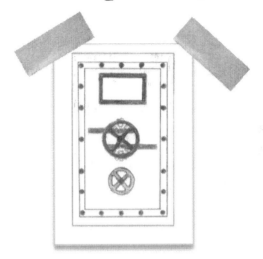

Orlo fought the sleep that was overtaking him. Too much had happened. In one day he had been to classes, the Hall of Keepers, and then The Works. He was exhausted but fearful. What might the people who called the Postal home do to him if he closed his eyes? He was concerned for Poppy and Knox and silently prayed that the Mysterium would protect them. It hurt to keep his eyelids open any longer, so he shut them, convincing himself that he was only going to rest his eyes, but instead, he fell asleep.

When he opened them again, he was no longer in The Works. He was back in the Slub.

I shouldn't be here, Orlo thought. *This isn't right. How did I get here?*

He had spent more time in this Hall than anywhere else in the Conclusus. When he was not out on a delivery, he was here, waiting to fulfill the next order. He knew everyone that came and went from the Slub—the other deliverers and the pullers and pickers that dropped off packages to be delivered to other gardens. He knew the timers that came here to sit and discuss with other timers the proper time to plant and to pick.

But today it was different; the room was silent, empty, and void of the conversations that brought it life. A strange sense of dread overtook him, as if he did not belong today. It was too quiet and too dark.

A hot breeze swept over him. He looked around as if someone had brushed his shoulder. No one was there. A creepy sensation sent shivers up his body. Something was not right.

He ran to the large, metal doors that would lead him out into the Conclusus. He tried to push them open, but they would not budge. Locked. Nothing was ever locked in the Conclusus because stealing was against the law. *This is wrong*, Orlo thought. *This is a dream.*

"Orlo…" the voice echoed.

"Who's there?" Orlo called out into the Slub. "Banyan? Is this a trick? Show yourself!"

"Go, Orlo," the voice softened. "Go."

"I cannot go!" Orlo argued.

"Orlo…" the voice beckoned. The warm air circled around him, pulling him into the darkness of the Slub. It wrapped around his feet, guiding his steps one by one back through the rows of benches, past the empty window where the clerk gave him his assignments, past the holding where his cartagon rested, and to the very wall where Davy created the doors to the other gardens. He and his cartagon had sat in this very spot hundreds of times, but a feeling of anxiety overcame him—a feeling that he was about to see something he had never seen before.

Orlo was afraid that if he tried to turn around, the voice would rotate his body and make him face the wall again. "Where am I supposed to go?" he yelled to the blank wall. "There's no door!"

The voice did not answer.

"Show yourself!"

There was no response.

"I should be going. I have to get back." An odd sensation swept over him—like he could not go back, not because he did not want to, or because he did not know how, but because he was not allowed.

Again the voice said nothing.

Orlo thought back on the words he had spoken to determine if something he had said might have encouraged the stranger to be silent. Then Orlo had a thought, almost a memory, of a voice he had heard when he had stumbled across two flat pieces of metal that made the wings of Poppy's ladybug. Had he heard this voice before? Had it told him how to build the ladybug?

No, Orlo thought, this voice is different. *It's...* He tried to think of a way to describe it, but it was as if something was fighting against him. *It's dark.*

The warm air from the cave wall blasted in his face. Orlo squinted his eyes at the bareness in front of him. He looked again, stretched his arm outward, and then instantly jerked it back. There was a door! *A door*, he thought. *There shouldn't be a door. Davy is not here to make it.* Then, he realized that beside it there was a second door. *This is not right! There should never be two doors at one time!*

Simultaneously, both of the doors swung open. In the distance, beyond the first door, he could see the glittering Conclusus. Home. But behind the second, he saw hazy, dreariness of the *The Works*.

The voice called to him, again. "Orlo!" He had to leave; he had to get away from the voice, but which door should he pass through?

Which one? Which one? Why was this so difficult? The Conclusus was his home, however the Works felt...safer. Orlo took a step toward the door to The Works just as a hot wind blew past him, sealing it closed.

"Orlo..."

With no where else to go, Orlo inched deeper into the tunnel. The image of the Conclusus vanished, taking with it his only source of light. Without the steam-lit lamps on his cartagon, he was unable to see where his feet were stepping. *My goggles would be helpful.* As he said it, his goggles appeared in his hand. Orlo slid them over his head, secured them over his blue eyes, and adjusted the focusing knobs on each side. They were not fancy and did not provide light, but Orlo hoped that by adjusting them he could see farther objects up closer and avoid an impending attack from whatever lurked ahead of him. *He was thankful to have them.*

Suddenly, he could no longer remember where he was going, nor could he remember if he had eaten lunch that day. What if his hunger was causing him to hallucinate? He had heard of hallucinations once before. In classes one day, Knox's apprentice had insisted that the oil he used for motion sickness gave him the ability to see through the tiny cracks in the Conclusus ceiling, all the way through the earth's top layer and into the World. A healer's apprentice had laughed at him and claimed that it was a hallucination. At first, not knowing what a hallucination was, Orlo thought it might be similar to a dream. The educator ended their conversation by declaring that hunger was making them all hallucinate their silliness and sending them to their towers for lunch.

Orlo adjusted his goggles once again as the tunnel began to brighten. There was a light up ahead. He slowed down as the warmth from the pipes on each side of him increased. The dampness from the mist escaping from the cracks in the pipes settled on his skin.

He thought he could hear the sound of stomping, then a steady upbeat clapping. A rhythmic *ploing, ploing, ploing* and then the fast whining of a stringed instrument accompanied them.

Orlo moved quicker. He ran.

He should be there by now, to the music, but there was no end to the tunnel.

He ran faster, pumping his arms back and forth to gain speed, but as hard as he ran, he could not reach the music.

Was something holding him back? He took his goggles off of his head and tossed them to the ground. He unbuttoned his waistcoat and tried to slow his breathing, but it was getting hotter. He listened for the voice that had called him to this moment, but it was silent.

Then he heard her. "Hello, Deliverer."

The sweet voice of Elder Bednegraine startled him. "Please do not be afraid." She glowed in the faint light around her—illuminating her smooth skin, the few strands of auburn hair that purposefully fell from under her headdress, and the symbol of the interpreters embroidered on her yellow sash. "It will be okay, Orlo. I know everything. I want to protect you," she said.

She circled around him, eyeing him tenderly, and then touched the place where the frozen pipe had burned his hand. The bandage was gone, and so was the wound. "This doesn't make sense," Orlo mumbled.

"No, Orlo," she said, removing the yellow gloved hand from his, "it does not make sense. They should not have ordered you, sweet Orlo. It was not fair to bring you into this. They have broken the law, but you know the truth. You are a good boy. Now please, give it to me so you can return to your household."

"I don't have anything." It would have been against the law to deny the request of an elder, and if he indeed had whatever she was requesting, he would gladly give it to her.

"I believe you do. Hand it to me." She nodded to his chest. Orlo touched his chest to find that he was holding a package. He had not seen it since he went to bed that night in The Works.

"This is a dream," Orlo said, beginning to understand what was going on around him.

"Everybody dreams, Orlo. And you have such brilliant dreams, do you not? You were not supposed to, but no matter." She lifted his once damaged hand in hers. "We can give you what you most want, if you give me the package." The small parcel did not seem like much. "It holds a truth too large for you. We will keep it safe."

"But that's what I want," Orlo replied. "I want the truth." He did not know why he had said it, or what he meant by it.

"It is not meant for you, Deliverer. You desire the knowledge of the inventors do you not?"

He did. He always had. Yes, that was what he wanted the most. He wanted to be an inventor. He had known the woman in front of him for as long as he had known Poppy and Knox. She was a friend to their household. She could help him.

Orlo held the package out to her. "Orlo, I knew there was something very special about you. Thank you. You have served us…"

Before she could take hold of the parcel, a cloaked figure appeared. Its masculine voice shouted, "Run, Orlo! Run!"

Chapter 16

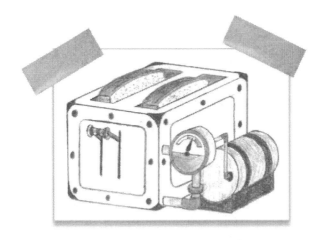

Orlo woke panting, sweaty, and clutching the package to his chest in the little metal pop-up bed Banyan's mother had prepared for him. The mist outside was beginning to rise, and a faint *ploing, ploing, ploing* filtered in rhythmically. At his left, a set of beds stacked one on top of the other held a sleeping Banyan and his younger brother. Orlo checked his hand—still bandaged. Banyan's mother had applied a concoction to it that definitely included lavender.

"Urgh," he muttered. Lavender oil certainly made him sleep deeply, but that dream was so strange and so...real feeling. He liked his first one better. He pulled the book in tighter, praying to the Mysterium that he would never have another dream like that again. It had left his heart pounding. He looked around again to be sure he was back in the place he had fallen asleep.

After Orlo had read Sima's note, Banyan and his family welcomed him into their home. The family had fed him well, had not asked him any questions, and had assured him that he could stay with them until he was sent for. But he did not trust them. If the pain in his hand had not been so intense, and he had not left the prescribed treatment in his satchel, he would not have let the tow-headed woman touch him. His entire life, he had been told that The Works was a holding place for lawbreakers. He had strived to avoid this place, and now he was being forced to stay. The music outside grew louder. Banyan and his brother were beginning to wake in their beds.

Orlo got up and slipped back into his trousers and waistcoat. As he folded the blankets he had slept under, he hoped it was the last time he would need them. He quietly slid out of the room and into the open area of the second floor where Banyan's mother and father were already having breakfast.

"Morning, Deliverer," the mother said with a smile. She reminded him of Poppy—not by her looks, but by manner. She seemed genuinely kind and willing to make Orlo's time in The Works more comfortable. Things here could not be as they seemed. He reminded himself to keep his guard up. Most likely, this woman was not as she seemed.

"Would you like something to eat?" she asked. "We've had pastries brought in from down the street." The sweet scent of sugary pastries wrapped around him. He had smelled similar aromas coming from the Confectionary in the Conclusus, but had always had to settle for Knox's yearly birthday cakes as such treats were reserved for the special Gatherings of the Upper Decorum.

"No thank you," Orlo said, politely. The delicacies were tempting, but his insides felt unstable and queasy from the uneasiness of his dream. He pulled the package to his chest. "I heard music this morning."

"Feel free to step outside and have a walk around," Pa said excitedly. The idea of walking freely around The Works felt a bit dangerous. Any one of them could snatch the parcel right out of his hands, and he would never see it again. Sima would probably make him live down here. The concept of his situation was like another dream. He half expected—almost hoped—to wake up in his own bed tucked under the quilt that Avia had given him.

"We gather today!" the father said.

"You gather?" Orlo asked.

"Course we do, Deliverer! Now, I'll tell you, it's not as grand as your Gathering in the Conclusus, but we like it just fine."

A puff of black smoke escaped from the small box the mother had been using to toast the bread. "Drat! Crazy thing!" She used her apron to fan the smoke out of the window. "Well, the boys will be eating soft bread with their jam this morning."

Orlo stepped over to the device and examined it. He pushed the lever down on the side and watched it pop up. He had never seen anything like it. "Design's from the World," Pa said, recognizing Orlo's curiosity. "Our inventor whipped it up last year. Guess we've worn the thing out."

"What do you mean *inventor*?" he asked. He had never heard of an inventor being released into The Works.

The mother and father looked at one another sadly. "Deliverer," the father said walking over to him. He placed his hands on his shoulders and looked him in the eyes. Orlo did not see an ounce of rebellion in him. "Take a walk around out there. Then remind yourself of this, whatever is true, whatever is honorable, whatever is right, whatever is pure, whatever is lovely, whatever is admirable, if there is anything excellent and praiseworthy, that's what you think on. Do you understand?"

Orlo nodded. He had heard those words spoken by Sima. Why would this man tell him the same thing? He shook his head and started for the door.

"We'll have lunch after we gather. We'd be honored to have ya," the mother said sweetly.

"Thank you," Orlo said as he stepped down the metal spiral stairs and into the Postal. He was numb, confused, nervous, and trying hard not to speculate about the fate of Poppy and Knox.

121

Maybe the open steam of The Works would help him sort out the past twenty-four hours.

Stepping out into The Works was not at all like stepping out into the Conclusus. There was a grittiness about The Works and all of its piping. In fact, it reminded him more of the Slub. The mist that filled the Conclusus was filtered and pure. Here it was raw, mineraly, and not masked by the strong floral aroma that pervaded the Conclusus. There was a sense of beginnings here, like a piece of coal before it became a diamond.

Orlo could hear voices accompanying the ploing, ploing, ploing, as well as drums and other instruments whose sounds he had never heard before. Pa had told him to walk around; his best bet was to head for the music. He could almost make out what they were saying as he passed the crudely constructed towers with their sparse gardens growing in their glass shelters. The steam leaking through the cracks in the pipes illuminated the town.

The music kept playing, the voices kept singing, and he kept walking. As he walked deeper into The Works, he realized that, unlike the towers separated by alleyways in the Conclusus, the towers here were practically touching. Twelve-story buildings squeezed up against towers no bigger than the one in which he lived.

Children sat with their legs hanging off the edges of the lower buildings. They reminded him of his first dream—the one he actually enjoyed—when he'd sat on top of the inventor's tower watching Knox and Poppy below. He squeezed his way through the crowd taking note of everything from their clothing that looked like it had been pieced together from remnants of various assignments, to the way they stomped their worn out boots.

Before he knew it, he had moved further into the heart of the tightening participants. All around him was clapping, dancing, singing, spinning, and swaying. He weaved in and out, holding tightly to the package. He could hear languages he had never heard spoken and the voices of interpreters interceding in conversations. Out of the corner of his eye he saw a small group of people gathered around a boy.

He watched as the woman placed her hand on him, whispered in his ear, and motioned for others to do the same. Orlo was mesmerized until the boy bounded to his feet, hugged the woman, and let the crutch he had been holding drop to the ground. Orlo rubbed his eyes in disbelief, but he had seen it. Right in front of him, a boy had been healed. He had always been told that the lawbreakers were stripped of their giftings during the removal ceremony. Despite the lack of ordained order, it was hard for him to deny what he had seen. He tried not to assume that the oils they had used were stolen, but the more he thought about it, he did not recall them using oils at all. Orlo had to restrain himself from running over and asking how they had done it.

He shook his head. These people had broken the law. He could not forget that.

Pa's words repeated in his mind: *Whatever is true, that's what you think on.* What was true? He saw the joy on the boy's face, the openness of giftings, and the contentment of the people. And the music...it was happy and made his insides stir. If he were to be honest with himself, he liked it. In the Conclusus, the Gathering day music wasn't so...free. The elder musician would schedule which songs were to be sung and the appropriate length for each one. It would be disrespectful to the gardener for them to sing any longer.

The music came to an end. People all around took seats on the ground, children crawled up into their mothers' laps, and others found odds and ends of what seemed to Orlo to be useless crates and boxes to sit upon. Orlo looked around for a nearby place to sit. The rusted watering bucket by his feet did not appear to be a comfortable seat, so he backed up to lean against the wall of a tower.

Listen. A voice, not the deceptive voice of Elder Bednegraine, but another—one he could not hear with his ears, coming from somewhere else—spoke to him. Orlo looked from side to side to see if anyone else had heard it, but apparently they were too engrossed in the person climbing to the crudely built platform. He looked to his hand. It was bandaged. He was awake.

A lady with a toothy grin and gown far too big for her gave him that comforting one-eyed blink and nodded her head toward the stage as if she were gently instructing her own child to pay attention to the speaker.

Orlo felt like he was preparing to listen to the gardener speak at a Conclusus Gathering. The thought was ridiculous. A gardener would have never been removed to The Works. The mere idea of liars and thieves gathering to hear the words of the Mysterium was laughable.

The lady beside Orlo gave him another friendly glance and then blinked at him with her right eye. Orlo was beginning to wonder if this was a type of communication that only those who lived in The Works knew about. He had trouble recalling if it was a law or if it was highly suggested to not make strange bodily movements at others.

Orlo held on to the package to protect it from these strange blinkers, giggling children, and waving citizens. Their blatant kindnesses made him question their motives. He would have to stay sharp, especially with the gap-toothed woman waving him over to sit with her.

Orlo turned away from the woman to get a better glimpse of the man who had positioned himself at the middle of the crudely constructed stage. The gentleman's dusty red garments shone under the steam-lit streetlamp. Orlo squinted and shook his head. Maybe this was another dream. *It can't be him*, Orlo thought. *What's he doing here?*

Chapter 17

Orlo watched, stunned, as Davy lifted his mechanical arm, bowed his head, and prayed. "There are not enough words to express our thankfulness to You. You are the Creator of light, love, joy, and happiness."

He's a messenger! He cannot act as gardener! Orlo thought frantically.

"Friends," he said, addressing the smiling faces in front of him. "I got to tell you what's on my heart. They call Him Mysterium; we call Him God. I've learned that He's the One True by whatever name we call Him."

The people nodded and said words like *amen,* and *that's right.*

"His Way is right. I know that now. He has filled me with the knowing of His will in all spiritual wisdom and understanding so I can walk in a manner worthy of Him, to please Him in all ways, bearin' fruit in all good work and growing in the knowledge of Him. He strengthens me with all power accordin' to His glorious might, for the attainin' of steadfastness and patience. I give thanks to Him alone, who has formed me to share His word. He rescued me from the domain of darkness, and transferred me to the kingdom of His beloved Son, in whom we have redemption, the forgiveness of sins."

The people raised and clapped their hands.

Orlo's mouth hung open. Poppy had once said that his face would stick that way if he did it for too long. He had immediately shut his mouth, terrified to open it again, until Poppy had said that it was a figure of speech.

If there were a list of laws that resulted in banishment to the mines, surely what Davy was doing had to be at the top of the list. He was in The Works pretending to be the gardener! Orlo felt like he was in a series of bizarre overlapping dreams. He half expected to wake up in L923 having tea with the boy who had burned his garden down to dust.

Davy's earlier words repeated in his head: *They're just people. Trust me.*

Orlo felt tricked and…cheated—that was the word Poppy had used—by his only friend. This could not be happening to him. He looked up at the messenger on the stage spilling words about darkness, a kingdom, and a Son. Orlo no longer saw the man on the stage as the messenger who let him in and out of gardens; he saw a lawbreaker—a lawbreaker who had shown him the way into this mess of a place on orders from the gardener.

Does the gardener know what Davy is doing? If the gardener knows and does not report it to the elders, he would be breaking the law. The thought seemed absolutely absurd. The gardener would never break the law. Davy must have tricked the gardener, too!

The music started up again. Orlo could not see Davy anywhere.

"Young Orlo!" His old friend's gruff voice surprised him from behind. "What under the earth are you still doing here?"

"Stay back!" Orlo commanded.

"Come on now, I know there's some explainin' to be done. No need to get all in a fuss."

"What are you doing here, and up there? And the gardener, does he knows? And the laws, and…" Orlo's words were spewing out of his mouth before he could properly organize them. "You…you were acting like you heard Him…"

"You ain't ever heard Him before?" Davy asked. "Course you haven't. That's a shame. They don't teach The Way up there. What was I thinkin'? Well, I guess it looks like we both have some explainin' to do. Let's step away from these fine people so as not to bother them. Shall we?"

Orlo did not see another option. The man in front of him was his only way back to the Conclusus. As they moved away from the Gathering, Orlo could hear the voice of another up on the platform talking about The Way. Some of the participants stayed seated, others got up to walk around. In the Conclusus, there were very strict laws about what time everyone was expected to arrive at the Gathering, where everyone was to sit, and when it ended. Orlo felt like he was breaking some law by walking away.

"I hear old Knox is on his way to a promotion. Can't wait to see what the sport whips up for the festival. Have you seen it?"

Orlo shook his head. As far as he knew, Knox had not yet found a starting point for his tournament entry. And how could Davy just going on talking as if so many things weren't wrong right then?

"I thought about entering once after I busted up my arm. It was the year that they were lookin' for something to invent for the musicians," he explained. "Wouldn't do me much good. I sound like an air balloon running out of steam. *Eeeeeeeeewwwwwwww*," he mimicked in a high laughing squeal. He was always happy. Even with his damaged arm he was happier than anyone Orlo had ever met. Davy may have been the happiest person he had ever met.

"You're a messenger!" Orlo said, boldly gesturing to Davy's red hat and pants. "You have the gifting to open doors. You've been assigned. You aren't the gardener."

"You are correct. I'm not the gardener. Nor do I desire to be—praise be to the Mysterium!" Davy said emphatically. "And you, young Orlo, are not supposed to be here." He glanced down at the package and then back to Orlo. "They send you down here for another one?"

Orlo was at a loss for words. He felt bound to the confidentiality of the Conclusus, but Davy was, or at one time had been, his friend. He was so confused.

"Wait a minute." Davy's expression changed. "You haven't been back. That's what all the hubbub's been about in the Slub. You've gone missing!" Davy's hands were now pressed to his cheeks. "But the door, I left it for you! Created it special so you'd go right back to your room! Did you leave it open? Oh this is bad, mate! Old Davy's gonna be in a garden of hurt."

"Davy, there was no door. I went and it was gone. Then I got a note. It told me to stay until they came for me."

A strange smirk crossed Davy's face. "Somethin's a-goin' on up there, young Orlo, and they got you in the middle of it, haven't they?"

"I don't know."

"Well, I know this. If you didn't shut that door, then someone else did."

"Someone here, most likely," Orlo said confidently.

"Of course not! No one here's gonna cause you harm. What did I tell you, young Orlo? They're just people. People who want a different life than what they got up there."

Should he be furious or scared at the way Davy was talking? He felt betrayed, fooled by this man who he looked up to as a member of the Decorum of the Conclusus.

Davy must have sensed it. He looked sincerely into Orlo's eyes. "You have been many places, young Orlo. More than most have ever believed to exist. You go and then you return, but you don't stay to see that in every one of those gardens, people move differently. Do you understand?"

"No. I don't understand, and I don't understand what you're doing here! Davy, did you break the law?"

"Fair question, young Orlo, but a tricky one to answer. I don't come here because the elders make me, but if they knew, I'd drop through the floor faster than you could tip your hat, and I'd never be able go back. Make sense?"

Orlo did not speak. He was without words to answer.

"Guess I better try somethin' else. Sometimes it's easier to show someone what they don't know instead of tryin' to tell them about it. Look around Orlo, and tell me what you think of the Liberum?" Davy's voice was calm and honest.

"The what?" Orlo asked.

"There I go again. The Works is what the Decorum calls it, but truth is, the rightful name is the Liberum! Has a nice ring to it, don't you think? It means free."

Orlo thought Davy was just attempting to change the subject, but for the sake of being able to get back to the Conclusus, he thought he better go along with it. "I think…" He was about to say unruly, but then he remembered the music and what Pa had said. "I think…" He hesitated to say what his mind thought about the haphazard collision of colors, sounds, and people, because his heart saw it as a beautiful invention.

"Here you can say what you feel. Our laws aren't their laws."

Orlo ignored his comment about the laws. "I think it's complex." *Complex* was not the word he meant to say. "Interesting." That was not it either. He searched his heart. He looked toward truth, his heart, what he honestly believed. "Fascinating. It's like a whole other garden." His true thoughts had spilled from his mouth. He wanted to add in lawless and chaotic, but that did not truly explain how he felt. It was what he thought—based on what he had been told, but it wasn't what he knew.

"Me, too. That's why I visit when I can."

Orlo raised his eyebrows.

"I've got other reasons, but enough of that right now." Davy slapped himself on the forehead and then rubbed it, looking as if he'd just realized it would probably have been wiser to not slap himself with the highly mechanized substitute he had for a left hand. "Hungry?"

Orlo nodded.

"I'll answer your questions, but only as much as I know. No lies, you have my word."

Davy stopped in front of a short building. A cloth covering of sorts stuck out over the door. The sign above it read in big pink letters: BAKERY.

"There is a lot you don't understand, and I can't make you, nor do I want to try to at this point. I'm not doing anything wrong *here*," Davy said. His emphasis on the word here didn't slip past Orlo. "The Liberum is different. The laws are different…come to think of it, I don't know the laws. They follow The Way, and that's all."

Orlo had heard that from Davy before—The Way.

"How 'bout this? You can ponder on all of this later, and we get you that bite to eat?"

"All right," Orlo said. He clearly would not—perhaps could not—get the answers to all the questions in his brain. His mind was a jumbled mess of Conclusus law and The Way spoken about in the Liberum.

"Come on in. This will certainly pop off your cap!" Davy exclaimed, pushing open the wood framed door.

Inside, the bakery shelves were piled high with twisted breads, plump rolls, fruit-filled pastries, and icing-drizzled sweets. Orlo's mouth began to water.

"Take what you like, but only what you can eat. It's their day off, too, even if we must eat."

Take, Orlo thought, *it's the way of thieves.* Davy went straight to a basket full of cinnamon bread. Orlo watched him take two pieces and then step aside. It felt strange to Orlo to take something before asking permission, but what if what Davy had said was true…both Pa and Sima had told him to think on what was true.

The truth was that the door was wide open for anyone to enter, the shelves were fully stocked, and Davy did not seem to be a bit concerned that someone would catch him.

Orlo walked the perimeter of the room. Before him were foods that could have been prepared by gifted cooks and bakers in the homes of the Upper Decorum. He leaned into a muffin and smelled—lemon and poppy seed. He lifted the delicacy from the shelf and cupped it in his hand.

Davy chuckled again. "Now, let's discuss this adventure you have found yourself wound up in."

Orlo smiled with his mouth full of lemony crumbs. "The door was gone. They sent a note. I had to stay," he muffled as several tidbits of the muffin fell from his lips.

"All right, I'll be going topside this evening. I'll let Knox and your guardian know that you're fine."

"No one is supposed to know I'm down here."

Davy crossed his arms. "I guess that creates a bit of a problem for us, doesn't it?"

"Sure does," Orlo said, consuming his last bite of muffin.

"These orders of yours are between you and the gardener. I'll tell you this: he's a good fella. If he says to stay put, I'd do it. It seems to me like he's almost protecting you."

"Me? From what?"

"Don't know, but I'm sensin' that somethin' is brewin' up there. I've been feelin' it for some time now. I've a good mind what it might be, but I ain't sayin'. No need to put thoughts under that cap of yours. I'm figurin' it's got somethin' to do with what's in that package you're guardin' with your life. How am I doin'?" Davy looked down at the package. "You say it was delivered to the Postal?"

"It's a block or two away. It's where I'm staying."

Davy grinned. "I know exactly where that is. Let's pay them a visit, and then I got to show you somethin'. Young Orlo," Davy chuckled, "you're gonna have a lot to dream about tonight."

Orlo was not only amazed that Davy had been coming to this place he called the Liberum often enough to "pay his hosts a visit" but also with his overall knowledge of the city. The man moved easily through the streets, waving at people, tipping his hat to ladies, and blinking one-eyed at the children.

"What is that one-eyed blink?"

131

Davy laughed loudly. "A wink they call it. Just a way to show friendship."

Orlo blinked his eyes to see if he could do it.

"Keep workin' on it." Davy chuckled.

When they arrived at the Postal, Davy used his mechanical appendage to open the glass-paned door. A delicate *jingle, jingle* trickled down from the brass bell that had been attached to the frame. "Anybody home?" he called. The *cling, clang, cling, clang* of footsteps running down the metal spiral staircase resounded from the back of the building.

"Uncle Davy!" Banyan shouted, running up and shaking his birth hand.

Uncle? Orlo thought. He recalled what he had learned about family order in classes. That would mean that Davy was either Banyan's mother's brother or his father's brother. He stumbled back. Davy had family in The Works! He was related to a lawbreaker and keeping in touch with them. It was unheard of. Once a lawbreaker was removed from the Conclusus, the family was not to look upon them anymore unless the lawbreaker would seek forgiveness from the Mysterium. But since the gardener was the one who heard from Him, it was nearly impossible for family to ever see them again.

"Hey, mate!" Banyan said, giving Orlo a friendly punch on the shoulder. Orlo rubbed his shoulder and forced a smile. Hitting was against the law because it inflicted discomfort. "We're about to leave for the Gathering. It's goin' into the night I hear!"

"You heard right! Still goin' strong out there," Davy said with a wink. "Is your pa home?"

"Paaaaaaa!" Banyan hollered. In seconds, Pa emerged from the home above.

"Davy!" he said. "It's good to see you, brother! Did you share at the Gathering this morning?"

"When there's a chance, I take it!"

"We'll have to start calling you *Gardener* before long." The two men laughed. The comment disturbed Orlo. Davy was not and never would be the gardener, but here it seemed like anyone that had something to say could step up and speak. And, the people weren't treating Davy like a gardener. The gardener in the Conclusus would never walk around with a deliverer.

"Enough of that nonsense, brother. Just glad I can share what's on my heart."

"I see you ran into the deliverer."

"Indeed. He showed me that package; figure I'd run him over to the Hall of Keepers," Davy said.

"Is that the reason you're visiting the Hall?" They both grinned at what sounded like an inside joke between the two of them.

"Enough of that, brother," Davy said, eyes bright. "You know it don't work that way."

"I know, but it can…" Pa said.

Davy's cheeks had taken on a pinkish tone. "Maybe one day." He winked at Orlo. "Anywho…I thought I'd stop by and see if you needed me to take anything over."

Pa laughed out loud. "Davy, you don't have to have an excuse to go to the Hall of Keepers. Tell her you're showin' the boy around. That's good enough, and it's the truth."

"Pa! Tell him about the crates!" Banyan said excitedly.

"Strangest thing," Pa said to Davy. "The Arc's been visiting quite a bit lately, dropping off crates. They looked like they were marked for the Conclusus. I didn't know where to put them."

Banyan scratched his head and twisted his face. "We opened it."

"You what?" Orlo snapped. "The law states…and the…did you think?" Orlo responded with a stuttering concoction of words about gardeners and assignments, but Davy stopped him.

"Banyan knows nothin' of your Decorum, young Orlo. The gardener is no more to him than someone who helps them with their gardens. He doesn't understand your concern." Davy stepped up and put his arm around his nephew. "Anything good in there?"

Orlo was appalled at the brashness.

"Just some books. They're storing them at the Hall. We didn't have room for them here."

"Books?" Davy asked. "Are you sure, Banyan?"

Orlo had heard Poppy talk about books, but he had never seen one. Banyan sounded like it was nothing of importance.

"Yep. Whole crate was full of 'em!"

Davy had a look of concern on his face that Orlo had not seen before. "I have to take him there. He deserves to know."

"They all do, Davy."

"I know, brother. That time will come."

Chapter 18

The Hall of Keepers in the Liberum was as beautiful as any of the buildings in the Conclusus. Polished pipes surrounded the building, pumping out great amounts of steam that fell on the tower and made the lush greenery that spewed over the top sparkle like giant emeralds. The gigantic tree trunk Orlo had seen the day before grew out of the top of the building.

Orlo grabbed hold of his thoughts. He was not a puller, a picker, or a keeper; it was not his assignment to know whether a tree could grow that high, but in all of his journeys he had never seen a tree quite as large.

They stopped in front of the arched entrance. At the top of the arch were the words: WE WILL SERVE ONE ANOTHER.

It did not say WE WILL SERVE the Conclusus, the Decorum, the elders, or the Liberum. It said "one another." Around the perimeter, etched into the stone, were symbols—one from each of the assignments. There were dozens of them, many that Orlo knew well, and some that he had never seen before. He ran his finger over the engraved harp; the symbol for the musician rested between the emblem of the puller and timer. He followed the intricate designs around the arch until he came to the one he hoped to see. There, at the bottom, between the leaders' tree of life and one of the shapes he had never seen before, was the tool of the inventors. The symbol was not bigger than any of the others, nor was it embellished in such a way to make it more important.

He reread the words, WE WILL SERVE ONE ANOTHER. "They're all equal. We're supposed to serve one another," he mumbled. Shivers shot through Orlo, despite the warm air of the Liberum. He felt as if he instantly possessed knowledge far greater than he had ever known before. "The people here, they serve the Conclusus while they serve one another. There's no one down here making these people work, yet the Liberum serves them willingly."

"They serve the Conclusus 'cause they love the people. The Way gives us that freedom. Besides, if they didn't, we'd all be freezin' up there," he chuckled. Davy placed his hand on Orlo's shoulder. "It's a lot to take in—might be frightening for you."

"I'm not afraid," Orlo said strongly. "I'm angry." It was against the law of the Conclusus to be angry, but he was not in the Conclusus. He felt like he had been misled, deceived—that the Conclusus, like the words on the fountain, was only telling part of the truth. Was this what he had to see? Was this what he deserved to know? That there was another way...a way where they were all equal? A way where they served one another? Where the Lower Decorum was as important as the Upper Decorum? A way where they were not divided by their color or the location of their tower?

Reminders of his short time in the Liberum swam through his mind: Banyan's eagerness to help a stranger; and his mother's insistence on bandaging his arm, making a bed for him, and offering him dinner. He had seen this service to one another in the Gathering, in the unlocked bakery, the hospitality at the Postal...

and in everything Davy had done to get him here. This place, the Liberum, was not about selfishness and deceit. It was about a new way, serving one another. No wonder nobody ever comes back, Orlo thought. *If the Decorum and the elders knew about this, our lives could be so different.*

"Young Orlo, I've been thinkin' about them sendin' you here and that package you got there in your hand. Maybe someone up there wanted you to see this for yourself."

"Why me?" Orlo asked. "Why not an elder?"

"Come on. I've got somethin' else to show ya." He motioned Orlo through the etched archway.

With Davy behind him, Orlo walked into the Hall of Keepers in the Liberum, unafraid, open-minded, and excited to experience what other revelations he was about to encounter.

Orlo expected to find two rows of apprentices lined up in anticipation of one day becoming whatever the Liberum's equivalent of the gardener would be, but instead he felt as if his breath had been ripped from his lungs. He had never seen anything, nor imagined, or heard of anything like this. Not even Poppy, in her knowledge of the World, had ever mentioned anything like what surrounded him.

The trunk of the large tree grew down into the ground beneath his feet, strong and sturdy, and then upward, bursting through the cave ceiling above them. The Conclusus was above him, but he knew of no tree this large anywhere. The walls of the open room reminded him of the Apothecary, except instead of illuminated vials of liquid, they were lined with tightly bound stacks of parchment. Around the top of the shelving, engraved into the wood, were more words: *For the Mysterium gives wisdom, from His mouth come knowledge and understanding.*

Orlo stared at the words, his insides a dry well soaking up the meaning behind the phrase he had never heard nor seen before. The knowledge of the assignments was passed down through the elders, but he had never thought about where they might have learned it. Nobody had ever taught him to fidget, but his fidgeting had led him to inventing. He thought back to the ladybug and that inner desire he had to fix, to build, and to create. Could the Mysterium have given it to him? Is that why Sima knew he could have won the tournament? Did she know about this…these words…this place? Is this how she knew he would be safe?

"There's more, young Orlo," Davy said softly. "So much more it'd take ten lifetimes over to understand it all. But, thankfully, we have the books." Orlo turned in a circle to see the book-filled room. There were books of every color, stacked high from floor to ceiling.

"Those are books? All of them?"

"Yes, young Orlo."

Poppy would love this place. Once, she had explained to him that, in the World, students learned history. The idea of learning about the past seemed useless to Orlo. Why would anyone care about what happened yesterday, if life was happening today? It was then she had told him about books. He had nearly laughed out loud and had to apologize for seeming rude. The description of books was as hard for Orlo to grasp as the idea of studying the past. There were no books in the Conclusus, but in this structure, there must have been thousands.

The room smelled crisp like the brick walkways in the Conclusus after the mist had settled for the night. He could hear sounds he had not heard before—sounds of paper moving in the books, and the voices around him reading.

"The books—free to everyone—contain all the knowledge of the gardens, and everything about all our giftings," Davy informed him. "Copied—every letter that makes a word and every word that make a sentence. Bound by the Binders, spoken by the Creator Himself. They speak The Way, Orlo."

"You weren't talking about the books when you said I had a right to know. Were you?"

"No, young Orlo. It's what's in the books that you have a right to know. It's that truth that matters. They sent you down here for that package…didn't tell you what you were walking into…but they had to know that you would find out. So, what I'm thinkin' is, the gardener sent you here for somethin' else." He shifted on his feet and crossed his arms across his chest. "You can borrow one, if you like," Davy said changing the subject. "The hard part is choosin'. I like to read the red ones," he said with a wink.

"Choose?" Orlo asked.

"Ah, I've been comin' here a little too often I guess," Davy said. "It means you get to pick for yourself." Orlo understood, and the idea of that kind of freedom unsettled him. "Come on, I have someone I'd like you to meet."

Across from where they had entered, a long wooden desk was piled high with a rainbow of books. A lady wearing an oddly striped black-and-red blouse with ruffled collar and puffy sleeves, appeared to stacking and sorting the books. She could have been Poppy's twin had she been wearing the plain draping's of a collector. Her hair hung loose and unsecured over her shoulders. A band the color of which Orlo had never seen wrapped around her mid-section and pulled her waist in tight. It was blue, but almost green—and not exactly either.

"Why, Davy! Are you back for more?" she asked, standing and leaning over the counter to give him a wink. Davy winked back. Her long skirt hung close to her body and did not rustle when she moved like the women of the Conclusus.

"Hello, Keeper!" he said.

Orlo wondered if there were once keepers in the Conclusus. *Maybe that's why they called the it the Hall of the Keepers—no, there must have always been gardeners.*

"Enough with the formalities, Davy," she giggled. "You sure do know how to make a lady blush." He looked at her the way Knox looked at Poppy.

Poppy had once told Orlo that he would look at a lady that way one day. Orlo had no doubt that he was a long way from that day.

"Fine, fine, Miss Rosemary," he said, taking her olive-skinned hand in his cold hard mechanized one and kissing it politely. "I would like to introduce you to Orlo the deliverer."

"A friend of yours is a friend of mine." She turned her warm brown eyes on Orlo. "It is nice to finally meet you. Davy has told me much about you." Orlo could not imagine what Davy would have said about him. His life was not dangerous like the messengers who went on missions to the World, or interesting like the healers who were always talking about the great numbers of people they had healed.

"Nice to meet you, ma'am," he said. Orlo attempted to wink at her to be appropriate, but his upturned lip and scrunched face did not cooperate. Instead, he extended his burned hand to shake. When she took it, Orlo winced.

She looked down at his hand and gasped. "Orlo, your hand! When did this happen?"

"A few days ago, ma'am."

"May I have a look?" she asked. Orlo hesitated.

"It's all right, she knows what she's doin'," Davy encouraged.

She unwrapped his hand with gentle care. It was red, swollen, and did not look much better than when he had first injured it. The fresh air felt good on the wound.

"Have you seen a healer?" she asked.

"Yes, ma'am," he replied, retracting his hand.

"I'm surprised it wasn't against the law."

Orlo did not know what to think of her comment. "They gave me lavender, but it's back at my tower."

"Well, it's a good thing! What if you had gotten an infection?" she exclaimed.

"Easy, Rosemary," Davy said in a soothing tone. "Remember how the boy is being raised."

"Sometimes, we don't get all the wisdom we require when the wrong people are believing they have it," she said with a confident nod. Davy flashed her a halting glare. "I'm not going to lie to the boy, Davy. I may not like all of their laws, but I don't break His laws either. Well, I try real hard not to." Her eyes strayed off into the distance as if recalling something from a long time ago. "Keep it clean, and make sure it gets some fresh air, all right?"

Orlo nodded.

"I hear the Binders have been sending a few more deliveries your way," he whispered.

"Davy, please don't get messed up in all of this."

"So you know then," he said with another wink. "I knew it'd happen sooner or later, just a matter of the right person havin' the guts to do it. I have a feelin' who it might be, but I ain't sayin' right yet." Orlo listened, putting together the pieces of his journey like the inner workings of the classroom clock.

"Stay out of it, Davy. If the elders find out you're using your assignment to come down here…they'll…well…"

"What? Send me to the wolves?" He laughed.

"You could just leave that place." She smiled and batted her eyelashes.

"Ah, don't worry about me. You know why I have to stay." He patted Orlo on the back. Orlo could not imagine Davy leaving the Conclusus. "Don't worry about me, Miss Rosemary. I'll be careful. So, ya mind if I have a look at those crates? I think it might do young Orlo here some good to have a peek."

She huffed, stepped around from behind the desk, and said, "Come with me."

There were people every way Orlo turned. Some were on ladders pulling out green books; others were putting orange and yellow books in specific places on specific shelves. There was an apparent rhythm about it all that mesmerized and pulled him deeper into the lifestyle of the Liberum.

At the back of the circular room was a thin door marked STORAGE. Rosemary pulled a key from underneath her blouse and used it to unlock the door. "Here you go," she said, swinging the door open wide. Stacked high were dozens of crates stamped CONCLUSUS.

Orlo brushed away the loose straw from an opened crate and lifted a soft purple book. On the cover was a single flower. He flipped open the cover and read, *The Book of the Observers*. Orlo dug into the crate, revealing more stacks of the purple books. Each one was embossed with a different silver symbol.

Rosemary propped her hands on her hips, accentuating her tiny waistline. "If I had the gift of interpretation, I'd imagine there's more to this crate than you know, young Orlo. But I don't, so I'll mind my own. It was a pleasure to meet you, Deliverer, but I must get back to work. Shut the door behind you, Davy," she said with a wink.

"You as well, ma'am!" Davy said, winking back at her.

"Until next time."

Once she was clearly out of sight he said, "Go ahead and ask."

"Ask what?" Orlo turned the books over in his hand.

"About Miss Rosemary." Davy rubbed his mechanical arm and sighed. "I know you are wonderin'."

Orlo was wondering about a lot, but Davy's relationship with Rosemary was not at the top of his list.

"She's not my bride, but I'll ask her soon. I promised her I would. I've got a few more things to figure out."

Davy looked at him as if his heart had been broken. He stared off through the cracked door to where Rosemary was joyfully handing a stack of books to an elderly woman. "She reads a lot of the books, Orlo. That's no gifting, it's wisdom. Miss Rosemary didn't break a law, she made a choice."

"She chose the Liberum?"

"Aye, she did. And I've learned this much—when the Mysterium gives us a gift, He doesn't rip it from us because we fall short. Our giftings can change yes, but that doesn't mean we lose all knowledge of the one we had before."

"But the gardener, the Mysterium tells him, and the elders—"

"We don't work like that here. I won't lie to you Orlo, but there are things you may have to learn on your own, and I have a feelin' He"—Davy created a large circle with his finger—"is about to show you, or you wouldn't be standing right here, right now. Whatever is goin' on up there, you're a part of it now. I'm not one to speculate too much, but I'd say that someone up there wants you to know what's going on down here."

Was it true? Had the gardener chosen him to come down to the Liberum? Did the gardener know this truth? Had he sent for the books?

"Why don't you choose one?" Davy instructed.

Orlo selected one of the purple books. He inhaled its scent and flipped back the crisp pages. His excitement took over as he rummaged through the crate, lifting book after book from the box until his heart told him to stop.

He sifted through the books he had already removed from the crate. He knew which one he wanted, but it was not there. He put the books back one by one, double-checking the cover of each to see if he had missed it. He looked around the room to see if he had overlooked a crate when he had an idea—an idea that…if he followed through with it in the Conclusus would label him a lawbreaker.

Orlo lifted the item he had been sent to retrieve; he placed his finger in the hole created by the little tear in the packaging. The rip expanded, revealing more of he purple underneath. This was wrong, but Sima said his future depended on it. *His future.* He knew which book he wanted, and he was sure that he was holding it.

Never. He had *never* broken the law of the Conclusus

He looked to Davy who was watching him toy with the damaged parcel. *Our laws aren't their laws.* It was what Davy had said. They were in the Liberum now. The laws of the Conclusus did not matter. Davy said to choose. With his hand aching, he untied the twine binding and ripped back the brown paper.

The smooth purple cover fit perfectly in his hand. Orlo rubbed his fingers across the shiny silver symbol of the inventors releasing a fragrance that smelled like the tree on top of his tower when Knox's balloon sailed back to the Hangar. He went to open it, but found that two intricate locks gripped the covering and prevented him from seeing the pages.

"This one," he said. "I choose *The Book of the Inventors.*"

Chapter 19

Orlo fidgeted with the locks—trying to decipher their complex workings and unique intricacies. "Deliverer," Davy interrupted his musings, "it's time to go." Orlo looked up to see that Rosemary had returned, this time with a note in hand. "They've called for you, young Orlo. Looks like I'm gonna be sending you back."

He held tight to the book as he followed Davy and Rosemary out into the openness of the Hall of Keepers. Here he had seen choice, the opportunity to choose, as Davy had put it—but what had he chosen? A book? A book that belonged to someone else? There had to be more. He looked again at the book in his hand. He wanted to stay and read them all—he longed to know what they said, why the one he held in his hand had been so important that Sima had sent him to retrieve it, and why his future depended on it. He ran his hand across the cover, realizing that he would have to explain why he had unwrapped the package.

"There is so much more I want to know! Maybe I can stay. You can teach me!"

Davy was silent before turning around. He scratched his scraggly hair with his mechanical hand. "It's not that easy, Orlo."

"Sure it is. If I lived here…in the Liberum…I could be an inventor, like Rosemary is a keeper, right? I want to stay, Davy!"

"Orlo, I can't agree to letting you stay."

"But you don't care about the laws! You don't care about the Decorum! Why do you have to do what they say? Leave me here. Tell them I decided to stay. It wouldn't be a lie."

"What about your guardian and Knox?"

"They can come, too! This place could use an aeronaut. And Poppy…Poppy would love it here! Oh and Avia, we'll bring her here, too."

"Is that what they want?"

"Freedom from the law, freedom from the Decorum? Who wouldn't?" Orlo said excitedly.

"So you're gonna up and run away?"

"Run away?" Orlo asked. He did not see it as running away.

"If you do this, what do you think all those people up there are gonna say?"

"It doesn't matter."

"Yes, it does, Orlo!" Davy snapped. "You stay here and the elders are gonna have to find a way to make it okay, meanin' they're gonna say you broke a law."

"But I haven't broken any laws!" Silence fell between the messenger and the deliverer. "I haven't broken any laws," he repeated to himself. "It would be a lie. The elders would be the ones breaking the law." Orlo felt the color drain from his face as he saw the brokenness of the Conclusus unfolding in his mind. "Davy, the elders lied, didn't they? The people of the Liberum chose The Way. That's why they were removed."

Davy lowered his head—neither acknowledging nor denying Orlo's sudden revelation.

"I have a choice, don't I? I can choose this, can't I?" Orlo asked, stopping Davy and Rosemary. Rosemary turned to face him, but Davy was motionless. "Davy, I can't go back! I choose to stay."

"Orlo, my heart's here, but it can't be my home…not yet," he said linking his arm in Rosemary's. "There's work to be done up there, and I'm not givin' it up until He tells me to. You think real hard about that. You got to trust that the Mysterium will bring you back at the right time. The books say that if we delight in Him, He will give us the desire of our hearts. If the Liberum is the desire of your heart, He'll guide those feet of yours back here."

"You're not a gardener, Davy," Orlo said, pushing past the only friend he ever had. "You can't tell me what to do."

"No, I'm not a gardener, but I am a messenger." Instantly a door embellished with all the symbols of the assignments appeared in front of Orlo. "It's my gifting to lead you where you have to go. You gotta trust me, young Orlo."

Orlo knew what his life on the other side would be like if he returned. "You keep saying that! Why should I trust you?" he asked. "You're no better than they are! You told me to choose, so I made my choice. Now you're telling me I can't have it."

"I never said you couldn't have it," Davy said calmly.

With the book tucked under his arm, Orlo gripped the golden door handle with his good hand.

"I feel sorry for the boy," Orlo heard Davy say to Rosemary as he turned the knob.

"He'll come 'round, Davy. I can see it in him," Rosemary said softly as Orlo pushed the door open.

Orlo was angry and disappointed—ignoring all the laws governing emotion. In the Liberum, he could invent, wear what he wanted, talk to whom he wanted, and live where he wanted. Two times in one week the opportunity for a different life had been pulled from his grasp. He would not allow it to happen again. He moved into the darkness; the door shut behind him as the light of the Conclusus came to life in front of him.

He prepared to walk back into the normalcy of the Slub, but what he saw was far from the dank dreary workplace. A narrow staircase materialized before him, filling his path. With one way to go, Orlo began his ascent. Step by step he thought about the Liberum and what life would have been like if he could have stayed.

The staircase wound upward, lit by tiny steam-filled bulbs on each side of him. He reached for the walls to steady himself. Orlo touched the walls again. They were hard and smooth, but not like the cave walls of the Slub. They were wooden, like the trunk of a tree. He climbed higher, reflecting on his conversation with Davy.

All of his life he had thought The Works—the Liberum—was a place for lawbreakers. They were not thieves or liars. They had not worried or offended anyone. They had chosen a life of equality and service to one another. Orlo's heart ached to go back. He had spent years dreaming of an apprenticeship with the inventors, entering their Decorum and becoming one of them, but the Liberum had changed everything. There, he could have what he wanted. *That's the desire of my heart all right*, he thought as he continued to climb the steps. *I'll go back. One day, I'll go back, and no one will be able to stop me.*

Lost in thought, Orlo ran face first into the back of a door.

He rubbed his head and looked at the door in front of him. With a shove, Orlo pushed the door open, throwing himself down onto the course ground. He stumbled to his feet and brushed off his trousers. Orlo gasped. Before him was an exact replica of the room he had been standing in—except the warmth and movement that had pervaded the Liberum was replaced with cold and silence. In a disheveled heap on the floor, rubbing her own head was Sima.

He reached down and helped her to her feet.

"What are you doing here, Deliverer?" she shouted. He looked up at the grandness of the large tree that burst forth from the criss-cross patterned brick floor and into a billowing display of bushy green leaves. One red apple, suspended, waiting to be plucked and enjoyed, hung from the highest branch of the tree.

"Deliverer," she snapped. "Pay attention!"

Orlo pulled his mind out of his distraction. "What are you doing here, Sima?"

"For the love of the Conclusus, Orlo! I asked the same of you! Where have you been?"

Orlo stepped away from her, admiring the ornately carved wooden shelving that towered all around the room, empty and dust-filled. "It's exactly the same!" he said, amazed. "It's almost like the one in the Liberum—I mean The Works! Except for these," he said, pointing to elegant banners that hung in brilliant colors between the shelving, each bearing the symbol of an assignment. Like the arching doorway, there were symbols that Orlo had never seen before—like an open book.

One section of the wall was left bare of shelving and replaced by columns of portraits. He had never seen someone's picture before. There were supposedly artisans in the Conclusus who could fulfill this type of order for the elders, but he had never seen the evidence. In each portrait, the individual was dressed in the brilliant blue-green color that he had seen Rosemary wearing in the Liberum. *The color of the Keepers,* Orlo thought.

He reached up to touch the cheek of a youthful lady. Her skin looked soft, her lips plump, and her eyes—he knew those eyes. It was as if the woman was standing right in front of him. He gazed up at the keeper, confident that he knew her. Cradled in her hands was a book. It was a brilliant purple with the symbol of the inventors pressed into a silver coin on the front—identical to the one he had brought back from the Liberum. Upon further inspection, he noticed that every person portrayed by the paintings held a book. Towards the bottom of the display, the books they held were more elaborate and more detailed with swirled etchings and—most noticeably—silver locks as beautiful and patterned as the book they protected.

"Deliverer!" Sima yelled, bringing his focus back to her. He should have been surprised to see her there, but he was not. "Where have you been? We sent for you days ago!"

"Days?" Orlo asked. She had to be exaggerating, but exaggerating was as good as a lie. "I stayed like you said, and I left there as soon as we received the message."

She placed her hands over her eyes and paced back and forth. "Something is wrong. Something went wrong. We waited for you here, precisely where our orders had indicated."

"Davy made a door to the Liber...uh, The Works, but it was gone when I tried to come back!" Orlo really did not want to think about Davy right now.

"What do you mean gone?"

"I got the package, and left, just as you told me to, but there was no door."

"But did you not get my message?"

"Sure I did, and I stayed like you said."

"How long did you stay?"

"Through the night."

"And the other two messages? Wait? You didn't get them." Her voice shook as she read his thoughts.

"Could you not do that, please," Orlo said boldly. A sense of equality soared through him. He no longer saw her as an apprentice, but a girl, like any other girl in the Conclusus.

"I must get to my father, right away. He has to know that the orders were altered! We have been intercepted."

"Wait! I did everything you asked! Don't you want to see the book?"

"You opened the package?"

"I..." He had no explanation for his action that she would understand.

"Of course you did. May I see it?"

He handed her the book and watched as her lips pursed and her eyes filled with tears. She carefully caressed the supple, purple cover, and then lifted it to her face to inhale the scent of new leather.

Orlo looked around at the empty shelving. "You're bringing them back—the books—aren't you?"

"One day," she said blankly with her sight set on Orlo's book. It was his book now, even if he'd been tasked with delivering it to someone else. He'd chosen it. "My father has told me stories of the books from his childhood, but I have never held one...until now." She pulled at the locks. Orlo half expected her to be able to open it. "It will not open."

"I know. I tried."

"Of course you did." She grinned. "Here," she said, handing it back. "You can open it."

"No, I can't!" he said emphatically.

"Trust me, you can." He was tired of people telling him to trust them.

"You *chose* it, Orlo. It is your book. You can open it."

"How do you know I ch—"

"Besides," she interrupted, "it is no good to us if you cannot get it open." She blew the loose strand of hair out of her face.

"What do you mean, *it's no good to us?* What's special about it? You said it's good for my future! You knew I would choose it, didn't you?"

"I do not have time to explain. I am glad you are well, but we need to get you back to your tower," she said solemnly. "Deliverer, there is something you must know. It is about the aeronaut..."

"Knox? Is everything okay? You did let him know that I was safe, right?"

"Well, not exactly. Deliverer, you must know..."

"They must be wondering where I am! Poor Poppy! Do they believe I ran away?" Immediately, Orlo thought back to his last conversation with Davy. "I have to go! Where's the door?"

Orlo slowly spun in a circle. There was not a door in sight. He assumed that the only way in and out was by messenger. He imagined that at one point in time, when the people in the paintings walked the brick floors, there was a messenger who sat at a desk like Rosemary waiting to let people in and out. Orlo's eyes scanned the room until they stopped at a banner that hung longer than the others. On closer examination, he could make out the brick arch behind it. "It's this way! Isn't it?"

She did not answer.

On the bluish-green banner was embroidered the open book. Orlo pushed the banner aside to reveal a grand metal door.

"Orlo, stop! I must tell you something!" she demanded.

"Not now. I have to get back!"

"Fine!" she said, irritated. "I will let you find out for yourself."

"Brilliant!" Orlo exclaimed, examining the complex mechanisms of the door. "It's like the safe in the Postal!" He rotated a knob to the left, and then back to the right. It released a great metal bar, which Orlo promptly lifted. He guided the door gently outward.

Orlo pushed aside another banner and stepped out into the wide hallway of the Hall of Keepers. He had been in this room a few days before. He turned back around to see the banner reading WE WILL SERVE. He stuck the book under his shirt in the back of his trousers, and lifted the banner to say goodbye to Sima, but the door had sealed itself shut.

Chapter 20

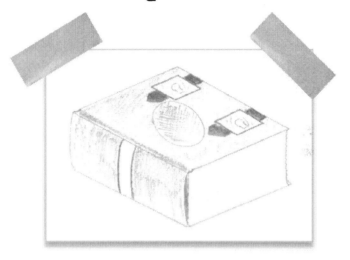

The streets were empty and the light dimming as night fell on the Conclusus. The soft hissing of the steam pushing up through the ground replaced the usual hustle and bustle of the city sounds. Knox would be home from assignment and Poppy cleaning up from dinner. Orlo figured their dinner conversation had most likely been on his whereabouts. He had been gone for nearly two days with no record in the Slub of his coming and going. On top of that, he had missed tea with Elder Bednegraine. He wondered if he had broken a law by not fulfilling an appointment with an elder.

He was too exhausted to think about it tonight, and though his hand was probably in need of more oil, he had already decided to refrain in order to have a dream-free sleep away from the elder, the cloaked man, and whomever else sleep decided to bring him.

Orlo ran past the towers of the Upper Decorum. Lights flickered off as his classmates were most likely crawling into bed. He could see the adults of the Upper Decorum enjoying an evening cup of tea in their rooftop gardens. It made him laugh to think that two days ago he had wanted that very life. Teacups and top hats no longer seemed important.

He had already decided to tell Knox and Poppy the truth about The Works. But where would he start? Its real name? The Way? Would they understand what it meant to serve others and not the Conclusus? Would they see the freedom in it that he had felt? He could imagine them embracing him, accepting all he said as truth. And then, they would choose the Liberum with him. They would all go together.

He would invent, Knox would return to his assignment as a messenger or stay an aeronaut—whatever he chose—and Poppy would become a healer. Their life would be perfect. He would introduce them to Davy, Banyan and the rest of his family. They would follow The Way and leave behind the Decorum. Maybe this was why Davy had told him to come back, so he could tell the others and they could choose as he had.

He turned right, passed the towers of pullers and timers, took a left down an alley, and then raced towards the cave wall where his tower had been built many years ago. All the lights were on inside, and the lanterns in the garden glowed. It was not much, but it was his home—for now.

Orlo flung open the door and found Poppy and Avia sitting by the fireplace.

"Orlo!" Poppy gasped. She rushed to him, fell to her knees, and gripped him tightly. In two days, he had forgotten how breathtaking the combination of citrusy oranges and sweet flowers smelled. "Orlo, Orlo," she murmured beneath sobs. Her dark hair hung loose and glistened in the generated light. Avia looked at him, her eyes dark and weary. Something had happened. He did not know what to do, or how to respond. He had never learned how to be affectionate.

He dropped to one knee and looked at Poppy's face. Her eyes were puffy and wet, and her face splotched with red. She would not stop saying his name. Then he realized what was wrong. This was what Sima had been trying to tell him. Knox was not there. "Poppy, it's okay. Where's Knox?"

"He's not with you?" her voice squeaked.

He took her hands and pulled her to her feet. She was shorter than most of the ladies in the Conclusus, but her petite frame made her appear long and stately. "No, ma'am."

She stepped back and gasped, clutched her hair and frantically said, "No! No! No! It's not true! I won't believe that it is true! Not my Knox!" She fell to her knees again and sobbed. Avia fell to Poppy's side, covering her body with her arms.

"Whatever is true, whatever is honorable, whatever is right, whatever is pure, whatever is lovely, whatever is of good repute, if there is any excellence and if anything worthy of praise, dwell on these things," Avia whispered over and over in her ears. "Whatever is true, we will dwell on these things," she repeated.

Had Orlo heard her correctly? Was she telling Poppy to think on what was true, as Sima and Pa had told him?

"What is true, Avia," Poppy said through teary eyes, "is that he is gone."

Orlo's insides flip-flopped. "Poppy," he asked gently, "where did he go?"

Both Avia and Poppy turned to look at him. "To find you," she said as if he should have known.

"Me?" Orlo asked.

"We thought…" Tears fell from her eyes. "We thought you ran away, or," her voice cracked, "the wolves had come for you." Orlo cringed at the thought. There were people who had gone missing from the Conclusus. In the Hall of Orphan Care, he had been told that the creatures surfaced in the night to take disobedient children to the mines. Maybe this wasn't true either; maybe it was just a way to cover up the disappearance of the children who had found their way to the Liberum.

Orlo stepped back. "But, I didn't run away. I had something to do, and I'm ready to explain. I wasn't permitted before, but now it doesn't matter."

Poppy slumped down in her chair as if the weight of the burden she was carrying was too much for her. "What took you a week that you could not tell us?"

"A week!" Orlo exclaimed. His face turned white and his hands shook. It had never occurred to him that time in the Liberum would move slower than in the Conclusus. He had seen it on his deliveries in other gardens and set his dashboard clock accordingly for the time lapses.

Avia squeezed his cheeks between her hands. Her eyes searched him. "Concern, discomfort, confusion," she said. "You don't know, do you? Orlo, you have been missing for one week, to the day."

"But where I was—it was not even two days! They told me to stay!"

"Orlo," Poppy said, staring off into the distance, "when you did not come back for tea…Elder Bednegraine—she said she had overheard your thoughts…that something was troubling you. We thought that you ran…" Her sobs filled her throat once again. He knew what she was going to say.

"No! I would never leave you!" he said, but in his heart, he knew that he almost had. "I can explain." He was trying his hardest to speak the truth.

Poppy shook her head. "He's gone, Orlo. He went to look for you. He said that he could do it. Something about his gift, that it had not been taken away."

Orlo stumbled backwards, his body hitting the door. He shook his head; this could not be true. For his sake, Knox had gone into the unknown.

"I'll find him. I will! I know someone who can help!" he cried. Sima had gotten him in this mess. He would demand that she get him out. He removed the book he had hidden under his shirt, slipped it into his fallen satchel, and flung the bag over his shoulder. He was ready to go.

Orlo turned to open the door. Poppy shot to her feet. "No, Orlo. I forbid you to go." Her eyes were stern. She had spoken louder to him than he had ever heard her speak. "No," she said softer, running her hand across his bare head.

"But, I can do it. I can bring him back. I have a way." She had never forbid him to do anything.

"No," she said again. She reached for his burned hand. Through sniffles and restrained tears she choked, "How is it, Orlo? Are you hurting?"

"It's better."

She turned it over and examined the wound. "Run upstairs and clean it with the olive soap by the sink. You may use my lavender oil if you are out. It won't be as strong as the one you received from the Apothecary, but it will help to heal the wound." She ran her hand across his head once again and left the room.

Orlo looked at Avia, stunned. "But, I can help! I can do this!"

"Orlo, you feel fear, loss, sadness, anxiety, confusion…too much for a boy your age. She feels a loss far deeper than anyone I have ever seen. She has carried it for a long time, but my son," she paused, "my son makes her forget. Now she remembers. She cannot go back to the World, Orlo. There is nothing left for her there. This is her life. You are her life. If she loses you…she can't lose you, Orlo." She spoke to him more clearly than he had ever heard her speak. She did not seem like the crazy lady who kept losing her letters, but like a woman overflowing with wisdom.

"We can't let him wander around down there. I can find him!"

"I believe that you could, Orlo. But she has spoken. It cannot be, at least not for now." Orlo was about to respond when a knock at the door startled the both of them.

With hope filling him, Orlo flung open the door expecting to see Knox, but instead, glistening like gold in the evening mist was Elder Bednegraine.

Chapter 21

"Oh, Orlo!" she said, embracing him. "I am glad you are safe! May we enter?"

"Welcome, Elder Bednegraine," Orlo said, respectfully ushering her in. "Would you like me to call for Poppy?"

Avia looked uncomfortable, frustrated.

"That will not be necessary. I have come to see you." The woman standing in front of him was as real as the woman in his dream. "Avia, may we have the room? I have a matter to discuss with Orlo." When she smiled, her teeth looked like white stones perfectly lined up under her reddened lips. Poppy had explained to Orlo that in the World some people wore straightening devices on their teeth as children to make them as straight as Elder Bednegraine's. He was fascinated by the idea, but at the same time terrified. He had asked Poppy if it was a punishment for disobedient children. She had said it was not.

"What are you going to do?" Avia grumbled, "Take his letters, too?" Her personality had instantly changed with the elder's company.

"I apologize, Elder Bednegraine," Orlo said.

"It is alright, Orlo. You all have been through so much. Avia, do you speak of the letters you mentioned at the Gathering?"

Avia snatched the cloth which she had been stitching and started up the stairs. "Don't let that woman do a number in your head!" she called down.

Orlo was about to apologize again when Elder Bednegraine raised her hand gently to quiet him. "The minds of the elderly are frail. They have a tendency to mix reason with nonsense."

Orlo knew all about her nonsense.

"Orlo, forgive my intrusion at such a late hour. I had received word of your return, and I absolutely had to make certain for myself that you were here." She wrapped her arms around him, smothering him in the cool taffeta of her yellow gown. "Oh Orlo, if anything had happened to you, I do not know what I would have done with myself. And to return to the news of Knox's disappearance! Please know that we have done everything we can to find him. I have insisted Poppy take a few days off of her orders. She may return when you believe she is able."

"Thank you," was all that Orlo could say.

"Such a tragedy, but we will honor him in our minds for his bravery in fulfillment of his duties to your household and to our Conclusus."

Orlo held tightly to his thoughts, cleared his mind, and tried not to think on the past events. Elder Bednegraine was a friend to the family, but her realistic manifestation in his dream made her presence uneasy. "If I may, where were you all of this time?" She walked around the room looking at the objects that Poppy had used to decorate their tower.

To not answer a direct question from an elder would be against the law.

"No need to answer. I can see that it is too much at one time. Do promise, Orlo, that you will tell me about your adventure. Will you promise?"

She was looking into him, searching. "Yes, I promise." He swallowed the lump of apprehension in his throat. He glanced at his satchel. He had not meant to, but he had—and she had seen it.

"Good. I will await the day." She opened the door to where her apprentice waited. "And Orlo…"

"Yes, Madam?"

"I must caution you that lately it seems a wind of discontent has blown through our dear Conclusus. Be vigilant that you are not led astray, and be wary of the company you keep. *I want to protect you.*" She stepped through the door and let her apprentice shut it behind her.

Her words unsettled him—I want to protect you. She had said that in his dream. Maybe he had heard her say it before. After all, he had known her for a very long time. Orlo grabbed his satchel and ran up the stairs to the kitchen.

Knox's failed attempts for the Tournament of Inventors lay on the table—bits and pieces of broken ideas abandoned for Orlo. *He left in a hurry,* Orlo thought. Orlo turned on the water to wash his pink and wrinkled wound. The warm water stung his hands as the dirt from his journey left him and slid down the drain. He turned off the faucet, but a constant drip continued to escape. Glancing under the iron sink at the piping below, Orlo thought, *I could fix that.* He extended the fingers of his left hand to the reach for the loose valve, when pain shot from the burn to his fingertips. The drip would have to wait.

Poppy kept the household oils—remains from past visits to the Hall of Healers and a few that Poppy had attempted on her own—in a cabinet by the stove. Orlo opened the small cupboard; it was like a mini-apothecary in their own tower. He lifted the vials, smelling each one until he came to the one that smelled like lavender. He stared at the tiny container, debating whether or not it was worth the crazy dreams. He turned it up and allowed the yellowish oil to drip on his hand. He rubbed it in gently as the liquid soothed his pain and the aroma soothed his mind. He felt selfish taking care of himself when Knox could have been taken by the creatures and forced to serve in the mines away from everyone he loved.

Orlo heard the gentle whimpers of Poppy escaping from her bedroom. What could he say to make it better? Now was not the time to explain where he had been, but he would tell her—when she was able to hear it.

Orlo grabbed a candle and an illuminating stick, picked up his satchel again and climbed the metal staircase to the roof. The steam in the Conclusus was sinking to the ground, leaving miniature droplets on the foliage in their tiny garden. The day was nearly done. He imagined the residents in the Liberum willingly turning the large valves and shutting down the pipes that carried the steam from the mines into the Conclusus. He saw Rosemary stacking up the beautifully bound books, and Davy leaning over the counter smiling at her. He envisioned Banyan and his family at the Gathering. "Ahhh! Why can I not stop thinking about them?" he screamed into the openness.

Orlo climbed the scraggly branches of the boswellia tree and positioned himself where he could see the high rooftop walls of the Hall of Keepers concealing the great tree that grew behind them. He could not believe he had been in there less than an hour ago—and before that in the Liberum. And gone for two days, but to the Conclusus, an entire week. He had experienced brief time lapses before between gardens, but never this long. He flipped open the top of the illuminator, producing a flame that he immediately transferred to the candle. On another day he might have mentally taken it apart to understand how it worked. It was a fascinating invention, but he had other things on his mind.

By the light of the candle, the leaves around him glowed in such a way that they took on the blue-green color he had seen on the woman in the portrait. He wished he could sit up there forever and let life pass by below him. He would live off of the food produced in their garden, and be happy observing the lives of the Upper from afar. But, it was not what his heart desired. He did not know what his heart truly desired, but a life without Knox was not it.

Orlo stuck the candle in a knot on the tree branch and reached in his satchel for the book. He wondered if he was breaking a law by having it, but then he reasoned that—since no one knew of the existence of books—it would be impossible to have a law forbidding it.

He ran his fingers over the tool embossed within the silver and the intricate locks. On each of locks there was a tiny hole. *Maybe they take a key*, he thought. He turned the book over in his hands. *Useless. I can't open this thing. I could've at least chosen one that opened.*

He lay back on the branch, holding the book tightly to his chest. The sweet aroma of the boswellia tree floated around him as his mind swirled with reminders of the Liberum, the Hall of Keepers, and his conversation with Davy. What is the desire of my heart? he thought. *Right now, I desire to open this book!*

A breeze blew through the leaves of the tree. The earthy scent grew stronger. Orlo lifted the book to his nose intending to smell the fragrance of aged paper and worn leather, but what he smelled was not that at all. It was the smell of his tree.

He examined the locks again, this time taking careful notice of their outward design instead of their intricate construction. On each one, etched, and clear when he turned the book sideways, was the boswellia tree. "Maybe," Orlo said, reaching toward a small hole in the tree where a sticky yellow substance moistened the bark. Orlo took a glob of the resin and pressed it onto the lock. A burst of light shot out and, with a snap, the lock popped open. He repeated what he had done with the other lock. Snap!

Orlo lifted the cover and read: *The Book of the Inventors*. "Ha ha ha!" Orlo laughed out loud. "I did it! She was right! I did it!"

"Orlo?" he heard.

The voice startled him so badly that he rolled sideways from the branch and hit the grass-carpeted roof. "Urgh," he moaned. "I've got to stop doing that." He sat up, rubbed his head, and scrambled for the book.

"I thought I might find you here," Poppy's gentle voice said before Orlo could hide it behind his back. "What's this?" She lifted it up and ran her hand across the cover. "I've never seen one like it." She rubbed the spine and examined the inside. "The binding looks as if it's been done by hand. And the artwork inside is exquisite. Is this why you were gone, Orlo?"

She was nearly breathless with awe. "No, ma'am. I mean yes, ma'am."

"Knox didn't quite understand when I told him about books." She sat down on the grass beside him, the skirt of her work dress circling around her like a puddle.

"Had he never seen a book in the World?" It felt strange to speak about him in the past tense.

"When we met…" she paused at the memory. "It doesn't matter." She exhaled, as if exhaling would release a portion of the memory she sought to speak, but by the law of her new world, could not. "I haven't held a book in my hands in many years. I've missed them—stories, adventures, and mysteries! There were a few in college I would have liked to toss off the back of a pick-up truck. But oh, Orlo, you have found a treasure!"

She opened the book, turned back the cover, and read, "In wisdom dwell with prudence, and find out knowledge of witty inventions." Her fingers thumbed through a few more. "All things came into being through Him, and apart from Him nothing came into being that has come into being." She looked up to Orlo. In the pale light, she looked beautiful and mysterious. "Orlo, what is this?"

"It's called *The Book of the Inventors*."

"Orlo, is this book stolen?"

"No, Poppy. I chose it."

She put her free hand on her hip. "You chose it?"

He took her hands in his. "Poppy, there's something I should tell you."

That evening, he told her everything.

Chapter 22

Orlo was not surprised that Poppy had asked him more than a handful of questions regarding his absence: Was it safe in the Liberum? Why did they have a library? Did the Conclusus have a library? Were Rosemary and Davy engaged? Should she send a thank you note to Banyan's mother? He had told her everything about the dreams, the crates of books, and how he wanted to stay—to which she responded that she did not blame him—and how Davy had told him that he had to come back. He ended with Elder Bednegraine's uncomfortable visit a few hours before.

When he had asked Poppy what he should do, she had looked at him through tired eyes and said, "Be careful, Orlo."

They had stayed up late in the night pulling strength from one another by sharing and comparing stories from the World and the Liberum. In the early morning hours, they agreed that it would be wise to stay home from the Gathering in light of Elder Bednegraine's warning. It was against the law to miss the Gathering, unless illness had overcome the household. Poppy said that she would explain their absence to Elder Bednegraine. Then there was the issue of the book.

At first, Orlo and Poppy thought it might be a good idea to keep the book hidden from Avia, fearful of whom she might tell, although chances were that no one would believe the ramblings of an old woman. But then, they agreed that its presence might lift the air of sadness that hung throughout their home.

That night, when Orlo brought out the book, Avia collapsed on the floor, gasping for air. Their first thought was to get her to the Hall of Healers, but Avia insisted that she was not going to a place where they would smear her down with their oils. "It makes me all slippery," she argued, waving them off, "and I smell like a flower bed!"

Once she had caught her breath, she stood, pulled her skirt up to her knees, and danced around the room. "You found them, Orlo! By His name, you found them! You found my letters! I told you! I said you would find them, and you did!" What followed next was an awkward concoction of clapping, stomping, hand shaking, and a bit of rolling on the floor. In all the excitement, Orlo forgot to ask her how she had known about the book or why she claimed it as her own.

Poppy could not hold in her laughter. "It is the first night since Knox's disappearance that life has felt somewhat normal. I will make us a treat!" That night, as part of the celebratory evening, she prepared her special peppermint tea with an added spoonful of honey—an expensive import given to her by Elder Bednegraine.

A late night knock at the door silenced their party. Orlo half expected it be Elder Bednegraine bringing them news of Knox. He opened the door as Avia slipped the book behind her back.

In front of him, dressed in a black top hat adorned with a red band and giant red feather sticking out from the side, was a messenger. His red velvet coat was long, hanging nearly to his ankles, and fastened with a brass circular buckle. On the buckle, the torch, the symbol of the messengers, was outlined in red rubies. It was not only late for a messenger, but Gathering Day. The law prohibited him from fulfilling orders.

The household knew the messenger's odd appearance must mean there was news of great importance. At his presence, Poppy cupped her hand over her mouth and Avia put her free arm around her daughter-in-law.

"Orlo the deliverer?" the messenger asked.

"Yes, sir," Orlo's voice shook with anticipation of bad news.

The eccentric messenger handed Orlo a note, tipped his hat, and walked away. Orlo flipped the note over—there was no seal. Without hesitation he opened the letter and read:

Orlo the deliverer,
In light of recent events, you are cordially invited to represent your household in the Tournament of Inventors at the Festival of Sevenths.

At the bottom of the note was the emblem of a dove and in its mouth an olive branch. Orlo had never seen it before. He turned the note over; there was not a seal to let him know from what sector of the Decorum it had come, or a signature to let him know who sent it. Poppy and Avia watched him, waiting in anticipation.

"I've been asked to represent our family in the tournament," Orlo said gently. He folded the note and stuffed it in his pocket. How could he replace Knox?

Avia stepped up to him and placed the book in his hands. "Orlo, the finder of letters, you must do it."

Poppy pulled the ladybug necklace that she had kept hidden in the fold of her dress from around her neck. "You must. It is what you were created to do. You were created for such a time as this."

Orlo stared at the book, and then up at Poppy. She nodded. In the Liberum, it would not take a tournament to prove his gifting. But in the Conclusus, winning would change the lives of those he loved. He could try to take Poppy and Avia to the Liberum, but they would never go, not while there was the hope of Knox's return. In that moment, his heart chose to stay in the Conclusus instead of returning to the Liberum. He understood what Davy had meant by *there's work to be done*. He chose the tournament—for the safety of Poppy and Avia.

The days that passed were long and filled with orders. His hand had almost fully healed, and days in the Slub had replaced those in the classroom, making it impossible for him to avoid "the company he had been keeping" as Elder Bednegraine had advised. However, he did make use of the alleyways to cut across the Conclusus in order to avoid her. He kept his eyes open for Sima and thought only of lunchtime food in order to avoid his thoughts being heard by the interpreters. At one point a puller had greeted him with "Good morning, Deliverer."

With thoughts of lunch on his mind, Orlo had accidentally responded with "And to you, Pickle."

Orlo backed his cartagon out of its holding. Thoughts of the Tournament of Inventors, invention ideas, and Sima's words—"you would have won"—kept him from concentrating on his orders to P10424. Many years past, the cartagon had won the Tournament of Inventors and secured its creator, a former puller, the position his grandson still enjoyed in the Decorum today. The puller's grandson would never be an elder, but he was very much a part of the Upper Decorum. The cartagon huffed and puffed and pushed steam from its underside. Orlo had not been told what he was delivering today, or where he was going. Well, the clerk may have told him, but Orlo had not been paying attention.

The night that the messenger had delivered his mysterious invitation, Orlo had spent the majority of the evening poring through *The Book of the Inventors*, but there was not a plan, blueprint, or set of instructions for an invention. It was all words...scripture, as Poppy had tried to explain.

And today, Orlo's mind fought between a whirlwind of ideas, finding Knox, and completing his orders for the week. Twice the opportunity to be an inventor had been in front of him, and twice it had been taken from him. And now it mattered even more. Without Knox there—without knowing where Knox was and whether he was okay—Orlo needed to do this for Poppy and Avia. Nothing would stop him this time.

Orlo pulled up to the wall. Anxious bubbles filled his stomach. Davy was standing at his usual post. They had not spoken since that day in the Liberum. His face was drawn, his jolly disposition displaced by distraction. Orlo got out of the cartagon and walked over to hand him the order that he had been given.

Davy hardly looked at him, as if their time together in the Liberum had never happened. "It's a good place," Davy mumbled. "I would guess you were deliverin' citrus, that garden can't grow citrus…too cold. And, I would also guess you were pickin' up roses. They have good roses there."

Orlo remembered, but he didn't say anything.

Davy spoke aloud, but not to Orlo. He placed his hand upon the wall as he had most likely done a hundred times in Orlo's lifetime. "Don't be gone long. The door won't stay open."

"I know, Davy," Orlo said.

"Glad you made it back."

"Thanks," Orlo replied. The air of tension between them was thicker than the humidity in the Slub. Here was a man he had once called friend. Elder Bednegraine would suggest this same man had been leading him astray. However, if it were not for Davy, he would not have *The Book of the Inventors*.

When Davy lifted his birth arm to the bare cave wall, Orlo saw that the highly mechanized mechanical arm was gone. In its place, Davy's dingy red jacket dangled. Had they taken his arm away? Was this his punishment for helping Orlo? Was Davy's loss Orlo's fault? The mechanical arm had been the first of its kind—given to Davy back when Orlo lived in the orphanage. Davy never talked about the accident, but Orlo knew it had happened on orders to the World. Knox had said Davy was a good friend, and if it were not for Davy, it would have been Poppy stuck in that door. That was all Orlo knew about the accident. It would have been rude to ask him any more.

Davy's head hung low and his usual smile was gone.

"Davy?" Orlo started to ask what had happened, forgetting the law governing rudeness.

Davy shook his head and frowned. Orlo understood. Davy did not want to talk about it.

Orlo turned to board his cartagon.

"Orlo?"

Orlo jerked back around. "Yes, Davy?"

"Sorry to hear about Knox. He'll be all right. His gifting will take care of him."

"Thanks." Orlo climbed into the cartagon and watched as the door opened in front of him. He felt more alone than he had ever felt in his entire life.

"And Orlo," Davy called. "It's not your fault." Orlo had told himself the same thing, but he had trouble believing it.

Orlo drove the cartagon into the darkness until it emerged in a green-carpeted landscape of yellow, red, pink, orange, and white roses. Davy had been right.

It was chillier here than the steam-warmed Conclusus. He unloaded the crates, which he assumed were oranges by the faint scent that reminded him of Poppy, and waited for the pick-up. He checked his pocket watch. He would do whatever it took to be back to the tower on time. Poppy had enough on her mind. She should not have to worry whether something happened to him as well.

Orlo pulled his goggles up on his head and sat down on the steps of his cartagon. He closed his eyes and imagined pieces of scrap metal coming together to form a handheld device that would remove the thorns from the roses before they were picked. "That won't be useful," Orlo mumbled. They did not have roses in the Conclusus, and when the roses were imported for special occasions, it was requested that the thorns already be removed.

In the distance, he could make out the movement of several small children walking toward him. He had planned to use every opportunity he could to search for Knox. When the children were in hearing distance he said, "Greetings from the Conclusus! I'm looking for a man, an aeronaut that goes by the name of Knox."

One of the children looked at him strangely and replied, "As for man, his days are like grass. As a flower of the field, so he flourishes." She bowed her head and handed a bundle of roses to Orlo.

"Does this mean that you have seen him? Are you saying that he is okay?"

The next child stepped up to him saying, "Consider the lilies, how they grow: they neither toil nor spin; but I tell you, not even Solomon in all his glory clothed himself like one of the these. But if God so clothes the grass in the field, which is alive today and tomorrow is thrown into the furnace, how much more will He clothe you?"

"No, his name is not Solomon. It is Knox! Does God know where to find Knox?" The child's words sounded like what he had read from the books in the Liberum, and she called Him *God*.

A third child, smaller than the others, leaned into him and spoke in voice as tiny as she was. "The grass withers, the flower fades, but the word of our God stands forever."

Orlo groaned at their cryptic responses. Their words were delicate, soft-spoken, and as flowery as their garden, but they did not make sense. He just wanted to know if they had seen Knox. He walked to the back, opened his cartagon, and unloaded the citrus. "Flowers go in the back."

Behind the girls, a trail of people carrying small crates of flowers lined up to load his cartagon. He decided to try again. "I'm looking for a man; his name is Knox. Have you seen a stranger pass this way?" Instead of answering, a man put a wreath of flowers on his sweaty head. "Umm…thank you, sir."

Orlo climbed back into his cartagon, laying the loose flowers beside his seat. Poppy would enjoy them. It was always a treat for her when he visited P10424. As strange as these people acted, they were extremely kind. And he wouldn't give up. He had another delivery today, and four more this week. Someone must have seen Knox pass by.

Orlo pulled his cartagon back through the door Davy had created for him, guided it into the holding room, and shut off the steam valve. He leaned back in his seat. It felt hotter than usual. If he did not get the roses out fast enough, they would wilt before the tournament. He wiped the sweat off of his head and went to unload the crates.

He had so much on his mind that focusing on one idea for the tournament was difficult. If all else failed, he figured he could enter the ladybug—he could call it entertainment, like a toy for the children of the Conclusus, as if they did not have enough to keep them entertained. For most of the Upper Decorum, hiring children to keep their own children occupied was not unusual. There was a constant exchange of children and goods.

It was the one aspect of childhood that Orlo thought was ridiculous. Poppy did not need to pay someone else to have their children play with him. He had been content to spend his free time with Poppy and Knox.

Orlo took his goggles off of his head and tossed them angrily at his cartagon. Where was Knox? Why couldn't things have stayed the way they were? *Because I didn't want them to*, he thought.

Orlo went over and picked his goggles off of the hard ground to see if his frustration had cracked the lens. "Sorry, God," he said out loud. Startled, he looked around to see if anyone had heard him. Had he referred to the Mysterium as God, and apologized to Him? *I'm a participant in the Tournament of Inventors now,* Orlo thought, *I have to get ahold of myself! One wrong move, and I'm out!* The participants in the tournament were watched closely, not only by eager people hoping to get a pre-show preview, but also by the Upper Decorum, who enjoyed being sure that participants were adhering to the laws. During tournament time, there were more removals than usual. At one time, Orlo would have seen it as a coincidence, but now he saw it as a way to eliminate the competition under the guise of helping to correct a fellow member of the Decorum. Now that he knew the truth, being removed to the Liberum seemed like a gift rather than a punishment..

Orlo unloaded the crates, positioning them on a long conveyer belt that would carry them through the Slub and into the Conclusus where a collector would haul them to their appointed destination. He pulled out his handkerchief and wiped his forehead. Lately it felt like the Conclusus was getting hotter. He wished there was some way to cool down without visiting gardens like P10424. Like a flash of light invading his brain, he saw it.

He had an idea—one he had never heard of anyone else entering before—and he had Poppy to thank for it.

Chapter 23

If Orlo had not been distracted by what he thought was a tournament-winning idea, he might not have left his last delivery with his pants wet to the knees from having to push his cartagon out of a swamp. He knew that his future included some minor repairs including pulling mangrove root from the underbelly of the cartagon. Poppy wrapped a blanket around his shoulders and set a cup hibiscus tea in front of him.

She took his hand in hers. "It has healed up nicely," she said pleasantly.

Orlo thought about his idea. It was a good one; in fact, it was a great one. But what if he did not win? The question had been weighing on him. "Will you stay here?" he asked her.

She sat back in her chair and rubbed her tired eyes. The band with the symbol of the guardians was wrapped securely around her arm. "Yes," she said flatly, her smile forced and her lip quivering. "This is my home, Orlo. You are my home. You know what they say, there's no place like home." She got up to refill his cup even though he had yet to take a sip. "Have you decided what you are going to make for the tournament?"

"I have, but it's a surprise."

"Of course it is. All right, Orlo, as you wish," she said glumly. He could tell by her solemnness that she was having a bad day. "Have you started on it?"

"Not quite." He needed parts—lots of parts. Orlo's insides stirred with excitement. There was one place in which he believed he could find the items he required…the Hangar where Knox stored the steam-powered balloon.

Orlo hurried out the door, but not before letting Poppy know where he was going. He had made that mistake once before and was positive that he would not make it again. The Hangar was directly behind their tower. Orlo had always thought that Knox's move to the back wall of the Conclusus had something to do with its proximity to the Hangar. As he had gotten older, he understood that it was not by choice that Knox lived where he did. Towers, like everything else, were assigned.

The one-story tower that partially extended from the cave wall had been specifically designed by an inventor years ago to roll back and release the steam balloon effortlessly into the air. The rest of the tower was fitted into the wall, out of sight from the Conclusus—like the Slub. Once Knox had the balloon airborne, passengers from the Upper Decorum were collected from their rooftop gardens and transported to their destinations.

The inside of the Hangar was colder than the outside, shielded from the warm steam by the walls. The deflated balloon looked sad and lonely. On his way home from the Slub, Orlo had overheard a musician complaining about the disappearance of the aeronaut and the inconvenience it was causing the Decorum. The musician, upon seeing Orlo, immediately followed it up with a verbal request for a moment of silence from those around him. Orlo doubted the genuineness of the musician's tribute.

Whether the empathy was genuine or not, Orlo had bowed his head along with the rest of them. The moment had no sooner begun than one healer had asked another if the aeronaut was to be replaced.

It would not be long until the black-and-white striped balloon would be soaring through the Conclusus once again at the guidance of Knox's apprentice. It occurred to Orlo that if Knox were to be replaced, there was a good chance they would have to move to a new tower, but where? There was not a portion of the Conclusus dedicated to guardians. He wondered if he would be forced to return to the Hall of Orphan Care and Poppy to the World. Avia would end up in the Hall of Resting, and Knox would still be lost, probably wandering in the darkness of the uninhabited worlds below. No. He would not let that happen—he'd take Poppy and Avia to the Liberum before he would let the elders separate his household.

Orlo walked to the back of the Hangar and looked through the pile of broken parts, failed inventions, and discarded materials that Knox had collected throughout his days. "Everything is useful, to somebody," Knox had once told Orlo. "Value is a matter of perspective."

Orlo scanned the scattered stuff. *It will be useful*, he thought. *I can make it useful.*

The walls were decorated with the original designs of current and past balloons. Orlo had asked Knox if flying the balloon was easy for him. "No," he had answered honestly, "it is not easy. But I can do it because it is what I have to do." Orlo stood at the long workbench replaying the conversation over in his mind.

"Shouldn't your new gifting make it easy?" Orlo had asked Knox.

Knox was evidently uncomfortable with the question because he answered by saying, "You would think that is how it worked, wouldn't you?"

Orlo felt like he had an understanding of something beyond assignments, the Decorum, and the Conclusus itself, but like the random parts scattered around him, he did not have the instructions to put them all together. Remembering what Knox had said made him wonder if Knox had been putting the pieces together as well. As a child, Knox had been groomed to be a messenger. One choice, as Davy had called it, demoted him to an aeronaut; another had sent him to look for Orlo.

Orlo stuffed in his satchel what his arms could not carry. The idea passed through his brain that it would be much easier to toss it all in the balloon and lift himself to their rooftop, but it would never work. The Lower Decorum was not privileged with air transportation, mainly because the Upper Decorum said that their towers were not tall enough. Like their own tower with the sprawling branches of the boswellia tree, the lower towers grew the trees—citrus, nut, and hardwoods. The balloon would never be able to get close enough. *An idea for another day*, Orlo thought.

Orlo held tight to the bundle of oddities. On his way out, he spotted Knox's goggles, long black coat, and utility belt hanging by the door. *Knox surely would have taken those items with him*, Orlo thought. The only place he ever went without them was to the Gathering. He wondered if he should share this piece of information with Poppy, or if the knowledge of it would bring her to worry. He felt torn between two laws—not lying and not inflicting discomfort upon another. He stepped out into the humid air and shut the door behind him by using his foot.

As the door slammed, he thought he saw a shadow move to a nearby palm tree. "Hello," Orlo called. "Is anybody there?" He turned to walk the fifty steps to the door of their tower when, out of the corner of his eye, he saw it move again. "Can I help you with something? The aeronaut isn't here." Hesitant, but curious, Orlo inched toward the shadow.

"Do not come any closer, Orlo," the voice of the figure said. "I am not what I seem, but I am here to come alongside you." The voice was familiar to him.

"I saw you in my—"

"Did you get the invitation?"

"Yes," Orlo stammered. "How did you—"

"Good. That is good."

"Who are you? How do you know who I am?"

"There is that which should be left unknown."

Orlo started to ask another question, but the stranger kept going. "You have been given the pieces to make it work again, Orlo."

At the stranger's words, Orlo looked at the pile of scrap gears, pulleys, screws, bolts, and pieces of metal that he was clinging to.

"He causes all things to work together for those who love Him." Orlo had heard that before...at the Gathering...from the gardener. "You have seen the possibility in the Liberum. You have felt it, Orlo. Your steps have been directed to this moment. It is who you were created to be. Make them believe in you, Orlo. Then, you can make it work again!" The dingy brown-cloaked figure from his dreams took off from behind the tree and sprinted into the forest that lined the far cavern wall.

"Hey!" Orlo yelled. "Wait!" He had questions, and he wanted answers. The cloaked man from his dream had been only a few feet from him. How was that possible?

The pieces in his arms as he ran back to the tower no longer looked like possibility, but rather a broken mess—exactly like his thoughts. Orlo tossed the rusty, dented, and broken items on his bed. He paced back and forth in his room, occasionally glancing out the window to see if the mysterious visitor was spying on him. How had the man known about the invitation? And he'd mentioned the Liberum—by name! What was it he had said about his steps being directed?

Too many thoughts crowded Orlo's mind. He did not have time for more unplanned visitors. The tournament was a few days away. He had to focus. I will think about it later, Orlo thought.

The Book of the Inventors lay open on his bed. At one time, Sima had said his future depended on it. He reached for it and flipped through the pages. He read, *And we know that God causes all things to work together for good to those who love Him.*

"Ahh!" He dropped the book to the wood floor beneath his feet. The cloaked man had spoken those words. With shaky hands, Orlo picked up the book. He flipped a few more pages and read,

Serve one another. The Hall of Keepers erected in the middle of The Work's dinginess proclaimed these words. It had been busy with excited people seeking the words that the books had to offer, but the empty Hall in the Conclusus with its billowing lush green leaves and single red apple was lifeless because the books had been taken away. The wisdom they possessed was gone.

Who would take it away? he thought.

It seemed that every word he read had been spoken to him sometime over the past several days. He set down the book beside his bed, placing it where he could see it as he worked and thought. Without thinking, he reached for a crank and twisted it into the center of a large gear. What was it the man had said about pieces and making it work again? Make what work? The more Orlo thought about the words in the book, the faster he worked—a screw here, a bolt there. *Unless…maybe…but it could not be.* He tightened and twisted. He could see the design in his head.

He examined the rectangular contraption in front of him. It was nearly done. He worked into the night, wishing he would have the next day free of orders to work on his invention. Occasionally, he would lean over and read what the book had to say, all the while tinkering and thinking. It was like the three went hand-in-hand. The more he worked on his invention, the clearer his thoughts became, and the more he read, the more he understood.

Sima had said to think on what was true. Why take the books away? Davy's words resurfaced: *The books contain all the knowledge of the gardens, and everything about all our giftings. Copied—every letter that makes a word and every word that makes sentences. Bound by the Binders, spoken by the Creator Himself. They speak the truth… The Way, Orlo. It's what makes it all work.*

Orlo set the box down gently on the floor. "They don't want us to know," he said to himself.

"It is a truth too large for you. We will keep it safe," he repeated the words spoken by Elder Bednegraine in his dream. She had been there, physically in his dream. She had tried to take the book.

The pieces had come together. *The elders don't want us to know the truth. If we know about The Way, we have a choice. We can choose who we want to be. We are the part that is broken. I have to show them the truth.*

Chapter 24

If Orlo could pick a day to be ill, this day would have been the day. He would have given anything to stay home and finish the machine. But he was not ill, and his hand was better.

He had not slept. It was not because his bed was covered in a mess of leftover gadgetry, but because he could not get Elder Bednegraine and the other elders out of his mind. When Poppy told him that she felt like it was time to go back to her orders, Orlo had jumped up from the table and shouted, "You should stay home!"

"Oh, Orlo!" she had exclaimed. "It will be good for me. I'll bring you a few grapes. We'll have them with dinner." She gave him a hug and walked out the door before he could figure out how to stop her.

Orlo bounced his knees nervously as he sat on the dusty bench of the Slub waiting for his name to be called. The image of the cloaked man and a broken Conclusus with a huge crack running straight through the fountain penetrated his thoughts. Everywhere he looked, he thought he saw the shadowy figure hiding behind a random stalagmite or under a bench. The man had said in order to make it work, he had to make them believe.

With a spot in the tournament and a nearly complete invention, Orlo had still not figured out how he was going to use the opportunity to bring the truth to the Conclusus. At first he thought he might yell it from the platform, but after Avia's outburst, he assumed the Decorum would see her craziness as contagious. It did not seem to matter if he won anymore. The prize he wanted was bigger than an apprenticeship. He wanted to be an inventor because he could choose to be, not because he had competed for it.

He stretched out his long legs and noted the patches on his knees. He examined the leather bracelet wrapped around his right hand, holding the symbol of the deliverer. He rubbed his sweaty palms on the calves of his pants and looked to the clerk to see if there was something holding up the calling of his name. A line of deliverers and carriers waited, checking their watches. Orlo did the same. He was already thirty minutes behind where he had anticipated. He needed to be back in time to finish his invention. He looked to the wall where Davy created the doors. There were already two other cartagons in line. It was not like Davy to be backed up.

"Orlo the deliverer." Orlo jumped up at the sound of his name. Normally, it would have meant he could grab his papers and leave, but he was asked to wait in line. Orlo checked his pocket watch once again. Poppy would be led to worry if he was not home for dinner. He hoped that word would get back to her that, for reasons he did not know, there had been delays today in the Slub.

"Excuse me, sir," Orlo said, tapping the shoulder of a man in front of him. "Do you know the reason for the delay?"

The man turned around. By the amount of sweat on his forehead and the indention left on his face by the goggles, Orlo knew this was not his first delivery of the day. "We gots a new messenger down here. Don't know what she's doin'. If I were a questionin' man, and I ain't, I'd say she weren't no messenger at all. Took her three tries to get my door open."

Orlo was having trouble processing all he was saying. Could it be that Davy had been replaced?

"Next!" the woman behind the counter called. Orlo stepped up. "Oh, it's you," she said with a frown. She took her stamp and slammed it down on the pad of ink, then onto the paper in front of her with a thud. Her lips curved downward as she stared at him over the top of her wired spectacles. She reached up and adjusted the sides to focus in on him. "M-hm," she said. "It's you. You know the routine. Don't speak unless you're spoken to. It's a drop off today. Nothin's comin' back. Your cartagon's already loaded. Don't look in the crates. It's not our business. Garden P327. It's a new one for you."

"Thank you, ma'am," he replied. What had he done to make her foul toward him? He took the assignment sheet from her hand and walked toward his cartagon's holding.

"Orlo the deliverer," she called. "It ain't your fault."

He grinned back at her to say thank you. Orlo figured that Knox's disappearance had replaced the whispered discussions of the burning of L923. He imagined that his name came up quite a bit. He did not blame them, because he blamed himself. He should've gotten word to them somehow.

Orlo pulled the nozzle of the water hose to the side of the cartagon. He lifted the lever, watched his pocket watch for three minutes twenty-seven seconds, and then shut off the flow of water. This was enough to get him to P327 and back. Inside, Orlo checked the pressure gauge on the dashboard of the cartagon and cranked the wheel, stoking the flame that would heat the water and producing the steam that powered the cartagon. He carefully backed his cartagon from the holding, and steered it in line behind the man who had told him that Davy was gone.

In the three years he had been making deliveries, Davy was the only messenger he had ever seen in the Slub. He was the only person of the Upper Decorum that he had seen in the Slub, with the exception of Knox, who stopped in periodically to see that Orlo was doing all right. And that pulled his mind back to Knox. In his sharp, black long coat, he had been a contrast to the dingy browns and tans worn by the deliverers. It bothered Orlo that Knox's goggles and utility belt had been left behind.

Orlo watched as the cartagon in front of him disappeared into the wall, and then pulled up to take his turn. As Orlo had been told, a short round woman with her hair tucked up under a tattered red top hat stood where Davy once fulfilled his orders.

"Elder Stockhart!" Orlo exclaimed. "What are you doing here?" She looked sad and uncomfortable in the velvety jacket. A red-and-black striped crinoline poked out from underneath. Around her neck was not the lamp that symbolized the teachers, but the torch.

"Oh, Orlo! I figured I would see you today. What am I doing here? Well, it seems I have been given a promotion of sorts."

"But you're a great teacher! Why would the gardener reassign you?"

"Now, now, let us not question them."

Them. This was the doing of the elders. What had they done with Davy? Orlo handed her his orders. She took it, read them, and looked into his eyes with dread.

She cleared her throat and tried to smile. "P327. It is a lovely place, Deliverer." Her voice was shaky and unsettled. "Be wary of critters. They have a nice variety of…" She stopped, placed her thumb on her chin and frowned. "I cannot seem to remember these days. Oh what is that species?"

Orlo pulled out his pocket watch without trying to let her see. He did not want to be rude, but Davy's disappearance had put a definite kink in his plan to get back in time to work on his invention.

"*Specus aranea!*" she shouted, startling Orlo. He dropped the pocket watch, thankful it had been clipped to his belt. "That is it! I do remember! Yes, I do! That is the species!"

"Yes, ma'am," he could barely choke out.

"They said I had the gifting, you know. I guess we all have a bit of it, do we not?"

Orlo could not discern if she was asking him a question, or confirming that the elders had gifted her with the abilities of a messenger. For most, moving up the Decorum from educator to messenger was rarely heard of. This was an honor. He wondered if they would make her promotion public at the festival.

Orlo could hear the sounds of other deliverers in their steam wagons piling up behind him. "Excuse me, ma'am," he said as politely as he could. "I believe I should get going."

"Yes, yes, of course." She did not take her eyes off of him as she placed her hand on the wall. "My mother was a messenger," she said sadly. The bright outlined edges of the large doorway began to form—ready to swing inward into the under land of P327, but the instant Orlo thought he could see the completed door, it went away. "Non!" she yelped. "Non! Non!" She placed her hand on the wall, scrunched her eyes, and grunted, "We will serve."

"One another," Orlo whispered.

"I beg your pardon?" she asked with a hand cupped behind her ear.

Orlo did not respond. There was not time to explain it all. She would find out tomorrow at the tournament. The door formed once again, this time coming to full completion and swinging open wide for Orlo to pass through. The woman wiped her forehead with the towel that she had stuffed under her belt loop. She looked completely exhausted.

"Thank you, ma'am." Orlo lifted his hat from his head and placed it back again. He adjusted his goggles and pulled into the opening. The door slammed shut behind him. This was not good. He drove through the tunnel thinking about the mysterious *Specus aranea*, and hoping that when it was time to return, she would know to open the doorway.

Seeing the light up ahead, he checked the clock on his dashboard and set the timer. *This should be an easy delivery*, he thought. He had made so many deliveries that it was hard to count them. In his time, he had delivered everything from seeds to oils. He listened for the gentle tinkling of bottles, but the *swish swoosh* of the cartagon was too loud.

When the tunnel opened up, Orlo was shocked to see that he had pulled out onto a wooden dock of sorts that extended over the water. He docked the vehicle and stepped out into the humidity. He removed his waistcoat, placed it on the seat, and checked the timer. He had less than an hour for them to unload. Beneath his feet, water slapped against the sides of the dock.

This garden was unlike any other. Large trees with sprawling roots grew upward into the sky of the cavern. Vines crawled across the cave ceiling hundreds of feet above him. The water was murky, but its soft glow brought light to the garden. Here it smelled clean and wet. He checked the time again. *Someone should be here*, he thought. He sat down on the edge, pulled his goggles up on his forehead and removed his hat.

It was hot. Not hot like the Conclusus, but hot like the Liberum. He unbuttoned his shirt at the neck and took his suspenders off of his shoulders. This was not a proper way to deliver, but the heat was unbearable. Where were they? Orlo stood back up and peered out into the wetland. Nobody. Then he had a thought—a thought that covered him in terror. *What if this is the wrong garden? What if she got it wrong?*

Chapter 25

The repercussions of this were too much for Orlo to handle—Poppy, the tournament, nobody would know where he was. He would be assumed missing like Knox and replaced—passed over as if he had never existed. With the heat and the plethora of strange events that had occurred in his recent life, he felt dizzy and disoriented.

He checked his cracked pocket watch once again. There was still time. In less than fifteen minutes, the door would appear, and he could back his cartagon out of P327 and into the Slub of his own J2415. He sat down and rested his head on the dock. It was hard to not think the worst, but he could not shake the notion that Elder Stockhart had made an error. Davy had always gotten it right, but now an educator who could barely make doors replaced him.

"No!" Orlo gasped. "They wouldn't have." The thought was too dark. "Think on what is true, think on what is true!" But he could not think on anything else. This was the truth. He knew it. He had been misdirected on purpose. "They planned this. This isn't P327! Help!" he called into the wetland. "Somebody! Help! I need a messenger! Help!"

I have to get back, Orlo thought. The heat and the gentle lapping of the water's movement pulled at his tired eyes. He forced them open. He had to stay awake—in case someone came for him.

But he knew no one was coming. Nobody knew where he was.

The heat was unbearable. His throat felt like it was closing up and his chest tightened. "Help…" he called again. Then, everything went dark.

When he opened his eyes he found himself back in the Liberum standing outside of the Hall of Keepers. *This isn't real,* he thought. *It's another dream.* He walked through the broad doorway halfway expecting Elder Bednegraine to pop out in front of him, but the room was empty. The shelves were full, but the people were gone. Rosemary, who should have been sitting at the front desk, was nowhere to be seen. He walked the room touching the books and inhaling their familiar aroma. All he had to do was wake up and he could go home. *Wake up!* he shouted at himself. *You have to get back!*

Time moved slower in the Liberum. He would miss the tournament. "Orlo."

Orlo jerked around to see the cloaked man. "It's you!"

"They know everything, Orlo."

"That's why they sent me away, isn't it?"

"They have known about you for some time. You have to get back. Make them see the truth!"

"I can't! I'm stuck. Nobody knows where I am!"

"Orlo, you must listen to me," he said more sternly. "You will have to create a door."

"I'm not a messenger!" Orlo said, his voice echoing in the empty room.

"No, you are not. But if you ask, it will be given to you; if you seek it, you will find it; if you knock, it will be opened to you. Ask Him, Orlo."

Orlo started to speak but the cloaked man put his hand over Orlo's mouth. "They have found me. I must go."

"Wait!"

The figure began to fade away.

"Who are you?"

But he was gone. Darkness fell across the Hall of Keepers. Orlo turned to see a new figure walking his way. He wanted to run but had nowhere to go. Wake up! Wake up! he told himself. The image moved closer. He ran to the tree hoping to find the door that would lead him into the Conclusus. The image moved silently in the darkness. He felt along the coarse bark knowing that somewhere in there was a staircase that would take him into the Conclusus.

There had to be another way in. *I'm seeking!* Orlo thought. He knocked on the bark of the massive tree trunk, hoping there was truth to the mysterious stranger's words. He felt the cold presence of the figure towering over him, but he could not see her.

Then he heard her voice, crisp and frightening. "Orlo…" She was in his head, calling to him. He had to go now. He had to make it back for the tournament. He had to get away from her.

"What do you want?" he yelled, continuing his search for a way out.

"You've broken the law, Orlo…"

"No!" he yelled. "I'm not a lawbreaker."

"You took it, Orlo. Tell them you took it. I will make sure you are pardoned…"

"I didn't steal anything!"

"Oh, but you did!" Suddenly, he saw a shadow of himself, standing by his cartagon. The shadow bent down and picked something up—the stone. "It wasn't yours to give, Orlo. You broke the law."

"It was a stone…a simple stone! I didn't steal it!"

"Tell them, Orlo, and your life can go back to the way it was. I can make it all go away…" Her words pressed into his mind. Orlo clutched his head. With his heart pounding, he briefly considered his simple life, but he wanted more—and not just for himself. The Conclusus, his home, deserved more. They deserved the truth.

Ask him. A new voice—the man in the cloak.

Hoping the Mysterium would hear his plea, Orlo shouted, "Will you show me the door?" A burst of light shot out from the tree. The darkness turned into light, and he found himself back in P327, if it was that garden at all, with a door, his size, directly in front of him.

Orlo gave the handle a swift turn and stepped inside, leaving the cartagon behind. He could hear the hum of the fans that cooled the room, and a soft buzz from the lamps that provided the light. He recognized those sounds. Then he could smell it—the faint hint of oranges and lavender.

"Orlo!" Poppy cried with open arms.

It was as if he were in another dream, a dream where the past repeated itself, except this time, Poppy was not in her work clothing. She was in her Gathering dress. On her arms were the gloves that Knox had given her, and around her neck the ladybug. Down her face a single tear trailed, but on her lips was not sadness. There was a smile.

Orlo's forehead dripped sweat. His suspenders hung by his sides, and he assumed his jacket was still on the seat of his cartagon where he had left it. It was like it was all happening over again.

"Am I back?" he asked, patting his clothing to see if indeed he were awake. He focused in on the elements of the room and the woman in front of him. Nothing seemed odd, out of place, or unusual. He turned around to see that their front door had shut by itself.

"Yes, Orlo!"

"Poppy, I…I…I was stuck," he stuttered. "I…" he patted his chest again to see if it was real. "I'm back. I created a door," was all that he could say. He studied the tops and palms of his hands. He did not know how he had done it, but he had acted as a messenger. Orlo felt as if the world he had known his entire life was standing up on its side and he was struggling to keep his balance.

She shook her head and pulled him to her. "No, Orlo. Don't be sorry. I had a visitor…in my dream," she said.

Orlo looked around nervously, hoping that no one on the outside had heard her. Her favor with the Conclusus had gotten worse as rumors of her staying without a husband were the new chatter. "Look at me, Orlo," she insisted, directing his eyes to hers. "In a dream. He said that Knox is alive. He is okay. The man—he said you would come back, too. And here you are!"

"A visitor?" Orlo asked. "In a long, brown cloak?"

"Yes," she said, startled. She took her handkerchief from the small pouch that crossed her chest and wiped the moisture from his face. He felt like a little boy again. "We have to go, Orlo! It's nearly time. Are you ready?"

"Ready for what?"

"The tournament!"

Oh, oh, oh no.

Once again, he had fallen victim to the time inconsistencies of the gardens. A day in the Conclusus had passed him during his time in P327.

"Where is it, Orlo? I will bring it down for you while you change."

"It's not done." Sadness tugged his shoulders down.

"Can you finish it?" she asked.

"I don't know," he said honestly. The cloaked man had given him an idea, but his invention would have to work.

"I can help! I fixed a thing or two in my past. What do you need?"

"Ice," he said flatly. "I need ice."

Chapter 26

With the help of Poppy and the not so helpful, but appreciated, advice from Avia, Orlo's invention was finished.

"What will it do, Orlo?" Avia asked. "Is it gonna make my dress bigger? I can hardly breathe in this thing." Poppy had asked what the contraption's purpose would be, but Orlo insisted he was keeping it a surprise. She was disappointed, but it was the only way to make the Decorum see the truth.

Elder Bednegraine would be watching, so he would have to make sure she did not overhear his plan. He didn't trust her.

"Can't you give us a hint?" she pleaded.

"Nope," he had replied smugly.

"How about a clue?"

"No."

"All right then, will you at least tell us how you came up with such an idea?" Orlo thought about saying that he had seen it in a dream, but he felt like credit should be given to God, because if God caused all things to work together for good, then his dream was God's way of dropping a hint.

"The Mysteri…" he started to answer. He had come to the understanding that God and the Mysterium were truly one and the same—called by a different name. Once the Decorum knew the truth, they would call Him God as well. "God, Poppy. God gave me the idea."

He thought she might cry. She took his hand and kissed it softly. "He loves you, Orlo."

Orlo had never heard that before. He scratched the back of his neck uncomfortably. "We should probably go."

The Festival of Sevenths was unlike any day of the year.

Anticipation for this day kept the children awake, and its preparation kept the Lower Decorum busier than usual. As they approached the inner circle, Orlo could see the rows of booths lined up around the fountain—each draped with a colorful silk cloth to provide a ceiling of sorts for the exhibitor. Large banners depicting the color of each of the seven higher assignments hung from the rooftops of the seven central towers. Imported exotic flowers from many of the gardens Orlo had visited decorated the fountain.

The children of the Lower Decorum danced through the streets holding sticks attached to colorful streamers. Interpreters walked freely among the people, sorting out their thoughts, and giving them reassurance in regards to their giftings. Messengers demonstrated their ability to open doors and permitted onlookers to have a glimpse at the garden on the other side.

Planters displayed baskets full of their finest picks, and seamstresses exhibited the latest in Conclusus fashion. Orlo had never cared much for fashion, but Poppy appeared to be entranced by the layers of frills the seamstresses were advertising as the next growing season's dress to wear. A few of the deliverers got in on the fun as well by selling rare items they had gathered on their deliveries.

A variety of music filled the air as each musician tried to play louder than the one beside them. As with the Gatherings, the Upper Decorum were dressed in their finest. As if their Gathering clothing were not fanfare enough, the clothing of the festivities was a show all of its own. Many of the ladies' dresses were so wide that passersby would have to say, "Excuse me" to not be accused of touching a lady inappropriately on the backside.

Along with the trading, exhibitions, and the tournament, other spectacular events were often added into the day as a surprise from the elders to the Decorum. In the past, there had been welcome home ceremonies for traveling messengers, celebrations of healing, and the promotion of a very young interpreter to the position she held even today as elder.

At the last festival there had been a demonstration of gifting by the children. It was fun to watch, as the children attempted to imitate their parents, until the daughter of two healers decided to try her hand at being a messenger. In doing so, she had created a door, walked through it, and never come back. The incident was never spoken of again. Neither she nor her parents were ever seen, and to this day there had been no more demonstrations by children below the age of apprenticeship.

Normally, this day in all of its beauty and excitement would have made Orlo forget that the next day he would be back in the Slub. But the day did not seem as bright as other years. It was as if a veil hung over the festival that he alone could see, a shadow that revealed all was not right in the Conclusus. He felt like he had obtained a new sense of vision—like the observers or the seers who saw what could be.

This day of celebration meant to commemorate the seven most extraordinary gifts the Mysterium had given to the Decorum looked more like a party of extravagance for the Upper Decorum. Orlo's mind flashed back to the Liberum—the dancing, the music, and the people. He looked up at the entertainment going on around him—it did not seem lovely anymore.

Traditionally, the Festival of Sevenths was supposed to be a time when the Upper Decorum could serve the Lower Decorum through the demonstration of their giftings, and for the Upper Decorum to show their appreciation for the talents of the Lower Decorum. It was a day when the Lower Decorum felt equal to those above them.

But what Orlo saw this day were pullers and pickers toiling to impress the musicians and the artists. He saw his fellow deliverers making trades so their families might be able to have an extra cup of tea or slice of sweet bread. He saw the smirks of the healers behind their hand painted fans at the booth of a timer who was explaining why it was better to plant leeks in the morning. Orlo wondered if he was the only one to notice what was really going on.

The wooden box that contained his invention was heavy in his arms. He needed to get it to the long wooden stage that had been erected at the base of the Hall of Keepers. He tried his best to see through the sea of taffeta and silks, and over the high hats of the men. The last time he had been this close to the Hall, he had been inside its abandoned library. He doubted anyone else knew a giant tree grew inside. There was a lot the Decorum did not know…but they would.

With his invention weighing down his arm, Orlo started to squeeze by an educator and artist fanning one another. The ladies appeared to be in such intense conversation that they did not realize that the husbands linked to their arms were yawning.

Poppy, who was behind him, shrugged; Avia, who had sworn that she had never missed a Festival of Sevenths in all her years and was not going to start today, was adjusting the bodice of her dress.

"Do you think she will be faithful?" the one dressed in orange asked of the one dressed in hot pink.

"Let us hope she does not decide to woo one of our men," the other said, hiding her face behind her fan. Orlo knew the "she" they were talking about.

"Excuse—" he started to say, choosing to face the consequences of rudeness over the possibility of Poppy hearing them. But the ladies kept talking as if he was not standing right beside them.

"I mean really, as if she has not been permitted to stay long enough!"

"Without that aeronaut, whose services I greatly miss by the way, Miss North has no reason to occupy a tower." The educator giggled. "Am I correct?"

At the word *North*, Orlo's face grew hot and his hands unsteady. If he had not been holding on to his invention, he would have yanked the flapping fan from her hand and shoved it in the other's mouth.

A gloved hand rested on his shoulder. Poppy had heard.

The artist spoke up again. "Should we not consider the law of the widows?"

"I do not believe it is specific to her case."

"You are wise beyond your years."

Unfortunately for them, Avia had overheard every word of their conversation. "That's enough of your yapping!" she said sternly enough for the women to hear her. "If you will so kindly mind your words and your skirts, we would like to pass by."

"Well, I never—" the educator started, until she saw Poppy. Her cheeks flushed, but she maintained her composure and moved far enough away from the other so Orlo, Poppy, and Avia could pass through their ruffles.

But before they were too far past the gossiping, Poppy said, loud enough for many around her to hear, "Orlo, you must know that I do not plan on going to the World anytime soon. Knox will be back before we know it." Her words were kind but firm, settling the debate that had blocked their way.

It felt strange to be at the festival without Knox. If he were there, the balloon would be bouncing from tower to tower high above them. The children of the Lower Decorum would jump up and down at the sight of it, pointing and waving. Knox would lean over and wave back. Orlo did not know of anyone in the Conclusus that did not like him, including many of the unmarried ladies—maybe that was why his unexpected marriage to Poppy was such a shock. Even though he had been reassigned from a messenger to an aeronaut, many of the Upper Decorum confided in Knox.

Orlo missed him and prayed he was safe.

When he found an empty space beside a cylindrical gadget, he set his invention down and peeked inside his box. Nothing was broken or out of place. He checked the block of ice secured in the center. *This will work*, he reminded himself, *unless she tries to stop me*. It would only be a matter of minutes, a slip in his thoughts, before Elder Bednegraine knew that he was there competing in the tournament. It did not matter if the elders voted for him, the Decorum would. Orlo pulled the lever on his invention. A faint *swish swoosh* and tiny puffs of cold air escaped from inside the box. He shut it off and let out a sigh of relief. It would work. Orlo looked at the scar the burn had left on his hand and grinned—a bit of inspiration. His invention would be ready by tournament time.

Orlo linked his arm in Poppy's and led her toward the heart of the festival where he hoped she would be free of the conversation of the ladies her age. It was the law for a married lady to have an escort, and as far as he was concerned, she was still married.

Apprentices from all across the Conclusus had set up demonstrations of their giftings in the booths. The apprenticed musicians attempted to prove their newly found knowledge of the instruments, and the healers revealed their abilities to use the oils produced from the plants of the Conclusus to cure headaches, cuts, gut ailments, dizziness, bone pain, sadness, and boredom. If they could diagnose it, they had a treatment for it.

Poppy excitedly pulled Orlo to the booths of the healers. She watched as they dropped and rubbed various oils on willing members of the Lower Decorum. A timer and a puller, arms crossed, discussed their part in the growth of the plant that had produced the oils. A frail healer, thin faced with a hat too big for his head, waited with wandering eyes beside a table set up for bone adjustments.

"You look like you could use an adjustment," the boy said. Orlo looked around to see if maybe the apprentice was speaking to someone else. "Yes, you, Deliverer. It will not hurt."

"No thanks." He was not in the mood to be treated like the Upper Decorum.

"Why not, Orlo? It might be fun!" Poppy insisted.

"Never had one, never needed one," Avia said loud enough for the healer who was shifting back and forth on his feet to hear. The healer smiled at her reluctantly.

"I am not going to hurt you, Deliverer," he said. "I am in my third month of apprenticeship, you know."

"Go ahead, Orlo. Give it a go," Poppy continued to encourage.

Maybe it will help clear my head. Orlo stepped up to the table.

"Face down," the boy instructed. Orlo swung his boots around and laid his face down on the table. He did not like being unable to see what was going on around him. The boy placed his hands on each side of Orlo's spine. With a quick thrust he pressed his palms into Orlo's back. There was a loud *pop*, and then the healer moved his hands to a new spot. Once again he aligned his hands, and with a *pop*, Orlo felt his back relax. Tingles ran through his body. The tension he carried vanished with each movement of the boy's hands until every ounce was gone. Orlo thought he could stay in the healer's tent all day and let the boy adjust his bones. The boy was about to start again when Orlo heard Poppy's voice. He turned his head to the side to see her.

"Excuse me, Healer," she said politely. "How did you acquire the vial that you wear around your neck?"

"Do you not recognize the vial, Miss…" the older healer said, clearly confused as to what she should label Poppy.

Orlo recognized the vial. It was like the ones in their cupboard at home, like the ones that Poppy used for her hobby.

"It is one of your own," the woman said. "It is not?"

"Mrs." Poppy corrected her.

"Excuse me?"

"Mrs. It's Mrs. I'm married, Healer."

"I suppose you are. Please thank your spouse…when you see him again…for his trade. It has surprisingly proven to be…quite valuable. Our elder looks forward to acquiring more." She nodded her head and returned to the observation of a student who was busy placing drops in the ears of a puller.

"I'd be happy to trade," Poppy responded.

"I don't think that will be necessary," the healer said smugly.

Poppy's face was frozen. The only boswellia tree in the Conclusus grew on top of their roof. Poppy tended to it like it was another member of their tower. Occasionally, she would make a small cut in the tree to allow the sap to seep out. Once the sap hardened, she would pull it off the trunk, purify it with steam and extract the oil. On those days, their tower smelled fresh and strong.

"Healer?" Poppy's voice was stern. "How do you plan to acquire more if not by trade?"

Orlo could see that she was upset. He sat up and swung his feet back around to the side of the table. As he did, he thought he saw the cloaked man walking among a mass of people moving toward the Hall of Keepers.

"The adjustment is not over yet," the boy instructed Orlo.

"I'm sorry. I have to go, now. Thank you," Orlo called as he wriggled his way out of the booth to where Poppy's face was now as pale as her dress. "Poppy, we have to go!" Orlo tried not to take his eyes off the man that no one else seemed to notice. He wanted to talk to him, not only to tell him thank you, but to tell him his plan.

"With all respect, madam, please answer my question," Poppy said.

"Poppy, we have to go!" Orlo insisted.

The healer did not answer. Her cheeks were flushed, and beads of sweat were forming on her forehead underneath the overhang of her wide blue hat.

"Orlo," Poppy's voice cracked, "they will take our tower. They will take the tree. She is right. It is very powerful." He had no trouble believing that this too was the decision of the elders.

His eyes searched the sea of passersby, but the cloaked man had vanished. "Did you hear me, Orlo?"

"Yes." He had heard her, but his mind was elsewhere. Orlo checked his pocket watch. There was another hour before the tournament was to begin. Something else was drawing the people to the tower. Orlo took Poppy by the arm to lead her away from the healer's booth before she could continue her interrogation of the healer.

Orlo pushed their way through to the front to see what was taking place. More inventions of elaborate design had been added to the display for the Decorum. The eager audience discussed the possibilities each one would bring, speculating their purposes—everything from seed planting to fan folding. The inventions were not only complex, but also beautiful—their tiny parts glistened like jewels in the high mist. It made him proud to see that several were pointing curiously to his plain box.

He knew the elders would never pick him as the winner, especially since he was supposed to be trapped in a swamp. However, if Orlo's invention worked the way he had planned, it would wow the Decorum in such a way that the people would begin to question the decision of the elders. If they questioned that decision, they would begin to question others and open their minds to the possibility of another way—the truth. Then, he would tell them.

"Did you hear?" someone asked him.

"Are you talking to me?" Orlo replied, looking around to see if she was speaking to one of the many others surrounding him.

"You are a deliverer, are you not?" She looked him up and down from his tweed cap to his laced boots.

"Yes, ma'am. I'm a deliverer."

"Well then, you must know." Her smug expression said she was proud of the knowledge that she possessed and Orlo did not.

"No, ma'am," he responded.

"Well," she said, leaning into him. "I have been told that they found him making unlawful doors."

"Doors?" Orlo asked. That very morning he had entered the Conclusus by way of his own door.

"I heard," interrupted a man in front of him, "that it was a door to the World." Those surrounding Orlo gasped.

"I heard," interrupted a woman to his left, "that it was not a door at all, that he was using a gifting that was not given to him." Orlo felt faint. This was another way to keep him from competing in the tournament. They were going to have him removed.

"It hardly matters where the door was created. The one armed man created it. You know whom I mean, Mildred," the lady said, fanning herself.

Orlo felt as if his heart would stop; they weren't talking about him.

"Oh yes! Such a tragedy about the accident and all. How gracious of the gardener to even allow him to keep his assignment all this time. What was his name?"

"Davy," Orlo murmured, aware that the door in reference was the door to the Liberum that Davy had created for him. Sima was right; they knew everything.

A roll of drumming hushed the eager crowd and directed the onlookers' attention to the stage. Orlo no longer wondered what special event would open the festival this year.

"Decorum! I welcome you to the Festival of Sevenths," the gardener announced, looking more worn than usual. Dark circles had formed under his eyes. His clothes were not as neatly presented, and his oversized green top hat was slightly lopsided.

"Today, we partake in a tradition that brings much sadness to me, and I am assured it will to you the Decorum as well." His speech was not as boisterous as it normally was, and his words were slurred and tired. "It has come to my knowledge by way of our elders, that one among us has become unlawful. It is not for us to discuss the details of such a manner, but to remove the one among us so his unlawfulness will not be spread to those around him." The gardener sighed. "Today, as part of our festivities we will once again fulfill the Passing of the Lawless."

This was not the first time Orlo had witnessed a removal. From the balcony of the Hall of Orphan Care, he had witnessed six removals at one Gathering.

Davy, escorted by two apprenticed messengers and the gardener's wife, stepped up to the platform. He held his head high and looked sorrowfully toward the Decorum.

"Davy," the gardener said, "do you deny the charges brought against you?" There was an odd exchange of glances between them, including—*was that a wink?*

"I do not," he said flatly.

"Will you please share your error with the Conclusus, so it will not be repeated by those among us?" the gardener asked gently.

"I've been creating doors without orders, Sir."

"Then, by order of the elders of our fair Conclusus, we will serve."

The gardener's wife placed her hand on the ground. A circular door appeared below Davy's feet. Orlo had not been able to tell him that he was sorry for the harsh words he had spoken. He wanted to run up on the stage and tell him everything.

But then, Davy's eyes found his. He nodded and gave a wink that Orlo knew was intended for him. Everything between them was okay. The gardener's wife lifted her hand and then lowered it, releasing the floor and sending Davy further into the earth to his new home.

The spectators did not cheer, but were solemn. "Tragic," the woman to Orlo's left said. "How awful his life will be among those people."

Orlo laughed when he heard the word "tragic" and then coughed so no one would think he was breaking a law by being disrespectful. To Davy, being removed from the Conclusus was not sad or tragic. It was a path directed to a place and person he loved. Orlo knew they were not removing him because he had broken a law; they were removing him because he chose the truth.

Chapter 27

As if the removal of one of his citizens had never occurred, the gardener stepped back to the middle of his stage. He raised his arms high in the air, looked proudly across the gathered Decorum and announced: "Ladies and gentlemen, let the Tournament of Inventors begin!"

The onlookers broke their reverent silence and cheered wildly.

"Participants, please take to the platform!"

"Orlo," Poppy said sweetly from behind him, "Knox would be proud to have you representing our household." Orlo agreed that Knox would be proud, not because he was entering the tournament, but because he thought Knox would be glad he was standing up for the truth. Like Davy had said, they deserved to know the truth.

"We'll find him, Poppy. We won't give up." Orlo took the gloved hand and kissed it.

"Go get 'em!" Avia shouted, pumping her fist in the air.

Participants from every assignment of the Lower Decorum climbed up on the platform and stood behind their contraptions. Among them was the inventor's apprentice, Lyla von Smoot. Her coordinated work clothing had been replaced by a bulging purple dress that was wider than she was tall. She waved to the audience by flicking her wrist back and forth, and blew kisses to her fellow apprentices standing ready to cheer her on.

Orlo had forgotten about her. He remembered her reason for competing now—to keep someone from the Lower Decorum from entering the Upper Decorum. A few families in the Conclusus claimed to have been around since the beginning of time. They and some others felt very strongly about the sanctity of the Decorum and keeping certain assignments within specific family boundaries—this was not a secret. Orlo knew that she already had the vote of the elder inventor before she had stepped onto the platform.

Let the elders vote for her, he thought.

Hello, Deliverer. Her voice was like a knife to his heart. She had been a friend to their family and a confidant to Poppy. Orlo could feel Elder Bednegraine sifting through the thoughts in his head from her perch at the top of the stairs. *I warned you, Orlo, but you would not listen! I wanted to protect you, but you chose...that is what they call it, is it not? Choosing? I gave you a way out and you refused.*

He had to focus. *I know you can hear me, so hear me well, Orlo. Our way brings order. It is how it has always been, and I will not let some clan of confused radicals and their delivery boy ruin it. The followers of The Way will be stopped, and the books will never make it back to the Conclusus.*

Orlo whipped his head around and glared up at her. She was smiling in her buttery yellow ball gown. A glistening band rested on top of her head. By appearance she looked youthful, sweet, and innocent, but he knew better.

Orlo turned back to the sea of Decorum faces in front of him. They had no idea what was going on around them. *Now I'm going to give you another choice*, she prodded. *End this or you will never see your aeronaut again.* Orlo's insides twisted, his hands shook, and sweat dripped down the sides of his neck.

They knew where to find Knox. What had he gotten himself into? What had Orlo gotten Knox into?

Focus, Orlo, he told himself. *They deserve to know the truth. Knox would want this.* He was not giving up. He knew too much. Now that he knew the truth about the giftings, faulty assignments, and choosing, he could not go back to a life that was a lie. And if the elders knew the location of Knox, that meant that he was alive— Orlo would find him.

On Orlo's left, a timer strapped a complex device to his wrist. On his right, an observer tightened a screw on a large box. Orlo stooped down to peek inside his own box. The ice would have to sit until it was his turn. The presentation of inventions could take a long time, and he needed his ice to stay intact. He looked down the long row of participants.

It looked like there were fifteen, sixteen counting himself.

As was customary, an artist would assist in the ordering of contestants. A gentleman with a long pointy beard and fuchsia coat with oversized golden buttons approached the participant on the end. He looked the puller in the eye and then wrote the number five. Other pullers in the audience cheered for their comrade.

The artists had always fascinated Orlo with their ability to draw what would best serve the Conclusus. It was said that the gardener and the elders worked closely with the artists in the process of assigning. The artist approached the next person, an elderly collector whose invention was slung across her chest like Orlo would carry his satchel—the artist drew a twelve. The artist smiled at her, nodded his head pleasantly, and moved down the line. He was nearly to Orlo.

The next in line was Lyla. She waved again, and blew a kiss to the artist.

"Three!" She squealed. Orlo's nerves flared. Condensation was beginning to form on the outside of his box. He tried to recall what numbers were left. The best he could figure, he had a shot at seven, fifteen, four, or nine. *Seven or four*, he thought. *A seven or four will work.* The observer had drawn the seven. It would be fifteen, nine, or four.

"Good fortune," the observer whispered to Orlo.

Orlo nodded. He believed he could be completely satisfied as an observer. He had never officially met an observer, but the few he had seen on the streets of the Conclusus acted humble, and without fail, they greeted him. Like the aeronauts, they were considered neither of the Upper or Lower Decorum. Observers lived simply, but were eligible for the privileges and fanfare of the Upper Decorum. Orlo wondered if they had chosen to live that way or—like everything else in the Decorum—it was chosen for them.

"Ahem." The artist startled Orlo by clearing his throat.

"Sorry, sir," Orlo stammered.

The artist looked at Orlo with curious eyes. "Interesting," he mumbled as he moved the ornately etched nib of his pen to the tablet. Orlo glanced down at the box. It was covered in tiny beads of water.

The artist's hand seemed to move slower than it had with the others.

Orlo shut his eyes. Timing could ruin everything. His hand moved downward. At this point, it could be a one, or the makings of a four. The artist's hand lifted from the paper and moved again.

"Four," the artist said loud enough for the elders to hear. "I believe this will work to your advantage. Will it not?" He winked at Orlo.

"Um, yes, sir," Orlo stuttered. Had the artist really winked? Did he know about The Way? Is that why he had drawn the four for him?

"Good fortune to you, Deliverer."

"Thank you, sir." Four, he thought. *I can work with four.* The artist knew what Orlo needed, and he had drawn it for him. *Serve one another*—it was part of The Way.

After all the numbers were drawn, the gardener once again approached the stage overlooking the participants. "Participant number one," he called, "you may proceed!"

Orlo noticed the gardener's eyes scanning the Decorum and his hands tapping nervously on his thighs. The elders who sat on each side of him leaned in to one another, their judging beginning before participant number one spoke his first word.

A night watchman, specified by the crescent shape on his hat, held tightly to a device composed of a system of wheels. "Elders," he said. His voice shook when he spoke. "I present for yer review a light enhancer. In the evenings when I'm a workin', it isn't always bright enough to see where I'm a goin' and who's a comin'. If I may…" He took a long wire, which had already been attached to a nearby lamppost, connected it to his device, and with pumped the handles on each side to turn the wheels. As the wheels spun, the light on the post began to brighten.

A calm *aaaahhh* swept across the audience until the watchman, taken by the responsiveness of the crowd, cranked the handles faster. Delight covered his face as he continued to turn the handles, one over the other, until sparks burst from the lamppost, sending most of the Decorum to their knees in fearful shaking fits.

"Oh!" the watchman shouted. "I rightfully apologize, sirs and madams. I believe I got carried away. It will work. It will! If I can try once more."

"Thank you, watchman," the gardener said into the voice-amplifying device. "We appreciate your service. Number two."

The second invention was a puller's endeavor to rapidly harvest rooted plants from the gardens. Orlo thought it was brilliant and knew that it would be very useful in decreasing the amount of labor put into the harvesting of those plants, as well as increasing the amount of produce provided to the Upper Decorum. The Upper Decorum did not seem at all impressed— neither did the elders.

The gardener did not have an opening to thank the puller. Lyla von Smoot had already stepped to the edge of the platform. She waved her hand and tilted her head from side to side. She bent down, not taking her eyes off of the audience, and opened the crate at her feet.

When she pulled the item from the box, the multitude went into a frenzy of whispers and gasps. Orlo had never seen the Decorum so astounded. Talk of the contraption's intricacy was passed down between the other contestants. It truly was a work of art. Fine lines and patterns were etched into its surface. Gemstones decorated the top of each tiny screw, sending a glint of dotted color wherever she moved.

A lump formed in Orlo's throat. He looked down at his very damp box. If presentation were to be scored, there was not a chance that anyone, including himself, could impress the audience like she had.

"I present to you, elders, my Decorum, the ability to cool yourselves without lifting a finger!" She placed a leather strap around her neck, allowing the device to hang on top of her purple gown. Orlo's heart sunk. She had nearly spoken the words he had rehearsed. With the flip of a switch, two tiny propellers lifted from the box and began to spin. Her hair blew back from her face.

A collective *ooohhhh* escaped from the mouths of the sweating bystanders.

"I can't believe she's wearing it," one of the other contestants said.

"Too bad the Uppers will be getting them first. I imagine it will be beyond my trading abilities," another replied.

The elders were on their feet clapping and nodding their heads in approval. Orlo noticed that an agreeable smirk had formed from the lips of Elder Archivald, the inventor. The girl had automated a personal cooling device, cleverly attached like a necklace that was not lacking in luxuriousness or practicality. Orlo looked down at his own wet box, then out to where Poppy was standing. She was smiling at him.

By her side was Sima. The girl winked at him, turned, and walked away.

"Well done, Apprentice!" the gardener congratulated. "Well done! Thank you for your service. Number four!"

Orlo stood up.

"One moment, four."

Elder Bednegraine, sparkling from head to toe, leaned in and whispered something in his ear. The gardener shook his head. He covered the voice-amplifying device with his hand to speak to her. Something was wrong; Orlo could feel it. Elder Bednegraine motioned harshly to Orlo with her hand. The gardener leaned in to the device. "Decorum, excuse us while we take a short break."

The elders were on their feet. The Decorum was in full-blown speculation, and Orlo was left standing.

He looked out into the crowd to see Poppy and Avia encouraging him with their hands clutched to their chest and proud smiles draped across their faces. The elders returned to their seats, frowning, and engaged in conversation clearly determined to deny Orlo's demonstration the courtesy of their attention.

"Number four," the gardener announced, "you may proceed."

Orlo stooped down and removed his device from the square box in which he had it kept. Its appearance of bolts, used parts and oversized gears did not have the flare and grandiosity of Lyla's cooling device, but the audience watched.

Orlo cleared his throat. "Elders and Decorum, I too have an invention that will cool us."

Eyes rolled and phrases like "a copy," "hard to beat," and "not a chance that it will be as good," were murmured.

Orlo opened his box and flipped the switch he had put in place to activate the device. With a scratch and a buzz, a blast of cool air escaped from a hole at the front of the box.

"I cannot believe that thing actually works," Lyla said, loud enough for Orlo and the entire front row to hear.

But then, it stopped. There was no sound of breaking or scent of an engine burning out; it simply stopped. *No! This can't be! What's wrong?* he thought. Too much had happened to bring him to this moment. His path had been directed. This was what he wanted. This was the desire of his heart—to share the truth!

"I am terribly sorry," the gardener said with genuine sincerity. "Thank you for your service, Deliverer."

"No! Wait!" Orlo said, taking the risk of speaking out of his place. "Sir, please, I can make it work. It will work. I don't know what has gone wrong, but it will work."

"I'm sorry, Deliverer, we must continue." Contestants one, two and three had taken a seat behind their inventions as the others waited their turn.

Contestant five proceeded with little applause, six and seven surprisingly had invented exact replicas of one another's, and eight had trouble remembering how to turn his on.

Orlo fidgeted, twisted, unbolted and screwed pieces back together as nine and ten presented. However, eleven's entry was hard to miss as a malfunction caused it to shoot flames backwards towards the elders. Orlo saw a spark connect with a musician on the side of the face. The elder healer immediately pulled a vial of oil from her waist pouch and smeared its contents all over his face. The other elders were busy checking to see if his or her hat had been singed. Orlo thought he smelled a hint of burning hair.

Twelve stepped forward after the healers attended to the other elders and the gardener had restored order.

If only I had the ability to heal my invention, Orlo thought. Thirteen was riding a large tricycle around the platform with an enormous shovel attached to the front. Two more participants, and it would be over.

Orlo stooped down to his invention. He took out his handkerchief and wiped the sweat from his forehead. He opened the top. The block of ice had melted to half its original size—not nearly as much as he had anticipated, but enough to make it work. He could see it all playing out in his mind—each gear, each turn. He looked at his handkerchief and wiped the condensation from the gray steel surface.

Then, he knew what to do. Orlo waited for fifteen to finish—so as not to be rude. He pulled out the extra, clean handkerchief that he kept in his back pocket and wiped the dampness from each gear of the device.

Suddenly, Orlo's invention whizzed and hummed. Cool air escaped from the front, followed by a tiny white flake. *Come on, Orlo* thought, *you can do this.*

"Start!" he commanded the machine. As if his words had spoken the device into life, a spurt of white fluff escaped from the opening and into the air. One after another, hundreds upon hundreds of tiny white snowflakes burst forth into the Conclusus, falling gently and then melting onto the felt hats, silken flowers, and frizzy hair that adorned the Decorum.

Several of the ladies dropped their fans and lifted their fingers to catch the tiny works of ice. Orlo gazed out into the stunned Decorum. Poppy lifted her glove-adorned hands in the air and twirled in the gloriousness of Orlo's snow.

Chapter 28

An air of peace fell with the flecks of snow. It silenced the musicians and subdued the applause of the audience. The temporary flurries hung in the air before descending and taming the humidity of the steam.

It was better than he could have imagined. He looked down at the device and then out across the stillness of the Decorum. He knew he had built it, piece by piece, but it did not seem real.

Little did the Decorum know that he had brought a piece of the World into the Conclusus, a piece that no one except Poppy had ever seen before, and a piece that—without his invention—they would never see again. He imagined Poppy dancing with Knox, twirling in the specks of ice.

Orlo stooped down and switched off the invention. As the last of the flurries melted in the air, a ripple of applause started from the back of the festival to the platform. He looked over the sea of Decorum faces in front of him, cheering.

"Orlo! Orlo! Orlo!"

For a brief second he thought he saw the brown cloak in the ocean of color, but like the snow melting as soon as it warmed in the rising steam, his watcher was gone. The moment was experienced, would be reminisced, and talked about for days to come.

His name grew louder. "ORLO! ORLO! ORLO!"

All he had to do was wait for the elders to declare Lyla the winner—because Elder Bednegraine would never give him her vote. The Decorum would be baffled. They would beg for the snow, but they would not be able get it unless Orlo was the new apprentice. They would question the decision of the elders, and then they would see, just as he had, that something was broken. Their eyes would be open to another truth. Yes, that was the plan. It would work!

No one spoke as the gardener and the elders stepped away from their chairs to convene in the Hall of Keepers. Orlo glanced over at the inventor's apprentice who was blowing kisses from her chair on the stage. Her confidence in her own performance was apparent. *She will be the winner,* Orlo thought. He tried not to look at her—careful to hold in the thoughts of his plan.

The other contestants toyed with their handiwork. He wondered what they were thinking, and if he were the only one who wanted to lose.

Orlo stretched his legs out in front in front of him, peered over his shoulder to see if the elders had returned, and then looked down at the snow-maker. He could see the hundreds of eyes watching him. He reached in his pocket, hoping to find a forgotten bolt or bent gear—anything with which to fidget in order to take his mind off of the wait. It was empty.

He inhaled deeply, puffed out his cheeks and released a long breath. Then, he pulled his hat down further on his head.

A ripple of chatter began as the elders occupied their assigned seats. The gardener stepped up to the voice amplifier, bringing the

Decorum to a hush of whispers. "Decorum, thank you for your patience."

Something was wrong. Orlo could hear the shaky nervousness in his voice. "Participants, thank you for the time and energy you put into serving our Conclusus, however, we have but one apprenticeship to fill." Orlo pulled his knees back in, and nervously bounced them. His plan had to work. He had to lose.

The crowd started up again, "Orlo, Orlo, Orlo!"

The gardener exhaled. "It is my privilege to grant the apprenticeship of the inventors, in fulfillment of tradition during our Festival of Sevenths, to…" the onlookers were eager. The only sound was the hissing of steam pushing out from the fountain. The gardener grinned. "Orlo the deliverer!"

The Decorum cheered, hats were tossed in the air, and the *bum, bum, bum, bum* of the musicians started up again. Orlo sat motionless as the other visibly disappointed participants removed their contraptions from the platform. *No,* he thought. *It can't be me. They won't see the brokenness. No!*

Go, Deliverer! he heard. He looked around until he locked eyes with Sima.

Orlo turned around to see the gardener motioning for him to climb to the top of the stairs. He looked back at Sima who was shooing him with her hands towards her father.

Poppy and Avia had already pushed to the front of the spectators. Orlo reached down and assisted Poppy by her glove-adorned hand to the stage. It took Orlo, along with the assistance of the night worker and the puller, to lift Avia up to the platform—and she promptly adjusted her bustle. It was hard to look at their delighted faces. He had let them down and they did not even know it.

Poppy hugged him tightly, and then cupped her hands on his cheeks. "Thank you, Orlo. Thank you very, very much. This is better than my birthday! I don't know what was better, the snow, or watching you beat that miss prissy pain-in-the-neck inventor."

Orlo rubbed his neck. Lyla had not caused him any pain. When he heard Poppy laugh, he knew that it was another one of her sayings. He took her by the arm and escorted her up the great staircase toward the gardener and the row of elders. With each step his head swirled. He had failed. The elders were not supposed to pick him. Why had they picked him? What were they planning to do with him? How could he make the Conclusus work again if he were serving the problem? He would rather be in the Liberum!

The crowd cheered louder with every step he took. When he got to the top he could see the elders with their fake smiles and pompous clapping. Poppy waved at her employer and friend, but a forced grin was all that she received in return from Elder Bednegraine. *Hello, Deliverer.*

"By order of the elders of the Conclusus," the gardener projected into the voice amplifier, "we present Orlo…the apprenticeship of the inventors."

This time, the Decorum lost all sense of order and cheered louder than before, once again tossing their top hats in the air and waving their arms at him, half anticipating that he would wave back.

Did you forget, Deliverer, we know everything? she hissed. Orlo's mind fought to focus on the voice of the musicians, the gardener's accolades, and Elder Bednegraine. The gardener placed a purple velvet sash across Orlo's chest. On it gleamed the embroidered tool symbolizing the finality of his entrance into the apprenticeship of the inventors. At one time, he would have embraced this memory and promised to never forget it. Being in the Upper Decorum was something he had dreamed about. Orlo saw the gardener look hesitantly at Elder Bednegraine.

She had heard his plan. *How could I have been so careless to think it?*

"Orlo, the apprentice!" the gardener announced as he lifted Orlo's arm and waved it for him. Orlo turned his head toward the interpreter, but she was gone. When he looked back, he realized that Poppy and Avia were no longer by his side.

"Poppy? Avia?" Orlo called into the chaos. "Where did they go?" he asked anyone who would listen.

A series of loud bangs echoed across the Conclusus. Terrified screams erupted from the spectators. The Decorum was running, fleeing from the stage. Everything around him looked darker. It was difficult to see what exactly was happening. Then, he saw the banners of the seven towers beginning to tumble—one by one hitting the ground and covering those unfortunate to be nearby. The Conclusus grew darker. The temperature was dropping. The steam that always puffed up in an invisible mist from the Liberum had stopped.

"Poppy! Avia!" Orlo's voice carried loudly across the Decorum. "My guardian! She's gone!" he yelled, turning to the gardener for assistance. But instead of facing the gardener, he locked eyes with Elder Bednegraine.

"Hello, Deliverer," she snarled, gripping his hand. "I do not know what you have done, but it is over. You will announce that this fearful display is your doing, a show of sorts, or you will never see the members of your household ever again."

She had them. All of them. "It's not me. I didn't do this."

"It is against the law to lie, Deliverer! Tell them!" Her voice echoed across the commotion.

"But that would be a lie! It's not me!" This was not how it was supposed to end. "Poppy!" he called out into the crowd. "Poppy! Avia!" he screamed, abandoning manners and most likely breaking several laws. The elders behind him were awkwardly bumping into one another in their hurried struggle to leave their chairs and avoid the unpleasant embarrassment of the chaos taking place in front of them.

"What did you do with her?" he screamed at the elder. "Where have you taken her? She belongs here! You can't send her back!"

A flash of light, followed by a deafening pop that made his ears ring and his head throb, shot up from the fountain. The Decorum fell to the ground, shielding their eyes and covering their ears.

Orlo felt the hand of Elder Bednegraine release his. A great force pushed him into the Hall of Keepers. The doors slammed behind him.

He turned, his face red, his eyes watery, and his ears aching. "Where is—"

"Shh, be still and know that He is in control," the gardener's wife calmed him. He shook his head. How could he be calm?

"Not here, not now. They will not know you are gone." Orlo looked at the gardener's wife and Sima who stood beside her.

"Gone? Gone where?"

"Shh! Please, Orlo. You must trust me. We will take care of you," she said with a wink. Orlo nearly stumbled back. "Come with me. Sima, go ahead of Orlo, and be ready."

"Yes, Mother." The gardener's wife looked around frantically, and then led Orlo to the huge banner that hung at the back of the Hall of Keepers. She threw it back, twisted and turned the knobs and handles in such a way to let Orlo know that she had done it many times before. She flung open the doors, pushed Orlo inside after Sima, and followed them, then thrust her body backwards to shut the doors behind them.

"Did she see them?" the gardener's wife asked, her voice unsteady and hurried.

"No, Mother, we were careful."

"Orlo, it is going to be okay, but we must not speak any more of it here. You must go, Orlo, but I will return for you. Your Avia we can protect, but I cannot make promises for your guardian...it would be too suspicious," she said confidently.

She placed her hand on the ground at Orlo's feet with much less fanfare than what had taken place during the removal ceremony. A wooden door emerged underneath him. He knew where they were sending him. He was adorned as an apprentice, but positioned as one to be removed forever. Elder Bednegraine must have convinced the gardener that Orlo had broken the law.

His hands shook and his legs were wobbly. He did want to go to the Liberum, he did. He had just wanted to tell the Decorum the truth first. They deserved to know. And *he* needed to know Poppy was safe.

Fear not, for I am with you always, Orlo. The voice was new to him, but familiar—not of an interpreter or of the woman who stood by his side. It was Him, the Mysterium...God. Immediately, his body steadied and he knew that everything would be all right.

"Until we meet again, Orlo the apprentice." The floor broke in two below his feet. He expected to experience the sensation of falling through darkness, but his feet instantly touched the hard ground. The light from above disappeared, and he was left in total darkness—alone.

Chapter 29

Quickly, Orlo! The petite voice of Sima spoke to his mind as her hand roughly grabbed his arm. *Don't think! Run!*

Orlo tried to understand what was happening.

I said don't think—especially about me. We are too close! We must get away from here! We must not allow them to hear us!

Orlo moved his feet faster in the darkness. The sprint was pulling at his sides and making his chest feel heavy. He could see the light ahead in the distance, and he knew where he was. This was the tunnel that would lead him into the Liberum.

Had the elders called for his removal? Had he been removed to Liberum? Elder Bednegraine wanted him to say that he had done it, but he had not. There was an explosion, and the mist...it had stopped. And the banners...they fell. There was screaming.

Poppy and Avia were gone.

The gardener's wife had said she would come back for him; nobody came back from the Liberum. Orlo could vaguely see Sima's black curls, and satin green dress bouncing in front of him. "Stop!" he called to her. "Sima, stop!"

"What?" She turned around sharply. Her eyes were moist and tired.

"What happened up there? Am I being removed?"

"Orlo, there is not time to explain! We have to go! You do not have much time! My mother will be back for you!"

"That's exactly what I have to think about! This! Your mother! Elder Bednegraine..."

"Orlo, if you will trust me, you will get your answers."

"Trust you? Why does everyone keep asking me to trust them? It's all a lie...the assignments, the Decorum. None of it's real! And you...you started all of this. If it weren't for you, I would have never come to The Works...I mean the Liberum. Knox would be here, and The Way, and the books, and the dreams, and the man in the cloak..." His throat tightened.

"You got what you wanted, Orlo!" she said angrily.

"What? This?" He tugged at the purple sash that hung across his chest. "No, this isn't what I wanted! I was supposed to lose!"

"Orlo, God is not done with you yet. Sometimes," she said, looking behind her, "sometimes it is not all about you. Your desire is a small piece to His greater design. Think on what is true. You have to believe in everything you have learned. Do not give up." Her eyes were anxious, shifting back and forth between the light at the end of the tunnel and Orlo.

He stood firm, convinced that he would not move any further. "Is it not better to live in the truth? Please, Orlo, we have to go! You have to trust me."

"Can you give me at least one reason why I should trust you?" he asked.

She was silent for a long time. *Other than my parents, you are the only one that knows about me, Orlo.* "And I sent you the tournament invitation."

"You? But the symbol on the back—"

"I told you that you would win. It was important for you to win. Can we go now?"

The puzzle that he thought he a put together once again felt broken—he felt broken. "Okay," he mumbled. Without being forced, Orlo followed Sima into the Liberum. In the distance he could see that Banyan, Davy, Rosemary, Banyan's father, and several others had gathered for his arrival. They knew he was coming.

"They are here to see you," Sima said, shyly stepping away from his side.

"Mate!" Banyan said, embracing Orlo. "It's good to see ya! How did we do? We didn't think we could pull it off, but we got ya here safe and sound!"

"You did that?" Orlo asked.

"Well, I can't control all the pipes, and I ain't takin' credit for the boom, but I had a hand in it all right. We got word no one was hurt...no one was hurt, was they?"

"I don't believe so. They might be somewhat shook up."

"Hello, young Orlo." Davy welcomed him with a wave of his new arm. Linked lovingly to his other arm was Rosemary. "Glad you made it out. We was gettin' concerned about ya up there on your own." Davy placed his good hand on Orlo's shoulder. "We need to get ya to the Hall of Keepers. There's much to explain, and someone who's been waitin' to talk to you."

Orlo's heart leaped. Had they found Knox?

As he walked, people waved, tipped their hats, and winked at him. They peered over the ledges, and leaned out of the windows of the rooftop greenhouses to wave. The gentle music of musicians filtered out from one of the alleys. His familiarity with the Liberum made it feel as comfortable as his own tower. The overwhelming sense he had before to stay, to escape the confusion up above was creeping back. He noticed that the gardener's daughter hung towards the back of the group. She did not seem entirely uncomfortable with her surroundings, but she did appear pleased to be catching the attention of several girls as the group paraded past the Postal.

Banyan pointed to the great pipes that were hissing and puffing all around them. "We turned them back on when you was safe. Ain't gonna let them freeze to death."

The upset in the Conclusus was meant for him?

The Hall of Keepers looked exactly as it had the last time he was there, not an inch of it looked different. Orlo searched the area, anticipating Knox's familiar face. He believed he would be here, but from where Orlo was standing, the only people he could see were the Hall's patrons, busy about their choosing.

Before he could take in the fullness of his setting, two arms hugged him from behind. Orlo whipped around.

"I told them you would find my letters, didn't I! I told them, and I told them! They thought my coils were loose, but here they are, Orlo! Oh, glorious day!" Avia cheered with her dress hiked up, dancing around in small circles. "Praise be to the Great Mystery! My Orlo has found my letters!"

Orlo looked at the others. The gardener's wife had done what she had said she would do; she had found Avia.

"Thank you, Orlo," Avia said. Tears filled her eyes and spilled down her wrinkled cheeks.

"Excuse me, Keeper," Rosemary addressed Avia.

Orlo looked at Knox's mother. The lady in the portrait and the missing letters—he should have put it together sooner. Avia had been a keeper in the Conclusus.

"He has requested that Orlo speak to him," Rosemary said. "Would you like to see the rest of the Hall?"

Avia clasped her hands in front of her chest. "I don't know the last time someone called me Keeper. Yes, that would be lovely." She had no more than had her arms around him and danced her jig than she was off pulling books from the shelving to sift through their pages.

"These are not her letters, Orlo," the gardener chuckled. "But the words inside are the same."

"Sir!" Orlo was shocked to see the man in his green suit standing in front of him.

"Are you well? Do you need anything?" he asked.

"No, Gardener. Thank you."

"I am no more a gardener than you are, Orlo. Call me Gregory." He turned his attention to the others who were eagerly standing by. "May I speak with the new apprentice alone?"

"Of course," Davy said. "We'll give you some time."

Gregory led Orlo out into the open air of the Liberum. No one stared at him or was distracted from their daily routine by having the head of the Conclusus walking their streets. "My wife is regretful that she could not join us at this crucial time. She thought it might be easier if you had a mother present."

Mother. He had one, and she left. He had been assigned another, and she was taken. "However, if it is okay with you, I have asked my Sima to stay with us, in need that she might interpret should my wording become too," he chuckled, "well, too wordy. Will that suit you? Habits are hard to break, you know?"

"Yes, sir," Orlo replied, stunned. This was not how the Upper Decorum treated those in the Lower Decorum.

"That is good. We are monitoring the time closely. The Hall of Inventors will be expecting their newest apprentice."

Did they expect him to go back?

"Orlo, may I speak frankly to you?"

Orlo nodded. The man he had revered was asking his permission to speak.

"We never imagined the magnitude of the gifting that you possess. What a gift from Him!"

Orlo did not know what he was saying. "A gift, sir?"

"Yes, Orlo!" Gregory stopped. "Orlo, you do not know who you are, do you?"

Chapter 30

"No, sir," he replied honestly.

"Why, Orlo, you are an inventor! It is who He meant for you to be! You were created by your Creator to create! My daughter accidentally overheard the thoughts of Elder Bednegraine several weeks ago. Apparently, on your way home from the Hall of Deliverers, you had a little bug on your brain. It unsettled her and the other elders greatly. But that was not all she heard."

"You made it," the girl by his side interrupted, "what was the word, Father?"

"Snow! You made it snow! It was marvelous, beautiful! Oh, what you are gifted to do, Orlo!"

"No, sir!" Orlo nearly shouted, stepping back from him. He considered that this was a trick, or a cheat as Poppy had said, to see if he would break more laws.

"I must tell you that I speak no untruth to you. I follow His Way. I will not lie to you."

Gregory had told him that he was gifted, but his whole life he thought it was fidgeting—until the ladybug. Could God have gifted him? Could he have been an inventor all along? Could his life have been different?

"Yes," Sima said, overhearing his thoughts. Her demeanor and overall countenance had changed. She no longer acted in charge, but rather a willing assistant to her father. "It is possible to be something more than what someone has told you that you must be. I thought you would have seen that, here."

"You mean, you did not send me here for the book?"

"Not completely," she said, stepping to her father's side. Standing there in her green dress, he could see what was being laid out before him, an error in the ways of the Conclusus—a girl trapped in an assignment that fit her no more than the goggles fit the young deliverers.

As he struggled to sort out his feelings, he thought he saw it snowing, but his machine was not with him. Had someone else invented the machine before him? Then the snow turned into droplets of water, pouring faster and faster down upon those entering and exiting the Hall. It did not wet their clothing, nor did it seem like they cared, with the exception of a few children who were running around catching the imagined tiny droplets on their tongues.

Orlo watched in amazement. "I thought if you could see it, you might understand," Gregory said. "The books say that we can do great things which we cannot comprehend. For to the snow He says, 'Fall on the earth,' and to the downpour and the rain, 'Be strong.' He seals the hand of every man, that all men may know His work."

"You did this?" Orlo asked as the water passed through his hands, hit the ground, and vanished.

"Yes. It is my true gifting."

"How? You're not an observer? You're our gardener! You assign... you assigned me!"

Gregory sorrowfully bowed his head. "I know this, Orlo. I was wrong, and I am very, very sorry. As I said, I am no more a gardener than you are a deliverer; I am indeed an observer. I have known for some time. Sima also overheard the thoughts of an artist...uninvited to be honest."

The apprentice bowed her head, embarrassed.

"About a secret, a room of books. But when we found it, it was empty." He removed from his pocket a purple book, and on it embossed in silver, a single flower—*The Book of the Observers*. "It was left on a branch in the tree. The elders must not have known of its existence when the other books were removed. Thankfully, I have a tree climber in my household. It was how I knew the truth. I confided in a friend, someone I knew that I could trust. Orlo, nearly everyone in the Conclusus has a relation in the Liberum, however not all are willing to admit it. My friend happened to have one as well—a brother by marriage, my wife's brother, who was willing to help in my quest to bring truth back to the Conclusus. I did not tell Davy about the books; he discovered them on his own. And once he knew, I could not protect him anymore."

"That's why he stayed in the Conclusus? To help you?" Orlo could feel the connections coming into place. He wished he had known the truth before he had spoken so harshly to Davy.

"Yes. I began to learn and to understand who I was. I observed others, like my daughter, whose gifting did not match up with their assignment...and then she found you. You see Orlo, you have a choice. We have the ability by Him to choose, but it was taken from us many, many seasons ago." Orlo knew Davy had made a choice. "We can choose to give that freedom back to Him if we desire, and in doing so, allow Him to guide us. Do you see?"

"Are you saying that my whole life has been a lie, and now that I know the truth, now that I know I can live here, be happy, and invent away from the laws of the Conclusus...I can choose to give it back? I can choose to go back to the way life was in the Conclusus—except it won't be the same?" He shook his head, completely confused. "I don't have a guardian, Knox is missing, and everything I have ever believed isn't real. Why would I do that?" he asked.

"Because we have faith that you can make it work again," Gregory whispered. Orlo could now see more clearly the weariness that had been overtaking the gardener. The hours of studying *The Book of the Observers* after the Conclusus had gone to rest must have taken its toll on him. "You have a gift."

"But lots of the Decorum have giftings."

"They do, Orlo, but they do not know who they were created to be. They are imprisoned in what the elders…and I, myself have told them. You know who you are. You know the gifting that is rightfully yours, and by winning the tournament you proved it to the entire Decorum." Orlo was beginning to see why his own plan had failed. "You are the first to live and exist truthfully in your assignment! Truth can return to the Conclusus, Orlo, and you have the ability to bring it! You can help us find the others. You can teach them, as I will teach you. We can bring the Conclusus back to life, Orlo. It is not gone—merely asleep."

The clock tower banged three loud resonating *gonnnnngs*. "Father, we must leave. You are to conclude the festival shortly. It will nearly be nightfall."

"Orlo, my wife will come for you late evening. If you choose to return, you will be returned to the dormitory in the Hall of the Inventors to begin your training…I imagine it will be you showing them a thing or two. Keep your eye open for others like you who are aware of the giftings of God. It might be hard at first to tell the difference, but I have a feeling you are beginning to see the distinction. Guard your thoughts, but do not be concerned about your safety. The elders would not dare harm the bringer of snow. Elder Bednegraine will be watching your every move and listening for your every thought—in the name of service to the Conclusus, of course. Do not give them any reason to have you removed. Do you have any questions?"

"Yes, sir," he said. Now that he knew Avia was safe, his guardian's location lay heavy on his heart. "Did they send Poppy back to the World?"

Gregory looked sadly at Orlo. He took Orlo's hand and placed an object in it. Orlo's fingers curled around the detailed creation. He knew what it was without looking—Poppy's ladybug. "I will not lie to you. Yes, Orlo, they have sent her back to the World. I promised her that this would find its way to you—so you would know that she believes in you, Orlo."

"It is not your fault," Sima said, reading Orlo's thoughts.

"The elders have not known how to acknowledge her since the day Knox brought her back," Gregory explained. "They feared that more would follow if they openly permitted her to stay. She was as much a threat to their way as you and I are, Orlo."

"What if they do try to remove me?"

"They would not dare remove a tournament winner. They would nearly bring about a riot. The Upper Decorum was enthralled by your design. They will each want one permanently installed in their tower."

"But I made it for her," Orlo said more to himself than the other two, "not for them." The first time Orlo had been in the Liberum, he had ambitions of a new life for those that lived in his tower. Now, it did not matter.

Orlo turned the tiny dial on the side of the delicate object that Gregory had given him. Its wings fluttered and its eyelids opened. Orlo clenched his fingers over it, stopping the movement. He was about to have it all—the adjustments, the friends, the tower, the top hats, the velvet coats, classes, feasts, and front row seats, but without anyone to share it.

"Orlo," Gregory said after removing his top hat, "do not forget that even in this you have a choice. We will not force your hand, but know that we all will make sacrifices." He looked down at his daughter. "Whether you choose to come back or not, I will do my best to secure Poppy's return. She was as close to living The Way as any woman I have seen. She deserves to have a choice as well. I must leave you now." Gregory placed the hat back on his head and hastily walked towards the direction of the Hall of Keepers.

The warm steam rose around them, glistening on the cheeks of the apprentice. Orlo imagined what she would look like in her true yellow instead of the green that she had to wear like her father.

Orlo liked the Liberum. It was safe here. Davy was here. Avia was here, and he hoped Banyan was the sort he could one day call friend. The aroma of freshly baked muffins and cinnamon pastries filled his nostrils. This was a nice place. He could do what he wanted to do, when he wanted to do it. He could make choices all day long. He could dream and talk to God without calling Him a silly name, and no one would stop him. He could watch the Arc sail in and imagine that it traveled to all the places he had once been assigned to go. He would fix Banyan's mother's toasting machine or invent a new one. In the Liberum, he could learn the teachings of The Way and how to serve one another.

Why would he choose to serve the Conclusus and follow the leading of a man who was called by one name, but was clearly another? He could have a life here, free of the lies and Decorum of the Conclusus. They could go about their way, living like he once did, happy and ignorant.

A tearful, but angry voice entered his musings. *Why would you not want to share this with them?*

Orlo turned to Sima who was storming off towards the Hall of Keepers. The pipes around him hissed as the workers hastily cooperated to regulate the amount of steam going into the Conclusus. Davy had said they didn't work the pipes because they had to; they did it because they loved the people. Orlo loved the Conclusus; it was his home. Why would he not want to share this with the Decorum? Sima was right. This decision was not about him.

Orlo looked around at those who lived labeled as lawbreakers. They had made their life here in a place where forgiveness and truth overpowered order and law. Davy had chosen the Liberum because he had gotten a glimpse of it, experienced it, and lived it. Didn't the Decorum have the right to choose as well?

If I stay, he thought. *I'm running away. The Decorum has a right to know. I figured out a way to show them the World so I could help them see the truth—and it's selfish of me to stay now and keep it to myself. I must show them The Way of the Liberum, too!*

"Wait!" Orlo called to Sima. "I'll return to the Conclusus, but…"

The girl stopped and turned towards Orlo. "But what, Orlo!" Her hands were on her hips and the snarky arrogance had returned to her face. Then she smiled. "Of course I will help you bring her back." Once again, she had read his mind. "Now why don't you invent me something to eat?"

Orlo took a final look at the Liberum. His new assignment would prevent his return, but it was what he had chosen until his steps were directed back this way. He had been given his heart's desire, an apprenticeship with the inventors, and learned who he was created to be. Now he had to take the life he had chosen, use what he had been given, and accept the challenge that awaited him as Orlo the inventor.

Meanwhile

"Is the situation under control?" the woman asked from the head of the table.

"Yes, Madam. The Decorum has been informed that it was a malfunction of the lawbreakers. The situation is under control."

"Good."

"And the apprentice, Madam, he guards his thoughts well," the elder in orange stated to the others who sat around the table with her.

"Possibly too well," a gentleman in a blue top hat added. "Elder Bednegraine, could it be that he holds them from you with purpose?"

"Most assuredly. However, I have it under control."

"Forgive me, Madam."

"Forgiven, old friend. You must not assume that what the boy believes will bring harm. His imagination is true to that of the inventors and other artisans. He knows of the Hall of Keepers and there is a connection to the apprentice Sima, but let us not make the assumption that we won't be able to turn him for our good."

"And the boy's father? What of him?"

Elder Bednegraine's eyes narrowed. "Find him and remove him. I believe R218 should serve him well." The table was silent. Nobody had ever spoken of R218 in the Conclusus. "Let us move on."

"Aye," the gentlemen in blue said with hand raised. "The gardener and his family?"

"Ah yes," Elder Bednegraine grinned. "He was called unexpectedly to the World. A matter of mission, I was told." The table produced a rumble of muffled laughter.

"Our next order of business," the elder messenger in her long red gloves stated, "is the security of the aeronaut."

"He is secure, for now," an orange-robed elder of the educators admitted.

"How we did not see it sooner is beyond me!" the messenger added.

"It is a good thing you discovered it when you did," the healer interjected. The elders nodded and agreed. "It will be the end of us if an aeronaut begins to believe himself a gardener."

"Orlo must never know of his whereabouts. Will you be able to see to that, Inventor?" Elder Bednegraine asked. An elderly gentleman looked up from where he had been listening. His long purple coat was buttoned to the neck. His eyes were darkened from sleepless nights and his cheeks sunken inward with age.

"Of course, Madam," he said removing his narrow top hat. "He will find me a reliable confidant. He may come to see me as…a father."

The ladies chuckled behind their fans and the men passed agreeing glances.

"But if I may, Elder," his scratchy voice asked, "is the boy stronger than we had assumed, or possibly stronger than you?"

Elder Bednegraine shifted in her seat. "No, Archivald, he is not."

"I must know what I am up against."

"I am confident your services will be up to par, Inventor."

"Elder Bednegraine," a girl dressed in bright pink, and of an age to be the daughter of most at the table, asked hesitantly, "I do not see where there would be harm in one who possesses a natural gifting occupying such an assignment."

"Elder Paulette, you have not been amongst our council long enough to see that when one is given choices, chaos ensues among those around them. Were you not at the festival? Those workers nearly ruined us! Our Decorum was established to maintain our faith, to keep it balanced, pure, and in order. It is a beautiful thing we do. The aeronaut chose his path when he brought in the woman from the North. The ways of the World collide with ours. We are blessed that she did not turn us on end. We cannot have a gardener who freely goes about on his own choosing. Do you understand?"

"Yes, Elder Bednegraine, I do."

"Then it is settled. The man we call Knox will remain in his current location until a suitable apprentice is chosen. Are we in agreement?"

"We are in agreement," the six said in unison.

"Excuse, one more question," Elder Paulette said with a hand raised. "But should our current gardener be found at fault, is his daughter not too young to step into his assignment? We cannot function without a gardener."

"You are correct." Elder Bednegraine grinned. "She is too young and has yet to demonstrate the true gifting of the gardener. By our law, one of us will have to step into assignment until evidence of the gifting is made present by her or one of his other apprentices."

"Should we not be prepared in the event of such an occurrence? Who among us would take on the honor?"

Elder Bednegraine rose slowly to her feet. "I humbly accept."

Thank you!

My Heavenly Father who has snuggled me through the entire process and whispered such wonderful ideas into my heart, my Jesus who has shown me grace through my doubting, and my Spirit who calmed me in the storms and reminded daily to not only think on what is true but also on what is lovely. Jamie—my husband, my teammate and best friend—I would not have put the first word on paper if you had not encouraged me. I love you more and more everyday. Kensi and Jack (my very first backer), you have taught me that encouragement comes in every shape, size, cup of tea, folded laundry, morning hug, and chocolate.I love you 20! Mom, I cherish my daily check-in and your faith filled wisdom. Thank you for being one of my biggest fans. Jordan, thank you for sharing your gift with my readers. (And Tori and Ben – thanks for lending him to me). All of my supportive family, I hear it takes a village, but with a family like mine, I believe I am covered on all sides. Tina, Missy, Lori, and Rachel, thanks for covering me in your friendship and prayers—hugs to each of you! Ryan Dunlap, thank you for going above and beyond to not only bring this project to life, but making it look its absolute best. Bethany Kaczmarek, you made my Orlo shine (and I love you to pieces!). Jason Dudley, you get me! The covers are beautiful—thank you! Julie Gwinn, my agent and personal cheerleader, thank you for believing in me so unselfishly. ACFW Middle Tennessee, we've got this! My Shanan family and crew of young writers (all of you!), you keep me going and I truly treasure our Mondays together. My Realmies who shared, liked and promoted their little speckie hearts out. Trish Corlew & the boys (Blake, Chase, and Gage), your faithful support has meant the world to me! Mary and The Books of the Gardener Fan Club (Esther, Hannah, and Nicole), you girlies are the best! And Dad, I so easily find a glimpse of you in everything I write…I miss you every day. Thank you.

And an extra special thank you to my backers,
you set this cartagon in motion. Thank you:

Chris Wells; Joseph E. McGuffey; Larry and Shirley;
Ash Greyson; Darren Tyler; Angela Herald;
The Marco Family; Rich & Ann Thompson and Family;
The Sartains; Keith and Patty Houske; The Penners;
Ron and Renee Yeo; The Casey Family; The Johnson Family;
The Taylor Family; Adair Family; Cathy Schwartz;
The Burke Family; Gabe Sandbrink; Larry and Lois Stone;
Caden, Grace, and Hannah Miller; The Milford Dumonts;
Jessica L Cornett; Emily; Matthew & Lindsay Fleming;
Weller Family; The Robertson Family; Brenda Johnson;
The York Kids; The Brown Family; Julie Sies; Trevor, Riley,
Tyler and Abby Cebulskie; The Petits; Joshua Kinzinger;
The Martinez Family; Henry Evan Adams;
The Lockwood Family; The Crawfords (all of you!),
Robin Brown; The Petterson Family;
and last but not least, James Johnson!

For more information, on *The Books of the Gardener*
visit: www.LaurenHBrandenburg.com

Made in the USA
Monee, IL
25 May 2020